W9-CDF-700

Lakshmi Holmström was born in India and came to Britain in 1958 where she obtained a BA and later, a research degree from Oxford University. She has lived in Britain since 1962 with long periods in Malaysia and various parts of India. Author of *Indian Fiction in English: The Novels of R. K. Narayan* and *Kannagi: A Retelling of a Fifth Century Tamil Epic*, she now works in multicultural education and towards the promotion of South Asian literature. She has two daughters and lives in Norwich.

H.039

THE
INNER
COURTYARD

•

STORIES BY INDIAN WOMEN

Edited by Lakshmi Holmström

Published by VIRAGO PRESS Limited 1990
20–23 Mandela Street, Camden Town, London NW1 0HQ

Reprinted 1991, 1993

This collection copyright © Lakshmi Holmström 1990
Copyright © in each contribution held by the author

All rights reserved

A CIP catalogue record for this title
is available from the British Library

Printed in Great Britain by
Cox & Wyman Ltd, Reading, Berks

ACKNOWLEDGEMENTS

I should like to thank all those who have helped in the compilation of this anthology. In particular my grateful thanks to the authors in India, who were able to spare the time to discuss their work with me; to Afzal and Jan Friese, Gita Krishnankutty, Vasanti Sankaranarayanan, and to Asha and Sunil Bijlani for their hospitality; to Rukhsana Ahmad, Tara Joshi, Chand Sharma and Asha Damlé for their help in researching particular details; to Eileen Urwin for help in typing the manuscript; and to Melanie Silgardo and Ruth Petrie for their encouragement and help throughout.

I am also grateful to the copyright holders for permission to reprint the following stories: for Lalitambika Antarjanam's 'Revenge Herself', to Narayanan Nambudiri; for Vaidehi's, 'Akku', to the author; for Kamala Das's, 'Summer Vacation', to the author; for Qurratulain Hyder's 'Memories of an Indian Childhood', to the author (this story first appeared in an English translation in the *Illustrated Weekly of India*, 1970); for Mrinal Pande's 'Girls', to the author (this story appeared in an English translation in *Manushi: A Journal About Women and Society*, 15 (1983), published at C1/202 Lajpat Nagar, New Delhi); for Lakshmi Kannan's 'Rhythms', to the author; for Ambai's 'Yellow Fish', to the author; for Ismat Chugtai's 'Chauthi ka Jaura', to the author; for Mahasveta Devi's 'Draupadi', to the author, and to Gayatri Chakravorti Spivak for her translation and notes which appeared in *Critical Inquiry*, Chicago, in 1981; for Attia Hosain's 'The First Party', to the author (this story first appeared in Attia Hosain, *Phoenix Fled*, Chatto & Windus, 1953, and Virago, 1988); for Anita Desai's 'The Farewell Party', to the author (first published in Anita Desai, *Games at Twilight*, William Heinemann Ltd, 1978 and Penguin Books, 1982); for Shashi Deshpande's 'My Beloved Charioteer', to the author (this story first appeared in Shashi Deshpande, *It was Dark*, published by Writers Workshop, Calcutta, 1986); for Shama Futehally's 'The Meeting', to the author (this story first appeared in *The Indian P.E.N.*, Bombay); for Vishwapriya L. Iyengar's 'The Library Girl', to the author (this story first appeared in *Imprint*, Bombay, 1985); for Padma Hejmadi's 'Birthday Deathday', to the author (this story first appeared under the author's previous name Padma Perera, in *Birthday Deathday, and Other Stories*, The Women's Press, London, 1985); for Rukhsana Ahmad's 'The Gate-Keeper's Wife', to the author; for Anjana Appachana's 'Her Mother', to the author (this story first appeared in *The 1989 O. Henry Festival Stories*, published in Greensboro, North Carolina, 1989); for Suniti Namjoshi's 'Dusty Distance', to the author (this story first appeared in Suniti Namjoshi, *The Blue Donkey Fables*, The Women's Press, London, 1988).

CONTENTS

INTRODUCTION

The short story seems to impose certain conditions: intensity, concentration, suggestiveness, surprise. However, it also allows a variety of approaches, from fantasy and fairytale at one end, to journalism and social documentation at the other. The authors presented here have drawn on all these. Moreover, the stories come from different languages, drawing upon different local experiences and traditions of story-telling; and there are some written by women who no longer live in India. I wanted to get away from the notion of a third world/women's story, which tends to be one of rural exploitation and victimisation or of urban loneliness, and to look instead for complementary and challenging representations of a variety of women's experiences.

Women in India have traditionally been tellers of tales. They have used not only the mythic materials of the epics in their local versions, the lives of the gods and the animal fables of the Panchatantra, but also the more realistic material of family histories and memories. But the short story as a literary form is a fairly recent phenomenon, mostly of this century. However it quickly established itself in India through skilled exponents who provided the models. Rabindranath Tagore was widely read in translation from Bengali, later Premchand in translation from Hindi, then R. K. Narayan who writes in English. A spate of journals in English and other Indian languages, established in the 1920s and onwards, published their works. Some of these journals were esoteric, some popular, a few exclusively for women. The best women writers of this time, while working within the early tradition of social comment, added a different dimension in two particular ways: they brought new material into their literatures with their strong portraits of women of their community; they also brought a refreshingly new spoken language, particularly the familiar language used between women.

The development of women's writing can be linked with the

development of the women's movement in India. Although the early decades of the twentieth century were particularly a time of social reform and comment, modern India's concern with the 'women's question' has a long history. This was first raised by men through a number of organisations which were to do with general political reform. Ram Mohan Roy who founded the Brahmo Samaj in 1828 strove for equal individual rights for men and women; Ranade who founded the National Social Conference campaigned against child marriages and fought for widow re-marriage.

By the end of the nineteenth century education for women began to be available; by 1914 Queen Mary's College, the first of its kind for women in Madras was set up; in 1916 Karve established the first university for women in Pune. The first autonomous women's organisations came into being in the 1910s and 1920s. They were concerned with a variety of legal reforms to do with women – property rights, dowry, polygamy etc. – but were always strongly linked with the Nationalist movement, whose first and primary aim was freedom from colonialism. This was a time when many autobiographies by women were published, thinly disguised as fiction: Raj Lakshmi Debi's *The Hindu Wife* (1876), Ramabai Saraswati's *The High-caste Hindu Woman* (1886), Shevantibai Nikambe's *Ratnabai: A Sketch of a Bombay High-caste Hindu Wife* (1894), Krupabai Sattianadan's *Kamala* (1894) and *Saguna* (1895). These were almost propaganda material, telling individual stories of struggle against repressive forms of orthodoxy, and pleading for better education for women.

In the 1930s, during the Freedom Movement, both men and women formed the left-wing Progressive Writers' Association, with a strong emphasis on realism and social comment in their work. By the 1930s and certainly in the 1940s there were some remarkable women short story writers: Lalitambika Antarjanam writing in Malayalam, Ismat Chugtai in Urdu, Ashapurna Devi and others in Bengali, Attia Hosain in English to name just a few.

The first wave of the women's movement came to an end with Independence, and with some gains: a secular state with the constitutional guarantee of equal rights of men and women in political and economic life; and also with the passing of the Hindu Code bill in 1959, a comprehensive reform of Hindu personal law. However, as women's rights activists have pointed out for some time, continued recognition of the traditional laws of religious communities often results in discrimination against women.

A 'second wave' of the women's movement can be clearly seen in the seventies when many women helped to found trade unions and co-operatives, to organise slum dwellers and tribal people. Meanwhile there has been a rapid growth in women's education, and numbers of women in all forms of work. Many of the younger women writers are part of this activist ambience. For example, Vishwapriya Iyengar writes, 'It requires infinite reservoirs of humanity not to be divided on the battlefront from those who suffer, not to let the poignant and violent moments of history be immobilized through the distinction of the chronicler from the victim'.[1]

Almost all the stories presented here were written since India became independent in 1947, though several women writers were well established before this time. I hope one early story will be of interest: Lalitambika Antarjanam's 'Revenge Herself', first published in 1938 in the Malayalam journal *Mathrubhumi*. One of my aims was to signpost some of the dominant themes in the writing by Indian women since Independence and to suggest their context. Thus colonialism and its aftermath, partition and exile and changing social conditions provide the specific background to universal themes of poverty and loneliness, childhood and age, sexuality, death and regeneration. I have not looked for overtly 'feminist' statements, but many of the stories are feminist in the sense that they present a woman's perspective and point of view in a particular way.

Most of the stories included here have a special kind of complexity. They are often concerned with overlapping worlds of experience (for example, the world of myth and fantasy and the world of high technology; the world of traditional ritual and

---

[1] Vishwapriya Iyengar, 'Memory and Identity in Fiction'. Paper presented at the Third International Feminist Book Fair, Montreal, 1988.

observance and a 'modern' sceptical world; the world of collective responsibilities and obligations and the world of the individual). Often a narrative is set against two such worlds. What is of interest is the tension or negotiation between such worlds and the sudden sharp slippage from one into another. Often too there is a protest implied either in that tension or conflict, or in the violence of the accommodation. The authors of these stories have found a variety of strategies to convey this.

Lalitambika's story, 'Revenge Herself' is an example. This story is based on an actual event in the late nineteenth century, which had an enormous impact in Kerala. A woman from the Nambudiri Brahman caste did indeed became a prostitute, and argued at her trial before a caste court that her partners in prostitution should be tried as well and if found guilty, should be excommunicated along with her. But why should Tatri, belonging to a caste which insisted so strenuously on the ritual purity of women, take to prostitution in the first instance? It became a kind of literary puzzle. Different versions of the story exist in Malayalam. Lalitambika uses the device of the ghost story in order to give a first person narrative of a victimised woman, which is framed within (and split off from) the first person comment of the narrator. In doing so, Lalitambika finds a way of voicing her own split response: sympathy because of shared understanding of unchanging daily ritual within a Nambudiri household, and sympathy too for Tatri's loneliness and frustration; censure because in the end the narrator is forced to see Tatri's individual protest against a larger historical process.

Other women's stories of Lalitambika's time suggest a similar ambivalence on the part of the author towards her protagonist.

Now the double perspective in Lakshmi Kannan's 'Rhythms' works in a different way, and is contained within the story. The narrator, a regular worshipper at the Mylapore temple, actively records her impressions of a normal evening of prayer. The distant dissonant sounds of protest gradually separate themselves from the harmony of her initial impressions, coming to focus in the paralytic's rage and incoherence at the end of the story. The irony of the ending is subtle, since individual rage comes to take a traditional form. It is given a place within a convention, a nindasthuthi (ironical praise) being an allowed form of dissent. So protest and tradition slide together finally, instead of splitting apart.

The stories which employ a child's point of view juxtapose a child's perceptions against an adult world, but in each case the emphasis is different. Thus in Qurratulain Hyder's 'Memories of an Indian Childhood' the child narrator mirrors the easy accommodation of fantasy and reality in the adult world (the interweaving of animal and human too) whereas the child's world and the adult world are more sharply separated in Kamala Das's 'Summer Vacation', and certainly conflict in Mrinal Pande's 'Girls'. Death broods over 'Summer Vacation'; the child Ammu perceives death and profound loss (of a whole way of life, a particular order) but also sees change and regeneration. Muthassi will undoubtedly die: Muthassi will never die. And it is birth that broods over 'Girls', actualised in the huge, threatening stomach of the mother, possibly containing the boy child. The adult world here is specifically a female one into which the rebellious child narrator refuses to be assimilated, moving instead into the world of imagination and fiction which will be both her refuge and her weapon.

Such possibilities of accommodation and manoeuvre are narrowed down in some of the stories. The young wife in Attia Hosain's 'The First Party' is forced to enter an unrestrained 'western' world precisely because all the rules of the ordered world in which she grew up enjoin her to do as her husband wants. By contrast, Talat in 'The Library Girl' is suddenly trapped within her burqa between one day's beginning and its end. The central image of sewing clothes in Ismat Chugtai's 'Chauthi ka Jaura' is significant in that it is one of shaping and contriving to match restricted means to huge aspirations and needs.

Other stories end with risks taken, sudden possibilities and visions as when the older woman in Shashi Deshpande's 'My Beloved Charioteer' confronts and shatters her daughter's illusions and her own past, when crazy Akku in Vaidehi's story turns her worst humiliations into triumphs, and when Dopdi confronts Senanayaka at the end of Mahasveta Devi's story.

This theme of displacement is the link between stories written by women from India who now live abroad and those who live there; the double perspective more sharpened – or perhaps just more visible because more self-conscious – in those who have migrated, as in Anjana Appachana's 'The Mother' and Padma Hejmadi's 'Birthday Deathday'.

Women of the Indian diaspora draw upon experiences other than that of migration, however. Asian writers in the west have come from India, Pakistan, Bangladesh, and by complicated routes of migration from different parts of Africa. By now they include some people who were born here and have never visited South Asia. What is shared by so disparate a group is the experience of migration and a colonial past. Rukhsana Ahmad's 'The Gate-keeper's Wife' draws upon this history in a sharp unusual way, using the point of view of a latter-day 'Memsahib'.

Among these writers of the diaspora, there is also a growing literature in Indian languages, as well as some interesting experiments in bilingual writing: trends which will be worth watching. That an Indian story comes from London or Norwich or wherever alters the entire notion of what an 'Indian' story is. Suniti Namjoshi's 'Dusty Distance' is a witty response to the literary establishment's tendency to stereotype, and serves as a comment on the whole collection.

The decision to include authors who write from within India and outside it; to represent those who write in the regional languages as well as those who write in English was deliberate. The point was to question the notion of a 'mainstream' of women's writing from India. However, this has meant that many important names have been left out. Out of the stories coming from India, I have given more space to those written in English in the first instance than to any other one language. This is because English, although used mainly by the middle classes in India, also crosses regional boundaries and addresses a larger audience. Overall, I have given more space to stories in translation. Yet, it must be remembered that only a few of India's sixteen main languages are represented here. There are many more stories which ought to be translated. A small collection such as this is bound to have its limitations, mainly those of finding good translations within a short time. It also happens that some of the best writing by women in some of the

languages such as Marathi consists of autobiographies and
'novellas'. Unfortunately it was not possible within the frame-
work of this book to include examples.

The relationship between author and language in an insist-
ently multilingual country is an interesting one, with a variety
of possibilities. Two of the authors represented here have
translated their own stories into English. A number of other
writers are fluent in more than one language but choose to write
their fiction in only one. Mrinal Pande spoke to me very acutely
of the creative tension she finds when writing in Hindi, the way
the language works on its own momentum, modulating what
the author wishes to say, comparing it to roller-coasting where
the rider's control – using the pull of gravity against the
movement of the roller-coaster – provides the excitement. She
said she cannot function quite in the same way in English and
chooses, on the whole, not to translate her own work. Yet
Kamala Das and Lakshmi Kannan write their poetry in English
while choosing to write their prose fiction in their mother-
tongue.

The reality of the multilingual situation in India is that many
urban Indians of today speak more than one language. The
fiction writer who is writing in any one language of India,
whether it is English or any other, has to reflect this reality. The
sliding of one language or language form into another, the
suggestion that different sorts of discourses are carried on in
different languages is yet another way of indicating concurrent
worlds; a technique often used by Indian writers in English,
and one which is difficult to translate. There is a wry self-
reflective irony in the reference to the English-speaking father
in Shama Futehally's 'The Meeting'. The reference to the Bengali
song at the end of Anita Desai's 'The Farewell Party' is a very
specific signpost pointing to the slippage from one social world
into another, at the same time suggesting the emotional tone of
each.

Many of the writers who choose to write in the regional
languages also spoke of the relationship between reader and
writer, the immediate recognition of shared responses within
the language community. This includes shared assumptions
about story-telling and expectations about what a story should

do (which an author may choose deliberately to confound). The non-Indian reader is invited to compare the regional language stories with those written in English bearing this in mind.

A word on the problems of translation. It is impossible to indicate in English local colloquialisms, the extent to which some authors such as Vaidehi and Ismat Chugtai have bridged the gap between ordinary speech and literary usage or, as in the case of Mahasveta Devi, have forged a new language composed of different registers.

The grammatical structure of a language such as Tamil allows the possibility of particular narrative techniques. For example, because of its agglutinative structure, a single word can make up an entire sentence consisting of a verb which indicates not only tense, but also number and sex of the implied subject (like English, Tamil has no grammatical gender). This allows for a terseness of style which needs to be indicated by other means when translated. More difficult are the implicit ambiguities: for example, the use of quasi-impersonal verb forms which leave the person and tense unstated; or the blurring of the distinction between narration in the first and third persons which can be sustained in many Tamil stories, so that the moment when a deliberate choice is made between the two is a significant turning point. Readers will notice that this also happens in 'Chauthi ka Jaura'. Similar to this subtlety is the way the single pronoun in English, 'she' can be indicated in two ways, 'this' she and 'that' she: ival, aval. The difference between the two pronouns is more than simply spatial distance: it can suggest social or psychological distance too, and there are corresponding more respectful forms ivar, avar. Often ambiguities cannot be indicated. The translator, opting for one choice, could lose a whole wealth of suggestiveness.

This is also the case when translating particular words which are ringed with resonances. However sensitively done, it is difficult to convey in English the exact implications of concepts (as in 'Rhythms'), the connotations of geographical space – particularly in relation to women (the coconut grove in memory of ancestors, the vadakkini and tekkini of 'Summer Vacation'; the inner and outer verandahs of the Nambudiri house in 'Revenge Herself'), and most particularly resonances of forms of address. In 'Girls', maamis and maasis cannot be generalised under 'aunts'; the difference in status between mother's sister and mother's brother's wife is significant. The first thing that the little girl notices when she enters her grandmother's house is that Naani has Maama's son on her lap – her son's son. The reader needs to educate herself to respond sensitively to these details. All the stories presented here have a denseness and richness of detail of the actuality of daily life.

The stories are in three sections: stories in translation from Indian languages; stories from India in English; and stories from the diaspora. Any pieces of information essential to reading the story are given in an introductory note; Indian words will be found in the glossary and notes.

Lakshmi Holmström, 1990

LALITAMBIKA ANTARJANAM

Lalitambika Antarjanam was born in 1909 in the Kottarakara district of southern Kerala, of literary parents who both wrote poetry. She herself had little formal education. In 1927 she was married to Narayanan Nambudiri. She was an active participant in the Indian National Congress and was later associated with the Kerala Marxist Party. All through her life she was a political activist and social reformer. Her published works consist of nine collections of short stories, six collections of poems, two books for children and a novel, *Agnisakshi* (1980) which won the Kerala Sahitya Akademi award for the best literary work of the year. She died in 1987.

In the Introduction I mentioned the actual event on which Lalitambika's story is based. Nambudiri Brahman women (of the protagonist, Tatri's caste) were also known as Antarjanam – literally meaning 'the secluded ones', more or less confined to the inner courtyard and verandah. The Nambudiris – unlike the Nayars and some other castes of Kerala which were matrilineal – maintained a patrilineal form of family organisation. A Nambudiri woman had no control or rights over her own sexuality, a Nayar woman – within certain limits, mainly of caste – did. A Nayar woman could have sambandam relationships with visiting husbands which could be begun and ended without formality. But a different ideal was required of Tatri, as an Antarjanam.

Lalitambika describes the lifestyle of a young Nambudiri woman in the late nineteenth century. She made ritual garlands out of karuka or herbal grass every day, sang songs in praise of Siva and Parvati to accompany the ritual folk dances of the Tiruvadira festival (dedicated to Madana, god of erotic love) and recited the story of Seelavati who ordered the sun not to rise so that she might save her dying husband. She was brought up to believe that her husband would be her pratyaksha

1

deivam, visible god; pati devata, husband god; a good woman was a pati vrata, his devotee.

The story also refers to Parasurama, one of the ten incarnations of the Lord Vishnu, who according to legend, threw his axe into the sea and raised a piece of land which later came to be known as Kerala.

Revenge
Herself

M idnight. I sat alone in my study. Sleep beckoned me with compassion, caressing my work-weary body and soul. But if I should put away my writing materials, there would be no returning until the next day – to the same hour, the same weariness. Silence all around, broken only by the occasional chatter of the married mice in the attic, or the snoring of the sleeping children in the next room. From the solitary lamp on the table a pale light was cast, somehow terrifying against the dense darkness outside. Somewhere owls hooted in warning. I am a coward by nature, let me admit it. I was more so that night, in those eerie surroundings.

I shut the window and bolted it, adjusted the wicks of the oil lamp, checked on the children to see if they were awake, came back and sat in my usual place. I had to write. But what should I write about? Where to begin? The problem overwhelmed me. It is not easy to write a story, particularly for a woman in my position. I want to write out of my convictions, but I fear to hazard my name, my status. When my stories mirror the reality of society, I am open to the criticism of all kinds of people. When they abuse me, how should I retaliate? I dare not even approach the question of religious customs. And yet in spite of all these scruples, whom will I displease this time? Which literary movement will I offend?

I threw my pen down in disgust, leaned back in the chair and shut my eyes. Many possible characters seemed to walk by: seen, unseen, alive, dead, women and men; suffering souls, voiceless, but with thunder and lightning in their hearts. Were they commanding me to record their lives? I was frightened, but exhilarated too.

Suddenly I heard the sound of approaching footsteps. What was this? I shivered and sat up. Had I forgotten to close the door and bolt it? I hadn't heard the sound of the door being opened. It was midnight, the time when spirits walk. And

3

though I am not naturally superstitious, I was afraid. I felt faint, my eyes closed. The footsteps seemed to come nearer and nearer, yet I could not move.

Minutes ticked by. Five minutes? An hour? I don't know. After some time I heard a woman's voice nearby, speaking to me softly but firmly: 'Are you asleep? Or are you just scared?'

I did not stir. Or rather, I did not have the courage to stir. The voice continued in a slightly sarcastic tone: 'You claim to be a writer, and yet you are afraid. I thought that experienced writers were accustomed to observing horror and tragedy without so much as batting an eyelid.'

My curiosity to see this person who knew this much about me, overcame my fear. I opened my eyes. Before me, as though from a dream, stood a woman, neither young nor old; ageless. Her expression seemed a mixture of sorrow, bitterness, hatred and despair. Her eyes seemed to burn with the intensity of revenge. I thought she was a figure from the pages of recent history – known but forgotten.

She continued authoritatively, yet with some kindness too. 'Mine is not a social visit. I thought you were in a dilemma, floundering without a theme for a story. I can offer you an excellent one: shelved and rotting, waiting to be written. With your permission – if you are not afraid . . .'

By this time I had pulled myself together somewhat.

'Yes,' I said, 'I am scared. Of this night. Of all that is happening now. Who are you? How did you manage to come here? Weren't the doors closed?'

'Who am I?' She laughed aloud. 'So you would like to know who I am. You want to know whether I am human being or devil; ghost or evil spirit. You have courage.'

Her laughter had the sound of a wild river that had burst its dam. Wave upon wave of that unearthly laughter filled the room, echoing, reverberating. By this time I was prepared.

'I admit I am a coward. But tell me who you are. Without knowing that how can I proceed? As human beings we need to know – even about the remotest stars – their names and station.'

'As human beings? I would rather you didn't call me one,' she cut in angrily. 'Once upon a time, I was proud to carry that name, and I struggled hard not to dishonour it. Now I no longer wish to be known as a human being, particularly a woman. One lesson I have learnt, and perhaps I have taught it too: the human condition is one of cruel betrayal and suffering.'

'Perhaps,' I agreed. 'But isn't suffering and pain the special gift granted to humankind – the golden chain that links human and divine?'

She dismissed the notion summarily.

'Suffering, a golden chain? What absolute nonsense! Just tell me one thing. As a means of bondage, is gold any different from iron? At least one knows where one is with iron. Gold hides behind its seductive façade. Iswara! That, after all, is the difference between devil and man too.'

By now, her face, charged with hatred, had taken on an inhuman aspect, though I could not quite understand how the change had come about. Sorrow, hatred, pride and revenge seemed to flit across it making it extraordinarily vivid, strangely attractive. I wondered what it was that she had endured in her past life.

'Are you waiting to hear my story?' she asked after a pause. 'Well, it is my intention to tell you. It is an old story, of true events that happened half a century ago. At that time it turned history on its head. You weren't even born then. Neither were these new-fangled social reformist organisations with their tall claims nor their leaders around then. Few characters from my story are alive now. But the echoes of those events have not quite died . . . Did you ever hear of Tatri of — ?'

I shivered. So this was she. Whose name our mothers had prohibited us from speaking. A name which to us had become obscene. I was speechless.

She saw my hesitation. Sadly she said, 'O yes, which Nambudiri woman hasn't heard of Tatri, "fallen object", "tainted goods"? Though none of you will so much as admit to that knowledge. But child, can you now try and understand why that hated one gave up her life?

'To begin with, she was as innocent as any one of you. She too once made karuka garlands. She too prayed like you, raptly clasping her black string. She fasted on all auspicious days. She was innocent, she had neither looked upon a man nor spoken

5

with him. Grandmothers used to uphold Tatri as a model of propriety to all the young girls who come of age.

'But you know that all those rituals are, after all, charades. You know that by the time we are seventeen or eighteen we are shrewd enough to control our most secret thoughts. On moonlit nights we sit in the inner verandah reciting prayers, our sighs suppressed. We sing "Parvati Swayamvaram" and "Mangala Atira" and dance, the catch in our voices unheard. And all the time we wait, with bated breath, for the men's voices in the outer verandah. We offer austere leaves of kuvalam in strict prayer, while our hearts are filled with the sensuous fragrance of mango blooms. And so we wait . . . days, months, even years . . . At last one day our mothers come with henna and silver ring. And our hands are given into the hands of a man – old or young, invalid or lecher. That is our destiny. That is our entire life.

'Mine was a lucky fate, or so people said in those days. He was in his prime, it was his first marriage, he had sufficient means. So I began my marriage with no worries. I soon found he was a man with aggressive sexual needs. I learnt in time to meet those demands, to please him in his taste for sex with the same attention and care that I gave to his taste for food. After all, one's husband is considered the pratyaksha deivam, the "seen" God. And it was to please that God that I learnt the art of the prostitute. If it were not for that, dear sister, I too – like so many women of our community – would have remained a mere wife, a neglected and ignored wife. Perhaps, too, none of the wretched consequences would have followed. On the other hand, it might be, that in learning to serve him, I unleashed my own instinctual being. I don't know. But I swear to you that at that time he alone was at the centre of my life.

'So it was that when he started drifting away from me, I was desolate. Often he didn't come home at night. I used to think, at first, that he was at a festival or a private feast. Perhaps he was at the variyam or was needed at the palace. I would cry and sulk on the rare occasions when I saw him. There was no one else to share my grief.

'He laughed in response to my heartbroken complaints. A man, he said, is as free as a bird. His life should be one of enjoyment. Surely a man cannot be expected to waste away his entire youth married to one woman, and that a Nambudiri wife.

'Sometimes I was filled with anger and bitterness. Sometimes I even wished to put an end to my life. I often cursed my lot as a Nambudiri woman, thinking, if only I belonged to any other caste of Kerala, one which would have given me the right to reply, to match his male arrogance with my freedom.

'But no. Each month, upon the recurrence of his birthstar, I bathed and prayed that he should have a long life, making offerings of tumba flower garlands and neivillakku lit with ghee. When I came of age I had prayed to be granted a good husband; now I prayed that I should be granted my husband's love.

'The steward of our estate was a kind man who made sure I had plenty to eat. But what about one's inner hunger, that other greed? Once kindled it is not easily quenched. It flows like molten lava, like fire through the very life-blood. He, my husband, knew this too. But he was a man and I a woman. A woman born in a cursed society.

'I too would have suffered in silence like all those other Nambudiri women except for what happened unexpectedly. One night he came home with a new wife. They were to sleep that night in the very bedroom I had shared with him. I could even bring myself to serve food to this woman, but to be actually asked to prepare their nuptial bed! Yes, I had chanted the "Seelavati charitram" again and again . . . But an Antarjanam is a human being too . . . I cursed her aloud. In my grief and outrage, I called her a whore. On that instant I saw him turn into a devil. He flung my words back at me. "I know perfectly well she is a whore – I love her for what she is. If you could be like her, I might like you better."

'I could bear the physical violence, but those words were a far worse assault. I was numb with the horror of it. A pati vrata, a woman of honour to be as much as told by her husband, "If you want me to love you, be a prostitute!" For a blinding moment, I was overcome by a furious thirst for revenge. Somehow I held myself together. But I knew I had had enough. I could not stay in that place a moment longer.

'I did not speak to him again. I withdrew into myself.

Desolate and grief-stricken, yearning for consolation, I returned to my own home. There followed days without love; uneventful days. There were no rays of light in the tunnel. All Nambudiri houses are dark prisons, after all. Is one any better than another? My father had died but his five wives were still alive. My brother was looking for a bride to replace his fourth wife who was now dead. My two widowed sisters were there too. The third one, driven insane because of the ill-treatment she had received from her husband, wandered about aimlessly. Two younger sisters, now grown up, were unmarried – a burden to the house and a grief to my mother. When I joined this lot, it was exactly like jumping from the frying pan into the fire. Living in such a bleak, claustrophobic world, who could be blamed for seeking some comfort? I was young, healthy, egoistic. I thought I was more beautiful than any of my husband's mistresses. In those days, when I combed my hair, freshened my face and glanced covertly through the windows, all I wanted was a glimpse of the outside world. I had an innocent desire to be seen and admired. There were some who caught those glances and smiled at me. I smiled in return. And that was all. Those aristocratic Nambudiris who were attracted to me knew well enough the consequences I would suffer for even this. As for themselves, they would have been ready for any kind of liaison provided it was discreet.

'Meaningful glances. Hushed whispers. Gossip and scandal. The inmates of the inner rooms turned out to be fifth columnists. My mother never lost an opportunity to curse me. "You sinner, born to be the ruin of your family's reputation. I wish I had never carried you in my womb."

'And one day my sister-in-law was peremptory with her order: "Don't step into the kitchen."

'I still cannot understand why I was punished so. I hadn't so much as touched a man other than my husband. I hadn't the boldness to nurture such a desire. There had been a few glances through the window. A few men had been attracted. Was that my fault? But the world was never concerned with reason or logic. The innuendos continued till they numbed my heart. Terror at the thought of dishonour threw me off balance; pushed me to the verge of the very abyss I dreaded. I was long past suffering. In all directions there was only darkness. It was as though through whirling coils of dark smoke my enemies waited, ready to strike, like snakes. To survive that final struggle I had to be a snake too. At last I gave way to those long quiescent storms of anger and revenge.

'If I should tell you what I decided to do, you would be appalled. But please remember, my sister, that it was done for you too, and for all Nambudiri women. As a matter of pride. As a show of strength. I enjoyed the humiliation of those men, for there never was any value attached to our own tears. Yet, after all, in the end I gained nothing, for even you women hated me, dreaded me more than the devil. Years have passed, but even to you of a modern time Tatri is no more than a fallen woman.'

As she spoke, her eyes filled with tears, and overcome with grief she laid her head upon the table. I watched her in silence, wondering what sort of future a woman such as she could have expected. If her life had been shattered and strewn around the wilderness like pieces of a broken bottle then was it her fault or that of society's? There could have been only two alternatives for her: madness or prostitution. Both tragic.

After a moment she sat up, her eyes dry once more and aflame with intensity. 'No, child,' she said, 'I shall not cry again. That was a momentary weakness.' She resumed her story. 'Nothing could shock me any more – neither the waves breaking the bounds of the sea, nor even the skies falling down. Life and death had all become the same. Yes, I made my decision. I thought that since I had chosen my destiny, it should also be an act of revenge on behalf of my mothers and sisters. If I should be victimised, it should not be on false grounds. If I should be made outcast, it should not be for being innocent. Women, too, I thought, can willingly choose the path of debasement. And if I should choose to fall, I would bring down with me several cruel men who were the means of that fall. I would see to it that in the clear light of justice many more men than I should deserve excommunication.

'On a certain night a new courtesan appeared on the festival grounds and temple precincts. She was beautiful and witty. Her modesty attracted men even more than her beauty. Princes, courtiers and Nambudiris, all sought her company. At first she kept them all at arm's length, saying she was a married woman with a husband who was still alive. She withheld a crucial detail about herself, however, – the community to which she belonged. They brushed aside her pleas to be left alone. They argued that in Kerala, the land of Parasurama, a woman was allowed as many husbands as she chose. The only women who were outside this rule were the Nambudiris. The rest, they said, were free to enjoy their pleasure. O these men who seem so honourable, so saintly! Men who expect unquestioning faithfulness from their own wives, but who are quite willing to ruin another's!

'So many men were attracted to me. So different from the ostracism of the inner rooms. I melted, I was moved. I could not have enough of their adulation.

'The new courtesan grew famous. Those who came to her went away happy. From each of them, in return for their pleasure, she received – or took – gifts and mementos. And so, gradually and deliberately, she gained possession of the honour of many men who claimed to be pillars of our society.

'There was one man who was yet to come. There was one man for whom she waited and watched. She knew he would not fail to come, once he had heard of this true pleasure seeker. We had not seen each other for five years. But I recognised him the moment I met him at my usual rendezvous near the temple. He, however, did not know me. How could he see in this proud and famous woman his old Antarjanam?

'I shall not forget that night. For that night I had debased myself; for that night I had lived and waited. From the moment he had last spoken, this idea had rankled, then seeded and grown in my mind. If a woman should go to the lengths of becoming a prostitute in order to please her husband, can she be called a pati vrata? For if that were so, I too was one; a veritable "Seelavati". Through my corruption I could please him, and yes, he was pleased.

'Just before he left me, he said, "In all my life, I have never met a woman so beautiful and so clever. I wish I could live with you always."

'At the very moment that he slipped the ring – once again –

on my finger, I asked him, "Are you sure you have never before met one like me?"

'Holding his sacred thread with both hands, he said, "No, I swear by my Brahmasvam. No. I have never before met a woman of your wit and intelligence."

'I smiled with triumph. I raised my voice very slightly and said, "That's false. Think of your wife. Was she any worse than I?"

'In the hesitant light of that pale dawn he looked at me once again. A strangled cry escaped him. "O my God, my Lord Vadakkunatha, it is Tatri. Tatri." And he fled from my sight, disappearing immediately.

'That's all I need to tell you. You know very well all that happened afterwards. As an Antarjanam I was brought to trial for defilement, and under threat of losing caste. It was a trial that shook the whole of Kerala. As it got under way, they were all terrified – yes, princes and Nambudiris too – that their names would be spoken by the prostitute. Then some went into hiding. Others frantically made offerings to the gods. Each hoped desperately she had forgotten him.

'I had more than names, I had proofs; a golden ring with a name engraved upon it, a golden girdle, a gold bordered veshti. And so, sixty-five men, priests among them, were brought to trial. I could have been the means of excommunicating sixty thousand men, not merely sixty-five. Any woman who was beautiful enough and clever enough could have done the same, such were the decadent landlords and Nambudiris of those days. I could have insisted on continuing the enquiry. But no. In the end, for all the submerged rage of all Nambudiri women, only sixty-five men were brought to trial. Those sixty-five were indicted. That was my revenge. Was it my revenge alone?

'And now, tell me sister. Which one do you think was worse, the man who led a woman into prostitution for his own satisfaction, or the woman who willed herself into prostitution to counter him? Which one should you hate? Which one should you shun?'

I had not uttered a word throughout her strange account, and now I was dumbstruck. She misunderstood my silence and spoke in a voice full of disappointment and despair. 'Why did I come here? I made a mistake. Why did I try to speak to a slave of a woman who has no self-respect or honour? Oh no, you will never change.'

I was not offended by what she said. At last I began to speak. 'My poor wronged sister, I don't blame you. I do sympathise with you. I understand that you were speaking for many – for the weak against the strong, for women calling out for justice, for all human beings whose emotions and instincts have been stamped upon. What you did was not just an act of personal revenge, it was a protest born out of grief and despair.

'But then, think of this, too. Was it not impulsive and headstrong to take up such a responsibility on your own? Individual effort cannot yield lasting results; sometimes it can be positively dangerous. Just think of that. That storm that you raised – what good did it possibly do to society as a whole? In the end, men used it as an excuse to victimise us even more: the memory of that event was a means of humiliating us, forcing us to hang our heads in shame. Remember too, that you hardly brought any consolation to the families and womenfolk of the excommunicated men.'

By this time, I too was stirred, my voice shook as I spoke. 'You must excuse me. But I have to say that for most of us, what you choose to describe as the sacrifice of Tatri was nothing more and nothing less than the trial of a prostitute. True, it created a storm, but it did not point to a clear direction for us. The end cannot justify the means, sister. Of course, I applaud your courage and your pride, but I have to denounce the path you took.

'But, all the same, we as Nambudiris can never forget Tatri. From your world of darkness and silence you hurled a random firecracker as a warning and a challenge. Nevertheless it ignited a torch for us in our generation, and there will be greater fires in times to come. Your revenge will be forgiven because of those radiant future fires.'

I held out my hands to her in love and compassion. But the face of the female form had paled, its eyes were lifeless, it vanished away into the morning fog, wailing. 'I must not let my shadow fall upon you. For you I am, and always will be, a sinner, a fallen woman, a devil.'

The cock crew. I woke up from that strange dream.

Translated from the Malayalam
by Vasanti Sankaranarayanan

VAIDEHI

Vaidehi was born in 1945 and lives in Udipi in Karnataka state. She has published three collections of short stories and a prize winning novel *Asprushyarn*. Several of her poems have appeared in leading Kannada journals. Her short stories and poems have been included in the anthologies made by the Kannada Sahitya Akademi.

'Akku' literally means 'elder sister'. The story takes place in a patrilineal joint family, in the house of the narrator's grandfather or Ajjayya. The head of the family is Doddajjayya, Ajjayya's elder brother. Doddatte is Doddajjayya's sister and the great-aunt of the narrator. Akku is Doddajjayya's daughter, she calls him Appiah, father. Siriyatte is Akku's younger sister. Chikki is the narrator's uncle's wife.

The vermilion mark and black beads are symbols of marriage.

Vaidehi often uses the dialect of the Kundapura Taluk of South Kanara in Karnataka, particularly in the dialogues of some of her stories. She describes this dialect as 'vigorous, subtle, with its own humorous and poetic expressions'. She writes: 'Grānthika [standard] Kannada stands as foreign when I handle such themes as Akku.'

14

Akku

Akku has a large vermilion mark on her forehead although she has no husband. There are black beads around her neck, but sometimes she will leave them in the corner of her box when she goes out. She has often devoured people whole, who have asked about her husband's whereabouts. Not always, though. Sometimes she will sit silent and tight-lipped. At other times she will burst out laughing through crooked mouth and nose-tip, shaking her head and looking at you from the corners of her eyes.

She always has a towel in her hand – actually a handkerchief, a man's handkerchief. No one knows how it came into her possession, nor is it worth bothering about. It is enough to say that Akku is never without it. And to her nothing is of greater consequence than misplacing it and looking for it all the time. Let domestic chores go to the dogs; she will carry on searching every nook and cranny for her towel.

Here, in Ajjayya's house no one is free. Perhaps Uncle Vasu is allowed a voice, and Bhanu Chikki actually dares to speak up a little. Doddatte, as Ajjayya's sister, and 'great aunt' to everyone, fears nobody. However, it is Akku alone who is under no obligation, no duress. She is mere chaff, empty. 'Let her wander around as she likes. She has to while away her time somehow.' Perhaps she wasn't always like this, without substance. But she is excused now. The rest of the household is there to churn butter, add spices to food, wear new saris and jewellery at weddings or whatever. The men look after the business and report to Ajjayya. They are all like the pillars of the house, never saying anything, however heavy their burdens.

Akku, held back by nothing, was not one to miss festive meals at other people's houses. The right side of her face seemingly squashed in, her dimly lit eyes moving, her lips forever trying to hide her jutting out teeth, she stood at a mere four and three-quarter foot tall. She would fill her nose with

15

snuff and then rub her towel sharply across it, this way and that, like a saw. She would pass her hand over her face and then wipe it on her sari which fell free from her shoulder, and then walk along, brandishing her towel. There was no shortage of people who spoke to her in riddles: 'O cloth that spreads, fan that sways, where will you eat today?' 'Where is the banner off to?' they would ask her to her face. She would answer if she felt like it. Otherwise she would snap, 'To your grandfather's death anniversary,' and leap away nimbly, like an evil spirit.

When she sat down to eat, she just slurped away quickly, head bent, oblivious to everything around her. She would clutch some of the delicacies in her left hand, wrap them up in the same towel that smelt of snuff and come home to sit alone in the verandah, stuffing herself, ungenerous even to a crow. She was expert at this.

She never missed the festive meals specially prepared to satisfy the whims of pregnant women, or to celebrate the naming ceremony of a baby. Once there, she wouldn't stir from the side of the pregnant woman who sat wearing tasselled flowers of seven kinds; weight upon weight. Akku, sitting there like an idiot would be sighted by strangers, or people from the husband's family. 'Who is this dishevelled creature, Devamma? Get her away from there.' The girl's relatives would come and plead timidly with her to sit elsewhere. But Akku was deaf to everything. It was the same at naming ceremonies too. She would let go of the ropes that held up the cradle only when she left for home. Sometimes she even sang a couple of lullabies after the guests had all left. And it seemed that people could never sleep in peace until they had finished mocking her. 'Akku, a whole flock of crows came to sit by the window to hear you singing like a cuckoo.'

Then Siriyatte got married. What happened on the day of the wedding is best heard in her own words.

'The bridegroom's party had arrived. No one had stayed with me, they had all rushed off to the pandal; I was very nervous, scared. Then Akku came in. "O, Akku," I said, feeling relieved. "Either Akku or her shadow," she retorted, sharply. She stood at some distance and stared at me. "Why have you dolled yourself up like this?" she asked. I didn't say a thing. Her voice sounded cracked and rasping. I just sat, numb, looking at her. "Come here," she said. "Why?" I asked. "Do as you are told," she said. I wanted to shout, call someone. Then I thought I'd better not. "Akku, aren't you well?" I enquired. She rushed straight at me and in a flash tore off the flowers from my hair. "This will do. No one who marries you for your beauty alone will keep you happy. You may write that on a wall." I tell you, honestly, I felt as if I couldn't breathe. Akku is attractive in her own way, although she is a bit short. But then she looked like a demon, just for a moment. I was very upset. Not because she tore off the flowers, but because of the way she stared, not blinking once. "How terribly hot it is," she said as she went out, fanning herself with one hand and wiping her face with the towel which she held in the other. If I had told this to Vasu, would he have left her alone? He would have thrashed her and locked her up in a room. Anyway, Doddatte came in then and told me off properly regardless of the fact that I was a bride. She re-did my hair and put the flowers in once again.'

Akku created a rumpus on the day Siriyatte left home after the wedding. 'Where has my husband gone and perished? Bring him back this instant.' Not a word other than that. She threw her towel into the air over and over again, repeating the same thing. Uncle Vasu who was standing there, cleaning his teeth with a small stick, said, 'Look there, in that enclosure,' and pointed at the cook, Babu Bhatta, who lay snoring beyond the bamboo screen, totally unaware of the commotion about him. Bhanu Chikki added, 'There's your husband. Nobody knows when he arrived, no one saw him. I heard him shouting, Akku, Akku, so I brought him in.' But Akku's tantrums didn't subside. The louder she shouted, the funnier it seemed. Satyamani, a boy just so high, couldn't control himself and ran to Babu Bhatta, and woke him up. Giggling away, he said to him, 'Babu Bhatta, they say you are Akku's husband.' 'I, married to her?' said Babu Bhatta. 'Good Heavens, she would break my limbs and put me in the fire – she'd sell me for a handful of puffed rice.' We were ecstatic, intoxicated with laughter. Meanwhile Thammaniah, black as coal, who was sitting leaning against the wall, breaking areca nuts and watching the drama unfold, joined in the fray. He was used to taking female roles

17

in the Yakshagana and now came swaying and beating his chest. 'Beloved, I am here, your husband. What do you want of me?' He looked around theatrically, smiling at everyone, but leapt back in pain as Akku rushed at him and bit him. She ran inside, got herself a glass of water and gulped it down. 'Thammaniah, get lost! Mind your own business. Don't interfere in mine. Shall I tell you now who your wife slept with the other day?' Her voice was as sharp as a flashing sword. Thammaniah's laughter was put out by the heightened merriment of those around him.

'Never mind, Thammaniah. Everyone knows she has lost her senses. Don't get upset,' Uncle Vasu said in an effort to console him. Thammaniah's wife, who had till this moment been watching happily, head resting on her bent knee, suddenly got up and ran inside, sari stuffed into her mouth as if she was holding back sobs. 'Bhanu, go in and see to her. Decent folk will be compelled to hang themselves because of this wretched creature,' said Uncle Vasu. 'Wandering all over the place and picking up filthy language!'

Akku who had shut herself up appeared only the next morning after the cowherd had taken away the animals for grazing. Anthanna who was around asked her, 'What happened, Akku? Did you find your husband or not?' This, in spite of being told that Akku should be left alone. 'I've just buried him,' she replied. Her face was distorted because of a sleepless night. She did indeed look as if she had washed her hands and feet after burying someone. 'What happens to your children then?' someone asked. 'What else is my lover for? He will look after them,' she spat out. 'What a predicament! The poor man,' someone else whispered and laughed. She appeared not to hear this.

Akku sat leaning against a pillar, her hair dishevelled, the vermilion mark bright on her forehead. Doddatte saw her and started rocking back and forth as she sat slicing green stems in circles. She was well known for composing songs on the spur of the moment and she sang now:

Akku's red mark on her forehead is lovely
and so are her curls.

She is indeed the loveliest
among all on earth.

Doddatte had dragged home her wandering husband and
lorded it over him. Eventually he died. 'It would have been
dreadful, had he lived. It's blissful now,' she had pronounced.
She spent her time teasing Akku, slicing vegetables and earning
her keep by doing chores; she was nearing sixty. Bow-legged
Doddatte looked all right when you saw her sitting down, but
her back arched when she stood up.

Akku listened to the song and blew her nose. She wiped her
fingers on her sari and asked, 'Where is my towel?' 'I saw it
going past the gate this morning. I was told it was on its way to
Manja's hotel for a cup of coffee,' answered little Satya and took
to his heels. Akku laughed, but did not make an effort to chase
him. Then she sniffed and turned towards Doddatte, 'Bow-
legged Subbi! I'll break your back and carry it over my shoulder
like a bow. Just you watch out!'

'My husband is in hell now, blessed woman. I would like to
stay in one piece as long as I live. Don't harm me in any way,'
Doddatte said in a tone of mock surrender. 'Poor soul,' she
added later, quietly to herself.

'Why do you say that? Poor soul indeed! Why do I need your
pity? I'm not a widow like you. Are you pitying me because my
husband went off to eat what he could beg at the roadside,
leaving me behind? Remember I was the one who pushed
Thimmappiah of the long house off me right into the pond. You
just listen to me, witch . . .' She would have gone on but for
the arrival of Doddajjayya. People ran helter and skelter as they
heard the sound of his breathing and the tapping of his walking
stick. 'Hey, Vasu!' Uncle Vasu came flying like Hanumantha,
the monkey God. 'Go on. Thrash her and cool her down a bit.'
Akku screamed as she sprinted away to shut herself up in the
corner room, as if Doddajjayya's words alone had raised welts
on her body.

Akku was Siriyatte's sister, but she was 'Akku' to everyone.
Even a newborn baby could call her that and not look for a
kinship term corresponding to the relationship. There must
have been a big age gap between Akku and Siriyatte, but all the

same Siriyatte looked older than Akku. And Akku had been as she was ever since Siriyatte was old enough to be aware of such things. 'It doesn't matter what you lose, so long as it isn't your sanity. Otherwise you are held in contempt not only by your own parents, but by the entire town,' Siriyatte used to say.

Akku had feigned pregnancy ever since her husband went away with a Sanyasi. Of course it never seemed anything but absolutely real to her. On one occasion she went around complaining loudly of a stomach ache. She made such a fuss of it that everyone who set foot into the house was told of her pain. 'I'll get rid of your pain once and for all,' offered Doddajjayya, brandishing a broom. 'Appiah, my baby will die. The sin will be on your head,' she screamed as she bent down and made sure her stomach would not be hit. After she had been thrashed, she stayed in her room, curled up, for a fortnight or so, without saying a thing. Her corner room was where all the junk was dumped. A broom had never been used there, it was filled with cobwebs. It stood in a corner, all alone. They even said that evil spirits lurked in that room.

Once, when we were all playing house, we heard a jangling sound from inside the corner room. Our throats went dry. We dragged our unwilling feet to tell the news to the others, and Uncle Vasu and Anthanna came hurrying to investigate. We were told off when we followed them. 'How dare you girls be so forward! Get back at once or else . . .' We were pushed back like cattle. We pretended to go away, but came back stealthily. Uncle Vasu pushed the door open slowly with one finger. 'Anthanna, what sort of ghost is this?' he laughed. We peeped in too. Akku was sitting by the brass cradle. The chains had been removed and placed inside. She was shaking them in an effort to rock the cradle. 'Quiet,' she warned. 'The baby has just dropped off after its feed.' Uncle Vasu laughed, screeching like chalk on a blackboard. Doddatte who came in swaying, said, 'Ask her if she had plenty of milk,' raising further splinters of laughter. And Uncle Vasu did ask, shamelessly. Akku arranged the folds of her sari and said, 'Yes; it will do for now.' 'Utterly mad! Well, never mind. When did you give birth to the baby?'

'Last night.'

There was talk the whole day about the ghost that had given

birth in the corner room. Uncle Vasu was afraid that if Akku was left there in that state, then a real ghost might come and strangle her. 'Don't you worry about it,' said Doddatte, 'This creature has already pushed away the ghost that really came to catch her.'

Akku was pregnant again the next day. Now the pregnancy was a permanent one. And her husband still did not return.

Then, one day, at last, news spread of Akku's husband's arrival, reaching even the people who were sitting upstairs in the house, reading quietly. Apparently he had been told of Akku's pregnancy on the instant he arrived and very nearly went away, shocked. However, on being assured that it was only a story, he changed his mind. Now he sat in the verandah with Doddajjayya, talking in a phlegm-ridden voice. He had neither a fat belly, a large moustache, a short body nor a rough face as we had imagined. Indeed he was skeletal, with limbs like sticks of wood. He sat hunched, wrapped in a dhoti which had enough mud upon it for the sprouting of seeds. Doddajjayya sat stiffly in his big chair, with an utterly joyless face. Even the tips of his moustache looked askance at this man, as if he were worth nothing.

Akku's husband was not able to sit still. He was squirming away like a watersnake. He had left her behind to follow the wretched Swami, remember? He had just walked off. The Swami had gone to Kashi and the Himalayas. So had he. Now he went on and on . . . He should not be considered a good for nothing. One could earn a tidy sum by staying with the Swami . . . Doddajjayya was not responding in any way. He wasn't even looking at him.

And then, where was Akku when she was sent for? She was not to be seen anywhere inside. 'Look for her. How can you say you can't find her?' the order came. Uncle Vasu, who went looking for her, had found her near the tank by the woods. 'Don't jump into the tank. Your husband has arrived,' he had said. 'Give him his bus fare and send him back. I came here because I saw him,' she had replied, quite indifferently. He had moved heaven and earth to bring her back. He now warned, wiping the sweat off his face, 'If you scold her and she jumps into the tank, there'll be nothing that I can do.'

Akku entered the house through the back door, but would not move from there for anything. She stood by the gaping paddy pounder, right heel against the wall, all crooked and wide-eyed. Doddajjayya, for his part, waited in the front verandah for a while, and then brought Sankappa, Akku's husband, inside.

'Akku . . .,' called Doddajjayya.

'Akku died three days and three nights ago. Did this wretch come to perform the last rites? Ask him that,' Akku said in a voice like a blazing fire.

Sankappa stood with his head bent, his face looking as if it had been partly consumed by cockroaches. Doddatte needled him further. 'So you have come back at last! Have you run through all the girls in town, or what?'

Sankappa stayed for two days. Akku continued to sleep in her corner room; and she did not come inside the house. Sankappa slept in the verandah, all curled up; a simpleton who knew nothing.

The next morning, Doddatte whispered to Uncle Vasu, 'Last night, I sat by the bottom step, waiting to see if this creature was really a Sanyasi. Would you believe it if I told you the fellow got up around midnight and quietly found his way to the corner room? It was only after watching him that I went inside to sleep.'

We girls were sitting there stringing flowers for worship and could not help hearing this. We felt like plugging our ears though when she added more loudly, 'These girls, they are all ears when they are growing up.' Was this not the same Doddatte who had goaded Uncle Vasu into asking Akku whether she had enough milk? She was the one who said whatever she chose, whenever she chose, unmindful of who might be around. And now she was being so sanctimonious. Was she not herself a woman too? These speculations began to mix with the flowers we were stringing.

Then Akku's voice exploded like a demon's.

'Hey, you whom they call Doddatte! Come here quickly. There is something I have to tell you. Bring some betel leaves with you . . .'

Doddatte heard the excitement in her voice, and rose to go,

saying that the slut was probably going to die. Behind her went the rest of the household, the servants and us. Akku sat there, rocking herself, one leg laid on the other. 'Hey, listen. He caught hold of me as soon as he came in. "Much better than a woman by the roadside," he said. "Get lost, scum," I said. "Don't touch me, I'm pregnant." "Who's responsible?" he asked me. "Thimmappiah of the long house," I said. He wouldn't leave me alone even then. I'll teach you, I thought, and pulled out the cradle chains. I hurled them at him over and over again. What do you think the wretch did? He wrapped a thin towel around himself and ran for all he was worth. Whatever you say, Doddatte, Thimmappiah was any day better than this creature. His chest . . . his lips . . .'

We could hear Doddajjayya's walking stick. Uncle Vasu put his hand over Akku's mouth and dragged her along to the large kitchen, where he pulled out a stick from a bundle of firewood and started beating her with it as if he were beating out clothes on a stone slab. 'If this fool wanders about all over the place, not only Thimmappiah, but his father too will get hold of her. Then the wandering will come to a stop once and for all.' The beating continued.

'He might not even have laid a finger on her, for all we know. If we believe this mad creature and go after him, we might very well get our faces slapped,' said Anthanna, rolling the betel nut from one side of his mouth to the other. 'Really! Thimmappiah of all people! Has any seed that he has sown ever sprouted?' His laughter grated.

'Drag Sankappa here. Let them both get out of here and hang themselves.'

So even the pillars of the house had found voice. Doddajjayya came in, trembling with anger. 'What did I do to deserve this,' he cried out, as if in pain. 'Hit her harder. Let her die. No one will regret it.'

'Appiah, Vasu is thrashing me. He is killing me and my baby too. Appiah ask him who he was after when he was sitting on Thimmappiah's verandah the other day . . .' Vasu hit her hard on the mouth as she screamed on. No one stopped him. No one asked him to let go. No one pulled Akku away. The audience grew; it seemed they wanted the scene to go on

23

indefinitely, as if they were prepared to listen endlessly to the perfect dovetailing of screams and blows. Bhanu Chikki stood, hands at her waist. 'She's nothing but a raving lunatic, and she turns everyone else into one.' She sounded as if she was sobbing.

'If I was beaten like that, I'd surely be dead by now. People say the mad are really strong,' a female voice spoke up.

But Akku's screaming did not stop. Neither did her accusations. And she did not die. It was Uncle Vasu who came out, defeated. 'Get away, everyone,' he cried, and bolted the door.

We thought she might run up behind him and scream for the door to be opened! We were wrong. Our desire to open the door for her surreptitiously, when no one was around, lost its edge. Akku stayed inside the room shouting and waving her towel.

'Thimmappiah's wife is waiting for you. Run to her. Run quickly, you shameless wretch. There! Are you going to beat me now?'

Translated from the Kannada
by Padma R. Sharma

KAMALA DAS

Kamala Das was born in 1934. Her mother was Balamani Amma, a well-known poet in Malayalam.

Kamala Das has published many collections of short stories under the name of Madhavi Kutty. She is best known in India for her collections of poems in English (*Summer in Calcutta*, *The Descendants* and *The Old Playhouse*). Her poetry has won her many awards and has been translated into Serbo-Croat, Swedish, French, German and Russian.

The house described in the story 'Summer Vacation' belongs to a tarawad of the Nayar caste of Kerala. A tarawad is a matrilineal household made up of a woman, her brothers and sisters, and the children of all the sisters. The term tarawad also refers to the family house and estate which were originally held in common by all its members, and administered by the eldest brother. To be a tarawadi, to belong to a tarawad, was also to belong to an aristocratic lineage and to possess certain attributes of honour and integrity.

Here Muthassi lives alone, helped only by the house steward. Ammu will be the last of the tarawad.

The old houses were built around a courtyard: the vadakkini and tekkini were the rooms facing north and south. The coconut grove referred to at the beginning of the story marks the boundary of the cremation ground where the ancestors were cremated facing south, in the direction of Yama, god of death.

Summer Vacation

It was always there, as long as I could remember, a small, emaciated tree, somewhat bent and with shrivelled up branches. That was a summer with no hint of rains. I watched the tree, its leaves, and above the few leaves, the spider's web hanging from a bare, sickle-shaped branch.

That tree was the only one of its kind, in a field full of coconut palms planted in memory of family ancestors who had been cremated on the southern side of the house. I wondered if it was telling us, 'I know I should not be here. But please take pity on me. Don't destroy me.'

I was walking one day with Muthassi – so I called my grandmother – picking up tiny dry miniature coconuts now and then and collecting them in the folds of my skirt. I asked her, 'What is the name of that lonely tree?'

Muthassi's eyesight had never been too good, not even in her youth. She blinked once or twice, straining to look in the direction that I pointed. She said, 'That one? It a nyaval tree.'

'Nyaval?'

'Yes, Ammu, nyaval. Haven't you seen nyaval fruit? Maybe you haven't. Deep purple in colour, about the size of a marble.'

'Can you eat nyaval fruit?'

'Of course you can. They have a slightly sweet and sour taste. I used to eat them a lot when I was a schoolgirl. And that reminds me of a girl, a certain Devu from Madathil House. She was famous for her black tongue. Once she remarked that my eyes reminded her of two dark nyaval fruit on a ceramic plate. I was really scared that I would go blind. I couldn't get a wink of sleep that night.'

Suddenly Muthassi bent down and picked up a gauze-like dry leaf lying under a coconut tree and said, 'I can use this as a strainer when I make oil out of scraped coconut kernel.'

I continued walking towards the nyaval tree and asked Muthassi, 'Where is that Devu you talked about now?'

'Oh, Devu,' Muthassi reflected with a wistful smile. 'She died a long time ago. Now I am the only one left. All my friends – they are all gone. Karthu, Vadakkemuri Chinnammu, Marath Kunju – all my companions, dead and gone.'

'Are they all dead?'

'Hmm.'

'So now you are alone, Muthassi, without any friends.'

I felt sad for my Muthassi, lonely in her old age, so I went up to her and hugged her close.

'Don't worry, Muthassi. Haven't you got me? I'll always be with you,' I consoled her.

'Yes, Ammu. That's more than enough for Muthassi.' She tightened her hold on my hand, and so we crossed the field and reached the courtyard in front of the house.

'Muthassi, just look at your hands, with all the veins standing out! I can't even see the veins on my hands. Why is that?'

'You are a small child, Ammu, whereas Muthassi is a worn-out old woman.' Muthassi threw the dry leaf into the front verandah, and we went on to the bathing enclosure next to the pond. A towel and a red soap dish with a piece of soap in it were lying on the steps leading to the pond.

Seeing the soap dish, Muthassi exclaimed, 'I forgot that I had left that soap here. I am lucky the crow didn't steal it.'

'Why, Muthassi, do crows eat soap?'

'No, but a crow might take it away, attracted by the colour.'

Dear Muthassi, I thought, how naive she is. That used piece of soap was not at all pretty. And yet she thought the crow would steal it. A piece of soap worn down by use, looking like a fragment of a tile! Was it likely the crow would be tempted enough to carry it off?

'So Muthassi, you think the crow knows what is pretty?'

'Of course. Is there any doubt? The crow has a keen eye for beauty. Otherwise why does it carry off the small oil bowls? Ammu, birds are very intelligent. They have more common sense and knowledge than human beings.'

'Why is that?'

'It is like that. That's all.' With that cryptic remark, Muthassi took my dress off, dipped it in water, soaped it and placed it on a stone.

'Muthassi . . .'

'Yes, Ammu.'

'When my school re-opens and I go off to Calcutta, who will come with you to the pond?'

'No one, Ammu. No one will come with me.'

'Won't you be afraid, Muthassi?'

She looked up from her washing, and said with a laugh, 'Why should Muthassi be afraid, Ammu? She is no longer a child. Do you know how old your Muthassi is?'

I shook my head.

'Sixty-eight. I will be sixty-nine this coming Chingam.'

'When will you die, Muthassi?'

'How am I to know the time of my death? It's all in the hands of God. When it's time for me to go, he will take me. No one from this Tarawad has lived up to this age. My mother died when she was forty; my uncle at forty-five. And grandmother, if I remember correctly didn't quite reach fifty. As for Kamalam . . . I am a sinner, that is why I stay alive. I often wonder what further sufferings are in store for me before I die.'

Muthassi wiped the tears that welled up in her eyes with one end of her mundu and noisily cleared her nose.

'But Muthassi, are you going to die soon?' I persisted.

She tried hard to laugh. I could see her small teeth, worn down and reddened. Her mouth had the fragrance of the betel leaves and nuts that she chewed. I put my arms around her neck, my face against her cheek and pleaded, 'Promise me that you won't die, Muthassi, promise me.'

Muthassi's eyes filled with tears once again. But she smiled and said, 'All right, Ammu. I promise I won't die. Is that enough?'

Some women came to visit Muthassi. Seeing me, they asked, 'Isn't this your daughter's child?'

Muthassi objected to this catechism. 'Who else could she be? Do you imagine I would keep other people's children in my house?'

The women laughed in a conciliatory fashion.

'Of course we recognised her, but we thought we should ask.

That's all. Who brought her home? Has Velayudha Menon come as well?'

'No. He brought her as far as Trichur. He wasn't able to get leave. Sankunni Nayar and I went up to Trichur and brought Ammu back.'

'Why did you have to travel all the way to Trichur, Ammukutty Amma? Sankunni Nayar could have gone by himself and brought her home.'

'Indeed! What an idea! Bharati, do you really think Velayudha Menon would have entrusted his child to a mere house steward? As long as I am alive such a thing is not likely. It is not a problem for me to go up to Trichur. I always tell the taxi driver to come and spend the previous night here so that Sankunni Nayar and I can set off before daybreak. We usually reach Trichur railway station at exactly the right moment to see the train arrive.'

'The child has grown since the last time we saw her,' the fat woman who wore a necklace studded with red stones said. She had a sleeping infant on her lap.

'She has grown a wee bit taller,' Muthassi conceded. 'But she hasn't put on any weight. She looks fatter because of the clothes she is wearing.'

At this stage, I put in, 'I am fat.'

The thin woman with protruding teeth covered her mouth with one hand and laughed. Then Muthassi lost her temper. She turned to me and said, 'You call yourself fat! You are just skin and bone. No, you haven't put on any weight, neither do you look pretty. Just look at your face – so dark and drawn.'

Muthassi made me sit next to her and began to smooth my unruly hair. 'Ah,' I protested, 'Ah!' All of a sudden the bald child lying on the fat woman's lap began to scream.

'Stop it,' the fat woman chided the child. 'He is a rascal! Screaming like that just when I am having a moment's rest.'

Muthassi said, 'He must be hungry. That's why he's crying. Why don't you feed him?'

'No, no, he's just had his feed. The rascal deserves a sound slap.' She tried to frighten the child by rolling her eyes in anger. 'I'll kill you,' she said. 'Just you wait. One of these days, I'll really kill you.'

29

I moved closer to Muthassi and asked her in a whisper, 'Will she really kill the child?' Meanwhile the child continued to scream at a higher pitch. I thought that his head looked like a huge rubber ball with a hole in it. Or perhaps it was more like a yellow balloon.

Muthassi couldn't hear what I said. She asked me, 'What are you saying? I can't hear you.'

'Will she kill that child?' I repeated.

'Who are you talking about?'

'That child's mother.'

Muthassi burst out laughing and said to the woman, 'Bharati, did you hear what Ammu is asking me? She wants to know whether you'll kill your child. She thinks you really mean to do what you say.'

The fat woman asked me in a horrified voice, 'Ammu, would mothers ever kill their own children? No one loves a child more than its own mother does.'

'Poor child! How can she know?' commented the dark woman with greying hair, who had been sitting silently chewing betel leaves until then. 'Just think of her fate. So very sad.'

The woman whom Muthassi called Bharati mused, 'Motherhood and moonlight are alike, so comforting, so essential to life. There can be no happiness without either.'

At this point, Muthassi suddenly stood up and straightened her mundu. She said, 'You must excuse me. It's nearly four o'clock. I must go to the kitchen and see if the coffee is ready. My servant Achutan is a slowcoach; he never does anything on his own. You come with me Ammu. Let's see what he is up to.'

Achutan was sitting on the kitchen floor, arranging parippu vadas on a plate. The mundu that he was wearing was as black as the kitchen walls. He got up as soon as he saw Muthassi and said, 'I couldn't get poovan bananas, so I got the Mysore variety.'

'Hmm,' said Muthassi, signifying assent. She lifted the lid of the coffee kettle with a kitchen prong to check whether the water was boiling. The fireplace was lit by a small hurricane lamp.

'Achutan,' Muthassi said in an exasperated voice, 'Can't you clean this lamp at least once in a while? Do I always have to remind you of everything?'

'I did try to clean and polish that lamp,' Achutan replied. 'The soot won't shift though. I think it is time to change the glass.'

'I don't think the glass needs to be changed. You are just looking for an excuse to avoid work.'

Then Muthassi bent her head to examine the bananas that Achutan had arranged on a plate. Achutan looked at me with a sly and knowing grin on his face. I had often caught Achutan watching me with that knowing look. I turned my face away in distaste.

'Achutan, bring four plates of bananas and vadas to the Tekkini. Let the child have her snack here.'

I asked, 'Can't I have my snack at the Tekkini too?'

An emphatic 'No' was the answer.

'Why, Muthassi?'

No explanation from Muthassi. Just a curt, 'That's the way I want it done. That's all.'

As Muthassi stepped out of the kitchen, she instructed Achutan in a lowered voice, 'Before you pour the milk into our coffee make sure you have set some aside for Ammu to drink at night. You don't have any discrimination Achutan, and sometimes your excessive generosity to outsiders can be trying.'

Achutan looked at me once again with the same sly knowing grin. As soon as Muthassi left the kitchen he leaned one leg on the wall next to the fireplace, removed a bidi from behind his ear, and said to me in a philosophical tone, 'Do you know where Achutan draws his life energy from? It's from this bidi. Not from tea or cooked rice or rice gruel – Achutan cannot function without smoking at least two bundles of bidis every day. Do you know that child?'

I did not reply. Achutan lit a bidi and started to smoke. He then lifted the coffee kettle off the fire, using a folded piece of paper.

'I will give you your milk first. Only after that will I serve the others their coffee. Satisfied? Don't you know that Achutan cares for you more than for anyone else in this house?'

I sat on the steps leading to the kitchen verandah. Achutan

thought that I hadn't heard what he said. So, biting on his bidi, he repeated with a peculiar slur, 'Do you know it?'

I laughed scornfully.

At this, Achutan removed his bidi from his mouth and put it away by the fireplace. He continued earnestly, 'Not merely in this house. In the entire village, there isn't a single soul whom Achutan loves as much as he loves you. Are you aware of that child?'

I shook my head, meaning that I didn't know. Wanting to change the subject, I asked him, 'Where were you born, Achutan?'

'Achutan's birth place! It's nowhere nearby. It is a place called Perindri, you must have heard of it. Oh dear, I can't afford to stay here forever indulging in small talk with you. I mustn't forget those greedy women waiting in the Tekkini. I have to serve that set of gossips their coffee and snacks, or else your Muthassi will kill me.'

'Achutan, you don't like those women, do you?' I asked in a lowered voice.

'No, I can't stand the very sight of them. I don't like women who go and gossip from one house to another.'

He put four vadas on a plate and gave it to me. 'By the time you finish eating those vadas your milk will be ready.'

Even the vadas smelt of Achutan's bidis. But somehow I didn't have the heart to scold him.

At noon Muthassi sat on the verandah, reading excerpts from the Ramayana. She used a pair of broken spectacles, holding them to her nose with her left hand.

I was very sleepy, so I stretched myself out on the bare tiled floor. I could see the sky through the railings of the verandah: a glistening, silvery expanse.

'Muthassi,' I called out.

'Mm?' She stopped her reading and turned to me.

'Will you be unhappy when I leave?'

'Yes.'

'Terribly unhappy?'

'Why should I be terribly unhappy, Ammu? You'll come again next year, won't you?'

'But . . . if you die meanwhile . . .'

Muthassi brushed aside my fears with a laugh.

'I won't die so soon, Ammu. I will live long enough to see you married and have children. Isn't that enough?'

'Muthassi, please tell me. Who will I marry?'

'Who knows!' Muthassi turned her gaze to the sky. 'I don't know. Only God knows.'

It was very comforting to put my head on Muthassi's lap. Gradually my eyes closed. I could hear the humming of a bumble bee from some part of the verandah. Muthassi explained, 'The bumble bee is building its nest.'

Very much later, I woke up to find that Muthassi was not there. I was lying on a woven grass mat with a pillow under my head. Where had Muthassi disappeared? I had the strange sensation of having slept for years together, during which time Muthassi had died. I sat up, startled. The bumble bee was still humming.

'Muthassi,' I called out.

From somewhere below came Muthassi's answer to my call. I got up, went slowly down the stairs and reached the Tekkini. Nani Amma who earned her livelihood by pounding rice was there with her five-year-old daughter. As soon as the little girl saw me, she hid her face with one end of her mother's mundu.

Muthassi was sitting by the inner courtyard, making cotton wicks for the oil lamp. She had stretched her legs out on a bamboo mat and was putting away the cotton wicks, one by one, into a biscuit tin.

'Nani, do you think I can go on having avil made just to provide you with a job? The avil you pounded last time is not yet finished. I know you have a lot of money worries, but I have no way of helping you if you come to me every other day with your requests.'

Nani Amma bowed her head. She stroked her daughter's hair and smiled. I was fascinated by the iron ring she wore on her right hand, a ring with intricate work on it. She wore a shabby mundu and torn blouse. And yet, I thought, she was lucky to be wearing such an unusual ring.

I went near them to take a closer look at the child. She came up to my shoulders, and was dark skinned – so dark that it was difficult to make out where the roots of her hair started. I would call that colour the very essence of black. The only clothing she had on was a skirt with red spots. There was a knotted black thread round her neck.

I asked her, 'What is your name?' She did not reply, but hid her face and most of her body behind Nani Amma's mundu.

Nani Amma answered, 'Amini – that's her name.'

Now Muthassi asked, 'How old is this girl, Nani?'

'She was born when that terrible storm struck our village,' Nani Amma said dramatically. 'Everyone was in a hurry to leave their houses with their beds and their cooking vessels. Only I remained, unable to get up from where I was lying. I told myself, if I am destined to die like this, then let me die.'

'But the fact is,' Muthassi interjected jokingly, 'that you didn't die. That means your time hadn't come, Nani.'

Putting away all the cotton wicks in the tin, Muthassi stood up. 'Come, Nani, come to the Vadakkini. Let me give the little girl something to eat, maybe the dosas left over from breakfast.'

The Vadakkini, as I remember it, was a dark room with a jackfruit in one corner, kept there for ripening, along with a basket of tamarind.

'Sit down,' Muthassi said to Nani Amma. Nani Amma whispered softly into the child's ears. She wiped the floor by brushing it with her bare feet, took the mundu from her shoulders, spread it on the floor and sat on it. The child stood behind her, only her shining eyes visible in the darkness. It seemed to me that there was no child, only those eyes suspended in the darkness.

I went to the kitchen in search of Muthassi. She was busy putting out pieces of dosa on a plantain leaf. The dosas were stale, having been left in the open, on the window-sill, since morning.

'Are you going to give those pieces of dosa to that child?' I asked Muthassi.

She nodded.

'Haven't they been left in the open for rather a long time? I saw flies hovering there. Don't you think the child might fall ill if she eats them?'

Muthassi hesitated for a moment. Then she said with a laugh,

'All right, Ammu. I won't give them to her. What about the snacks that were prepared this afternoon? Are you happy now?'

Half an hour later, I saw Nani Amma getting ready to go home, having had the food and tea. She was carrying a small basket containing the rice Muthassi had given her. She said to her child, 'Amini, just hold this basket for a moment. Let me tie my mundu properly.'

That child pretended not to hear her mother, and turned her head away in a different direction. This indifference infuriated her mother, who said, 'What are you doing, girl, star-gazing? Didn't you hear me asking you to hold the basket?'

With great reluctance the girl held out her hands to take the basket, but it slipped. The contents spilled out in all directions: first the rice, then the tamarind which had been concealed underneath.

'Useless girl!' Nani Amma rebuked her daughter and pulled her by the hair. She sat down, hastily gathered the rice and the tamarind into the basket and left the place in a hurry. Her daughter followed, weeping copiously.

I knew that Muthassi had only given the rice to Nani Amma. It became clear to me that she had stolen the tamarind. I was furious with her. I thought stealing was really low, dishonourable. I decided I should not let her get away with it.

I ran after her and called out her name. She turned her head, but on seeing me continued walking faster. Her child hadn't stopped weeping. Finally I caught up with her and questioned her. 'Nani Amma, why did you steal the tamarind? Is it right to take other people's property?'

'I didn't steal,' Nani Amma denied stoutly. She continued walking. The red sand kicked up by her retreating feet swirled around in the courtyard.

'I am going to tell Muthassi,' I said. 'You shouldn't steal things. Don't come to this house again. You are just a petty thief.'

That stopped Nani Amma. She held out the basket to me and said in a huff, 'Take it. Take back your precious rice and tamarind. I don't want anything from you.'

I was dumbstruck. I extended my hands to take the basket, like a lifeless wooden puppet. Nani Amma picked up her daughter and made to walk off. Then came her parting shot. 'We are poor people, child.' Her voice shook as she said, 'And you – you are the rich.'

I left the basket on the ground and ran back. I felt like weeping. I felt – as I had never done before in my life – that I had somehow committed a grave sin. I was too shaken to mention the incident to Muthassi. What happened to that basket? Did anyone pick it up? Did Nani Amma herself come back for it? I wanted to know nothing more about it.

It was time for me to go back to Calcutta. When we reached Trichur railway station, Sankunni Nayar said pompously, 'The train is due to arrive in precisely half an hour and two minutes. Velayudha Menon would have boarded the train at Cochin. The first-class coach will come in at the other end of the platform and the third class coaches will be at this end.'

'Will you please stop bleating, Sankunni Nayar,' Muthassi said, cuttingly. 'I am quite familiar with all these details. This is not the first time I have come to Trichur railway station.'

Muthassi got out of the car, gave an eight-anna coin to the taxi driver and said, 'It is the child's gift to you.' The driver put the coin into his pocket with a smile and saluted me.

Muthassi wore a gold-bordered mundu and veshti and had a gold tulasi mala around her neck. She looked regal and the people at the railway station made way for her in a respectful manner.

The clerk at the platform ticket counter asked her, 'So the child is going back after her vacation?'

Muthassi did not deign to answer. She had an air of aloofness which she reserved for strangers. She held on to my hand, crossed the revolving door and entered the station platform.

I wanted to go to the other end of the platform where the books were sold, but Muthassi would not allow me. She led me to the Ladies Waiting Room and made me sit down. She then seated herself opposite me, in a large easy chair. I could see a Brahmin woman in a red sari trying to catch Muthassi's eye. Later, when Sankunni Nayar came, she said to him, 'Sankunni Nayar, she wants a book. Please choose her a good one.'

Sankunni Nayar put the rupee note Muthassi gave him into the pocket of his green shirt.

'Don't buy any of those vulgar books.'

'What are you saying? Am I crazy, that I would buy vulgar books for the child?'

After he had gone, still muttering, Muthassi leaned back in her chair and smiled. 'When you come home next year you will have grown bigger.'

'What about you, Muthassi? Will you have grown bigger too?'

Muthassi laughed. 'At this age? Will Muthassi grow bigger? Oh no! If at all, I will grow smaller and smaller, until I am all shrivelled up.'

I suddenly remembered that small, lonely nyaval tree.

'Muthassi.'

'Yes, dear.'

'That nyaval tree. How long has it been there? Who planted it?'

'Who planted it? Who indeed! I don't know. It's been there as far back as I remember.'

'Will it bear fruit?'

'Will it? I don't know. Even if it does, the fruit won't be large.'

'Why?'

'That's the way it is. That's all.'

'Muthassi.'

'What, Ammu?'

'Perhaps the tree will bear fruit by the time I come home next year. Then you and I will pluck the fruit and eat them, together.'

After depositing my small leather suitcase and the Malayalam book, which Sankunni Nayar had bought for me, safely in the compartment, my father went and stood at the door. Muthassi's face looked flushed. She asked my father, 'Have you taken an oath not to come to our place? She was my only child – my daughter, my son, my all. She died. But you are still a son to me.'

Muthassi wiped her nose and face with the edge of her veshti. Tears still streamed down her cheeks.

My father said, 'I shall come next year, definitely. I don't yet have the courage. Please don't take it amiss. Remember how

37

we used to come, every year, the two of us, to that house. And now, how to come there, all by myself? Please don't misunderstand me, mother. I just cannot do it as yet.'

'I shall never misunderstand any of you. Especially my children. Never that.'

The train moved away from the station; my father pulled down the glass shutters of the window.

'Father?'

'Yes dear.'

'Will Muthassi die by this time next year?'

'No.'

'She won't, will she? Are you sure?'

'Yes. I am sure. Muthassi will never die.'

'Is that the truth?'

My father put me on his lap and kissed my forehead. He looked at me with tears in his eyes. I still remember the words he said. 'I promise. Your Muthassi will never die. She'll never die.'

'Will never die, will never die . . .' the wheels of the train seemed to chant.

Translated from the Malayalam
by Vasanti Sankaranarayanan and Asha Bijlani

QURRATULAIN HYDER

Qurratulain Hyder is considered one of the most important writers of modern Urdu fiction. She was still in her teens when she published her first novel, *Mere bhi Samakhane* (My Temples Too), but is best known for her novel, *River of Fire* (1959), which has been translated into the fourteen major Indian languages. In 1967 she received the National Sahitya Akademi award for a collection of short stories. She was the managing editor of *Imprint*, Bombay, and from 1968 to 1975 was on the editorial staff of the *Illustrated Weekly of India*.

'Memories of an Indian Childhood' was published in the *Illustrated Weekly of India* (1970) in the author's translation. It is set in Dehra Dun, and reflects the changing lifestyle and values in this most colonial of Indian towns in the days just before Independence.

Kamala Jharia and Kalu Qawwal were popular singers of the time. Rabindra Sangeet refers to the compositions of the poet Rabindranath Tagore. Kathak is the northern style of Indian classical dance.

Memories of an Indian Childhood

The emaciated old man in the threadbare, shiny black suit arrived punctually at three in the afternoon. With his walking stick he gently tapped the gravel in the front porch till a passing servant – usually Faqira – heard the familiar sound and went inside.

'Master Saheb has come,' Baji was informed.

The old man walked down the poplar-lined drive and reached the side verandah. Feeling each step with his cane he carefully climbed the wide flight of stairs and softly called, 'Resham, Resham.'

Resham came running, followed by Baji who gracefully carried the sitar. The way my fabulous Rehana Baji handled the sitar could teach a thing or two to Ravi Varma – were he alive – or to any Bengal-school artist worth his water colours who painted dark-eyed, sitar-playing damsels. Graciously she said, 'Adaab', sat down on the edge of the settee and took the instrument out of its purple brocade cover. The music lesson began . . .

After a light shower of rain a magical fragrance filled the air. A lone bird whistled through the leafy silence. Or a mountain wind rose and made the trees shed their unripe fruit. Often a dim, cold sun trickled through the rain and the garden turned to gold. On his way out through the orchard the old man sometimes found a peach – partly eaten by a parrot – lying in the wet, intensely green, cool grass. He picked it up, cleaned it carefully with his handkerchief and shoved it into his pocket.

Dog-like, Resham always followed him to the gate. Often she vanished into a rose bush looking for prey, or deftly climbed a tree. The old man looked up, briefly watched the trembling bough, bent his head again and went out of the gate.

Ever since Mrs Jogmaya Chatterjee of Calcutta took up abode in the bungalow next door, the inhabitants of picturesque, complaisant Dalanwalla had suddenly realised the acute lack of

40

Culture in their lives. Every drawing room had its massive gramophone and its Kamala Jharia-Kalu Qawwal records. Wireless sets were still rare and tape recorders had not even been invented. The status symbols consisted mainly of bungalow, car, 'English' cook and trained bearer. (There was many an eminent cook and bearer who considered it beneath his dignity to work for Kala Log.) Refrigerators too, were unknown.

But the strains of Rabindra Sangeet emanating from Mrs Jogmaya Chatterjee's house changed all that. Mrs Goswami, wife of a high-ranking (Government of India) official, said to Begum Faruqui, wife of another high-ranking (Department of Forests) official, 'Behenji, we all are really backward. Look at these Bengalis. So advanced in everything.'

'I have even heard it said, Behenji, that their daughters cannot get married unless they know music,' said Mrs Jaswant Singh, wife of a high-ranking (Royal Military Academy) officer.

'We Muslims disapprove of decent girls singing and dancing. But times have changed. I said to *him* the other day, I said, our Rashida must learn how to play the harmonium,' Begum Faruqui firmly announced.

This was how the winds of Art and Culture began to blow across Dalanwalla. A seedy, bidi-smoking guruji was acquired from somewhere and Dr Sinha's daughters dutifully learned the Kathak. Sardar Amarjit Singh, whose father owned a large business in Batavia, Dutch East Indies, took up the violin. The young Sardar also bought from Mr Peter Robert Fazal Masih, the pheriwalla, yards and yards of printed georgette for his turbans. With one of his colourful turbans on his head, his jet-black beard rolled with enormous finesse, the Sardar sallied forth, armed with his violin, and headed straight for the Rispana. Rumour had it that he went every evening to meet Mrs Feroza Khan, the lovely Afghan widow, who lived in a Christmas-card cottage by the stream. Evening after evening he informed his young Sardarni, Bibi Charanjit Kaur, that he was going for his violin lessons. But Mrs Goswami, Mrs Jaswant Singh, Begum Faruqui and my mother knew.

Such were the stirring times when my cousin, too, decided to take up music – partly because a sitar was handy, lying in its dusty cover in the store room. (My pioneering mother had learned – and forgotten – how to play it several years ago.)

A lot of things happened that winter. Resham broke her leg. Miss Zohra Derby, the Daredevil, arrived in town. Diana Becket was declared the Ravishing Beauty of London, Dr (Miss) Zubeida Siddiqui saw a black dog the size of a donkey at two in the morning. And Faqira's sister-in-law became a sparrow.

I must tell you about these important events in their chronological order.

My beautiful and brilliant cousin Rehana Khatoon had passed her BA that year – breaking a lot of records at Aligarh University – and was spending a few months with us. One afternoon as she sat drinking coffee with Mother and Mrs Goswami in the front verandah, somebody tapped the pebbles in the portico and a feeble voice said, 'Excuse me, I am told that a lady here wishes to learn the sitar.'

He was Mr Simon. He said that Mr Peter Robert Fazal Masih, the pheriwalla (he grandly called himself a travelling salesman and traded in cloth and gossip), had told him about Baji's musical intentions. He said that he lived alone in the outhouses of the late Rev. Scott's empty bungalow, and earned ten to twenty rupees a month if he was lucky enough to get one or two pupils. That was all he told us about himself, but being an ardent left-wing intellectual, Baji was greatly dismayed. Mr Simon, however, never accepted any help beyond his fees, he had that kind of dignity.

Mr Simon always wore a waistcoat – complete with an ancient watch-and-chain – a round black cap and round, thick glasses. He never entered the house (people like tradesmen and tutors were supposed to stay in the verandah) except on the first day of his employment when Baji asked Faqira to send him down to the back garden where she sat in the sun. It was a bitterly cold day. Led by Faqira, Mr Simon passed through my room where I played by the fireplace. He hesitated and stopped for a second, for a brief moment spread his hands towards the fire and quickly went out.

Resham, our otherwise arrogant Persian, became his great friend. 'Funny, how a snob like Resham has befriended poor

Master Saheb,' Baji remarked and added the observation in a typically feminine p.s. in her letter to Muzzaffer Bhai. She was allowed, as a gesture of modernity to correspond with our cousin and her fiancé, Muzzaffer, who was at that time engaged in the pursuit of knowledge at the University of Bombay.

While Baji wrote her letters Ghafoor Begum, her loyal anna, sat by her chair on the grass with her inseparable paandan. When Baji went inside Ghafoor Begum strolled down to the outhouses to chat with Faqira's sister-in-law or returned to her prayer settee in the back verandah. Ever since her husband (he ran a cycle repair shop at the crossing of Marris Road, Aligarh) had married an eighteen-year-old girl, our Ghafoor Begum spent her time on the prayer rug or in prescribing home cures for Faqira's ailing sister-in-law.

A good-natured Garhwali lad, Faqira had been discovered by Abdul, the cook, who found him in rags, knitting a sweater, by the Eastern Canal. For a few days he slogged as Abdul's masaalchi but was soon promoted to the rank of houseboy and worked under our very superior bearer (customarily called Sardar because he was the doyen of servants). A few months ago Faqira had informed Mother that both his elder brothers had 'turned to dust' in a ghastly accident and that he was going to fetch their widow from the mountains.

Tattooed and fair-skinned Jaldhara was an attractive, smiling woman of forty; she wore a gold nose-ring and a nose-flower and a necklace of Malka Tooria (Queen Victoria, to us) coins. Both her coolie husbands had fallen, together, to their deaths carrying some Badrinath pilgrims' luggage. Jaldhara suffered from some incurable disease and Faqira worried endlessly about her health. The day Jaldhara arrived in the outhouse Rehana Baji very knowledgeably discussed, at lunch table, the Institution of Polyandry in the Hills. Baji had obtained a first-class degree and my father was immensely proud of her.

In the afternoon I dashed off to my friends, Kamala and Vimala Rajpal, to tell them about Faqira's sister-in-law who was so rich that she wore coins round her neck. Resham followed me to the avenue. Afraid that she might get run over by a car, I picked her up, threw her across the hedge and pedalled off on my little bicycle.

Instead of falling in the garden, poor Resham got entangled in the barbed wire concealed in the tall hedge. Badly bruised and bleeding, she meowed and meowed till Faqira, who had come out to pick chillis for the kitchen, heard her desperate cries.

I returned to a sorrowing household. 'Resham is dying,' Baji told me tearfully. 'I still don't understand how she got herself entangled in those wires. Must have gone there looking for birds. The vet has just left.'

It was a terrifying realisation that I was responsible for Resham's terrible pain and possible death. Trying to hide my guilt from the world I hid myself in a cluster of leechis in the back garden. In woodpecker-like Mrs Warbrook's house the wireless set broadcast music from distant BBC. In the servants' quarters Ghafoor Begum was talking to Jaldhara and Abdul's wife. Baji was in her room writing to Muzaffer Bhai – probably about Resham's accident. The Persian lay bandaged in her frilled basket in the side verandah.

I lurked in the trees like a criminal and did not quite know what to do next. Finally I sauntered down towards my father's room and peeped in through the bay-window. Father sat in his armchair reading the *Pioneer*. I tiptoed in and stood behind his chair.

He heard my sobs and turned round. 'What is the matter, child?' he asked. I told him All, flopped on the floor and howled and howled till I felt a little better.

Every morning Resham was dressed and bandaged by Faqira and was sent down, once a week, to see the 'horse doctor' at the 'ghora haspatal'. Her leg had been shaved. Shorn of her glorious long hair she was now a humble, subdued and very unhappy cat. A few weeks later she could hobble about a bit and after a month limped all the way down to the gate to see Mr Simon off.

That was when, one Sunday morning, as I played hop-scotch on the drive Mr George Becket's head appeared over the henna hedge. A little hesitantly he beckoned to me and said, 'Good morning to you, young lady.'

'Good morning, Pil – Mr Becket,' I said politely and almost bit my tongue.

'How is your beautiful pussy cat? Mr Fazal Masih told me that she had had a bad accident.'

This was the first time that Mr George Becket had actually spoken to anyone in the neighbourhood. I thanked him for enquiring after poor Resham. He nodded, shoved his thumbs in the half-torn pockets of his shabby coat and shuffled off.

Mr George Becket was a destitute Anglo-Indian, generally known as Pilpili Saheb. He lived down the avenue in a broken-down cottage and was so poor that he went to the municipal water tap himself to fetch water. His only daughter, Diana Rose, sold tickets at an English cinema hall at the parade ground, and often passed by our house on her bicycle. She had golden, windswept hair and only four dresses which she washed at night at the water tap and wore with extreme care. But Mrs Goswami, Mrs Jaswant Singh and Begum Faruqui firmly maintained that Diana gadded about in such fineries because the Tommies gave her money. But if the Tommies gave her money (and I saw no reason why they should) why didn't her poor papa engage a water-carrier?

Dalanwalla was mostly inhabited by well-to-do retired Englishmen who lived quietly in their secluded, exquisitely furnished bungalows. Inside these peaceful houses walnut tables displayed piles of *Illustrated London News*, *Tatler*, *Country Life* and *Punch*. Bundles of *The Times* and the *Daily Telegraph* arrived by sea mail. In the mornings the ladies sat in their 'morning rooms', writing Home. In the afternoons they had their high tea in the verandahs. The mantlepieces were crowded with silver-framed portraits of sons who were engaged in further brightening up the Empire sun over such places as Kenya, Ceylon, Malaya and so forth.

Although these dear old people belonged to the twilight world of Koi Hai and Chhota Hazri, there were dedicated, self-effacing orientalists and scholars, too, among them. Mr Hardcastle was an expert on Tibeto-Burman dialects. Mr Green wrote learned papers on the Khasi tribes of Assam. Col Whitehead, who had lost a leg fighting the Pathans on the Frontier, was quite an authority on Pushtu poetry. Apart from these, Major Shelton wrote shikar notes in upcountry newspapers. Mr Marchman was a chess fiend. Horsey Miss Drinkwater called spirits on the planchette and woodpecker-like Mrs Warbrook painted lovely water colours.

One of the bungalows housed the 'British Stores'. Owned and run by a tall, hawk-nosed and very ancient Parsi, this was the historic place where the ladies met for shopping and gossip while their children hung about its Toys, Toffee and Lemonade counters (Coca-Cola too had not been invented).

In this comfortably smug and very English locality (Indians were accepted when they were 'upper class' and civilised enough to live in bungalows) Mr George Becket of the pale blue eyes was the only Anglo-Indian. Nevertheless, he considered himself a proper Englishman and rumour had it that when some years ago, George V, King Emperor died, Mr Becket solemnly wore a black armband and attended the Slow March Past at Kolagarh along with the mourning English gentry.

But, with the characteristic heartlessness of children, we referred to him as Pilpili Saheb and Vimala's teenage, Doon School-going brother, Swarn, had devised a novel way of teasing poor Diana. When she passed by the Rajpals' house Swarn placed the gramophone in the front window of his room and it blared out the following zany song:

> There was a rich merchant in London did stay,
> Who had for his daughter an uncommon liking,
> Her name, it was Diana, she was sixteen years old,
> And had a large fortune in silver and gold.
> As Diana was walking in the garden one day,
> Her father came to her and thus did he say:
> Go dress yourself up in gorgeous array,
> For you will have a husband both gallant and gay.
> O father, dear father, I've made up my mind,
> To marry at present I don't feel inclined.
> And all my large fortune every day adore,
> If you let me live single a year or two more.
> Then gave the father a gallant reply:
> If you will not be this young man's bride,
> I'll leave all your fortune to the fairest of things,

And you shan't reap the benefit of a single farthing.
As Wilikins was walking in the garden one day,
He found his dear Diana lying dead in the way.
A cup so fearful that lay by her side,
And Wilikins doth fainteth with a cry in his eye.

As soon as the song started poor Diana flushed deeply and bicycled away as fast as she could.

The winter's second important event was the arrival of the Great East India Circus and Carnival Company Ltd, which pitched its Big Top at the parade ground. The handbills announced:

The Great Marvel of the Century
The Lion-hearted Beauty
Miss Zohra Derby
In the Well of Death
Tonight and Every Night.

Faqira took Jaldhara to see the circus and came back in raptures. 'Begum Sahib, Bitya, Bibi,' he said, thrilled, 'This woman who rides the phat-phati in the death of well . . . harey Ram, harey Ram . . .!'

Next evening we, too, saw her as she sat in front of the Well of Death looking bored, chain-smoking Scissors cigarettes. She wore 'birjis' [breeches] of shining blue satin, and her heavily made-up face looked weirdly blue in the bright lights. (But those who knew declared that Miss Nadia of Hunterwali fame was not a patch on Miss Zohra Derby, the female Desperado.) A ferocious-looking man, also in blue satin 'birjis', sat next to her, twirling his waxed moustaches. A motor-bike roared at the back.

After some minutes Miss Zohra Derby and her ferocious companion entered the Well of Death on their motor-bikes and went roaring round and round, the Well shook and wavered and it was all very frightening.

After a week Faqira brought the sensational news that Master Gulqand and Master Muchchander, two stalwarts of the Circus and its star performers, had a fight over Miss Zohra Derby; she was knifed and slashed well and proper by Master Muchchander and was now in hospital.

But as was expected of him, Mr Peter Robert Fazal Masih brought the real scoop: Diana Becket had joined the Circus.

'Diana Becket?' Baji asked, wide-eyed.

'Yes Bitya,' Faqira put in enthusiastically, 'I too heard, at the water tap. In the circus Pilpili Saheb's Missya she will get a big fat salary and free tiffin, chhota hazri, everything. She says she could no more bear to see her old Papa carrying heavy buckets, he being so poor and all. And she says, as for the world, it harasses her anyway.'

All this was very sad-making. Then I remembered something and asked brightly, 'But the Tommies gave her money, didn't they?'

Ghafoor Begum glared at me. 'Run along,' she said. So I ran along.

A few days later the posters announced:

> Sensational European Belle
> The Ravishing Beauty of London
> Miss Diana Rose
> in The Well of Death
> Tonight and Every Night.

In the midst of these fabulous goings-on cinema also claimed my attention:

> The Greatest Film of the Year
> Starring Miss Sardar Akhtar
> At Palladium Cinema
> Tonight and Every Night.

> The Greatest Film of the Year
> Starring Miss Sardar Akhtar
> At Roxy Cinema
> Tonight and Every Night.

How could Miss Sardar Akhtar 'star' at two places the same evening? It worried me no end. But the problem was solved when my parents allowed Baji to go with Mrs Goswami and see *Achhut Kanya* (The Untouchable Girl). I was allowed to tag along with Baji. (About *Achhut Kanya* Mrs Jogmaya Chatterjee had informed Mrs Goswami that India had at last entered the era of cultural revolution because Gurudev Rabindranath Tagore's own niece had become a cinema actress.)

This was also the time when Mrs Chatterjee's daughters began singing the latest film songs like

Tum aur main aur Munna piyara,
Gharwa hoga swarg hamara

(With you and me and darling baby,
Home will be our Heaven)

The breeze wafted these ditties over to our garden. Ghafoor Begum shuddered, placed her hands on her waist or a forefinger on her nose, indicating censure, and said, 'What our elders used to say is coming true: A sure sign of the Day of Judgement would be when cows eat goat-droppings and virgins themselves demand husbands . . . This is Kaliyug . . . Kaliyug . . .'

Farqira, of course, took Jaldhara to see all these films. When she returned after a visit to what is now known as a 'New Theatres classic', Jaldhara developed high fever. The doctor said she was critically ill.

Now she lay all day long in the sun. One afternoon she said to Ghafoor Begum, 'My time has come, Annaji. One of these days I'll give up my life.' Ghafoor Begum tried to cheer her up and said good-humouredly, 'Nonsense, Jaldhara. You are going to be a doddering old woman. But tell me, Jaldhara, what is this spell you've cast over poor Faqira? Give me some mantra too for my faithless fellow. I am told you hill people know a lot of sorcery. Look how Faqira dotes on you, and you old enough to be his mother!'

Upon which Jaldhara seemed to forget her illness and laughed happily and said, 'Don't you know, Annaji, old rice is always better?'

'Old rice?' I repeated.

Ghafoor Begum turned round and glared at me. 'What are

you doing here?' she said sternly. 'Run along and play.' So I returned gloomily to my hop-scotch 'field' on the drive.

Bored with life, I decided to visit Kamala and Vimala. On the way to their house I saw Mr George Becket frantically running down the avenue. Just then Major Shelton emerged from his gate in his battered Model T Ford, and asked Mr Becket to hop in, which he did, and drove away in the direction of the European Hospital.

At the Rajpal's place a sad-faced Swarn told me that Diana Becket had had a serious accident. She was terrified every time she sat in Master Muchchander's arms as he went roaring round and round on his motor-bike. So the circus manager, 'Professor' Shahbaz, told her to start practising solo. That's how she bashed up both her legs. 'And I heard at the parade ground that she will have to spend the rest of her life in a wheel chair,' Swarn added.

We were too sad to play hop-scotch or anything. Swarn looked shame-faced and guilty. For some time he sat dangling his long legs from the bough of our favourite leechi tree. Then he jumped down and went off to play football with his cronies.

Chinaman John passed by, on his bicycle, carrying his usual load of household linen. We patiently waited for Mr Fazal Masih.

Mr Fazal Masih came round late next evening. He told us that 'Professor' Shahbaz was being interrogated by the police. The circus had quietly left town, Miss Zohra Derby had also vanished from the hospital.

Then Dr (Miss) Zubeida Siddiqui, a family friend, arrived to spend the holidays. Lean and in her thirties, Dr (Miss) Siddiqui stooped a little, inclined her head to one side like a bird and spoke in brief, abrupt sentences. She wore white, long-sleeved blouses and kept her head fully covered with her white cotton sari. She had studied in England and worked as the principal of some obscure girls' college somewhere in eastern India.

Dr Siddiqui said her prayers five times a day, and was also fasting, although it was not the month of Ramzan. The ladies of Dalanwalla were deeply impressed by her piety. ('England-returned and all, and yet so modest and spiritual,' Begum Faruqui commented with admiration. 'And such a strict follower

of God and the Prophet – peace be on him,' said Begum Ansari.
Begum Qureshi nodded.)

Dr Siddiqui was forever telling Baji some seemingly endless
tale in undertones. Once she went down to see Jaldhara and
uttered, 'What a fortunate woman.'

One evening Dr Siddiqui was especially morose, so Baji asked
me to come along and entertain her (as though I were a dancing
bear). She said, 'Let's hear that silly old Anglo-Indian song of
yours.'

Obediently I began:

> There was a rich merchant in London did stay,
> Who had for his daughter an uncommon liking,
> Her name it was Diana, she was sixteen years old
> And had a large fortune in . . .

Suddenly a lump rose in my throat and I ran away. Dr Siddiqui's
expression changed from moroseness to surprise.

One could not associate any kind of mystery with a dull and
prosaic person like Dr Siddiqui. Suddenly she became a figure
of high romance.

One foggy morning as Vimala and I haunted the Toffee
Counter in the British Stores we happened to overhear Mrs
Goswami at Tinned Food telling Mrs Jaswant Singh, Begum
Faruqui, and Mrs Sinha:

'This lady doctor poor thing (somehow they could never
remember that Zubeida Siddiqui was a scientist and not a lady
doctor), she has been jilted. And he is going to marry her own
niece who is very pretty and seventeen.'

'Men are like that, Behenji,' Mrs Jaswant Singh replied. 'Look
at our Amarjit.'

And Begum Faruqui said, 'The lady doctor is so God-fearing
and pious. Always praying and fasting.'

'For a woman – all depends on this,' Mrs Sinha tapped her
forehead with a forefinger.

'Let's hope Bhagwan listens to her prayers,' said Mrs
Goswami.

At two o'clock that night a dreadful scream rose from the

guest room. Everybody jumped out of their quilts and rushed to the scientist's rescue.

Lying prostrate on the prayer rug Zubeida Siddiqui was whimpering hysterically. I was promptly shooed away to my room but in the morning I 'happened' to overhear her talking to Baji in her usual drab undertone (very cleverly I had hung about the breakfast table after everybody had left).

'I hadn't told anyone,' Dr Siddiqui was saying. 'The pirji had ordered that I must recite this jalali wazifa. For forty nights. Last night was the fortieth. The pirji had said, come what may I must never look up or sideways and must concentrate fully or else the wazifa would have no effect. Last night, like a damn fool I looked in front and saw a black dog the size of a donkey sitting over there. Snarling. So I screamed. The dog vanished. My chilla was broken. Now. Nothing will happen. The time is up. Only a week. From now. Nothing.' She took off her glasses and began to cry.

Baji looked horrified.

'But Zubeida Aapa,' she said mildly, 'you are a scientist. Do you really believe in this – this hocus pocus? You merely had an hallucination. A black dog the size of a donkey!' And she began to laugh.

I have mentioned earlier that my Baji was a left-wing intellectual (one of the first crop).

'Rehana Khatoon,' Dr Zubeida Siddiqui said evenly, drying her tears, 'you are only twenty-one. You have doting parents. Doting uncles. Aunts. Safe and secure. Happy family. (I suddenly remembered the Happy Family cards we used to play in the nursery.) A splendid young man. About to be married. To him. You do not know the meaning of loneliness. Don't. Don't ever laugh again at somebody's loneliness.'

Suddenly Baji noticed my presence and with the flicker of her eyelashes asked me to get lost. So I got lost.

The same evening Dr Siddiqui left for Calcutta.

In the first week of December Jaldhara was removed to the hospital where she died the following evening.

Faqira went about howling like a child.

'Accept it, son,' Ghafoor Begum tried to console him. 'Accept it as Allah's will.'

'How can I, Annaji? She was mother, sister-in-law, wife, everything to me.' He howled some more.

But on the third day when he returned from the cremation ground, he looked strangely happy and at peace. He carried a clay pot full of poor Jaldhara's ashes. He said he was going to place the pot at the head of his cot at night and in her new form Jaldhara would leave her footprints on the ashes. Baji said she was greatly moved by Faqira's simple faith. At dinner table that night she discussed, with Father, the Theory of Transmigration.

Early next morning Faqira came rushing into Mother's room.

'Begum Saheb, Bitya, Bibi,' he said excitedly. 'My Jaldhara has become a sparrow.'

'Jaldhara has become a sparrow?' Baji repeated. Both of us went hotfoot across the dewy lawn to Faqira's quarters.

He brought the clay pot and showed us the tiny footprints of a bird. Obviously a sparrow had entered Faqira's room at night. They did, all the time.

'It's a sparrow, Bitya,' Faqira said simply and carried the pot back into his room.

Faqira began feeding the sparrows and placed cups full of water all over the garden. Whenever a sparrow entered a room through the skylight or a window he stopped all work, offered it millet seeds, uttering such cries as 'Che-che-che-ah-ah-ah-leh-leh-leh' or stood motionless with breadcrumbs on his palm. He also worried that Resham might catch a sparrow.

A few days before Christmas Baji received a letter from Zubeida Aapa:

. . . The day I reached here my niece was married to him. Posh society wedding. I have gone on strike against God. Married Dr Uppal the other day. Teaches in Burdwan.

P.S. Dr U. is a H. Convey the news to the Begums Faruqui, Qureshi and Ansari

Yours
Z. Uppal.

It was an exceptionally severe winter. Diana Rose was still in plaster in the hospital. Mr Becket was not seen at the water tap.

He dozed all day on a bench at the parade ground. His upturned hat, lying near him, looked like a beggar's empty bowl. Yellow leaves floated down from the trees and filled it to the brim.

Carol singers went round the quiet roads of Dalanwalla, singing 'Silent Night' and 'O Come Let Us Adore Him'. As the night deepened the haunting notes of some lone Garhwali's flute were heard in the distance. The water in the 'sparrow-cups' was frozen. Early in the morning ragged hillmen went about hawking coal. As the mist lifted the snow-covered Himalayas were lighted up by a weak sun. All day long blazing log fires roared in the grates.

On Christmas Eve Mr Simon told us that every Christmas morning he made plum pudding before going to church and spent the rest of the day reading the Good Book. On Boxing Day he promised to bring us some of his plum pudding. As Christmas presents he had brought a touchingly cheap Japanese trinket for Baji, a green ribbon for myself and a tiny rubber ball for Resham. Mother gave him a ten-rupee note. It was absolute wealth for him, he looked at it for some moments and carefully tucked it away in a waistcoat pocket.

Mr Simon did not come on Boxing Day or the day after. Faqira was, therefore, dispatched to the Rev. Scott's bungalow. He came back and hung down his head. Then he said slowly, 'Simon Saheb has become dust. Padri Saheb's gardener told me on Burra Din [Christmas Day] when he opened Simon Saheb's room he was lying dead and frozen on his cot. The winter killed him.

'He had only one blanket, Begum Saheb. And so he always slept in his suit.'

'It's very cold outside, Bitya. In our Garhwal folk often freeze to death. Can't be helped. How can one get so much warm clothing? Winter comes every year, anyway.'

For a week Resham had been sitting on the warm cushions of her cosy basket. That afternoon was less cold, so she limped down to the gate and posted herself at the little Chinese 'bridge'. There she began to wait for Mr Simon.

The sun went down. Bored, she decided to have a go at a sparrow before coming inside.

The sparrow flew off and perched itself on the branch of a

silver oak. Resham tried to climb the tree but with her broken leg came sliding down. The sparrow hopped on to a higher branch. Resham lifted her face and uttered a faint, helpless meow. The sparrow spread its wings and flew away towards the wide, blue skies.

All this happened during that winter in Dehra Dun.
After which, I grew up.

Translated from the Urdu
by the author

MRINAL PANDE

Mrinal Pande was born in 1946. She is currently editor of *Saptahik Hindustan*, the Hindi edition of the leading newspaper *The Hindustan Times*, based in New Delhi. She has a distinguished career in journalism and the media, and has published several collections of short stories as well as plays and novels.

In the story, Baabu and Ma are the father and mother of the narrator, Naani is her grandmother, Maama is her mother's brother, Maami the Maama's wife, and Maasi is mother's sister. Bari and Chhoti are elder and younger respectively. The dai is the midwife or birth attendant who will attend on her mother.

The ritual referred to at the end of the story takes place on the Chaitya Shukla Ashtami day of the Hindu calendar, usually some time in March or April, when young girls (kanyakumari, virgin goddesses) are worshipped as the living incarnations of Devi, or the devine feminine principle. A roli spot or tikka of red powder is put on the girls' foreheads, the aarti ceremony is done by waving the sacred flame around their faces, and prasad, food given to the devotees after worship, is distributed to all the participating women.

'Girls' was first published in 1983 in *Dharmayug*, and in English translation in the same year in *Manushi – a journal about women and society*, New Delhi.

Girls

The day we left with Ma for Naani's house, Baabu broke a surahi. I don't know whether he did it on purpose or by accident, but anyway the floor was flooded with water. Ma held up her sari and called Saru's mother – who was trying to eavesdrop from the adjacent room – to mop up the water, because if someone were to slip and break their bones it would be yet another problem. To Ma, everything in life is a problem. As far as she is concerned, whether we are at home or at school, ill or just playing around, we are a problem. While mopping the floor, Saru's mother looked up at Ma and asked, 'This time you'll be away for at least three months, won't you?' Ma put her hands on her thighs as if she were assessing their weight, squatted down and said, 'Yes, they won't allow me to come back sooner.' She turned to me and ordered me to go out and play. I always seemed to turn up at the wrong time and at the wrong place. As I was leaving the room I managed to pick up a piece of the broken surahi which I enjoyed sucking, and I overheard Ma addressing either Saru's mother or the cobwebs hanging from the roof: 'I hope it's a boy this time. It will relieve me of the nuisance of going through another pregnancy.' I could just imagine Saru's mother, in her usual manner, shaking her head and saying, 'Why not? . . . why not?'

When we reached the station, I scrambled on to the train, fought my way through people and luggage and secured a place next to the window. Triumphantly I stuck my tongue out at everyone and went 'Eee . . . Eee.' But when I noticed Ma's gaze turning towards me, I immediately started chanting the alphabet, 'E for Emli, E for Eekh.' Ma was not actually looking at me though, because she was preoccupied with all her problems. She had to mind the luggage, the wobbling surahi, the three of us, and cope with the exhaustion of pregnancy as well. At one of the stations we bought a lot of samosas filled with chillies. Just when we were buying them, a woman was making her child pee through the next window. The sight made me feel quite nauseous and I couldn't eat my samosa, so I gave it to Ma instead. Meanwhile I crushed a piece of potato which was lying on the seat into the shape of an insect to frighten my younger sister. She screamed, Ma smacked me and I started to cry as well. My elder sister was irritated and said, 'Oh what a nuisance you are!' Despite her irritation, I know that it is only my elder sister who really loves me; everyone else is horrible.

Maama was waiting to receive us at the station. On the way to Naani's I sat next to Maami and noticed the rubies in her earlobes bobbing up and down while she chewed paan. Every time the driver pressed the jeep's horn, my sisters and I would scream in unison, 'Poo-poo'. The driver was amused at our screaming, and when we reached the house, he lifted me and my younger sister out of the jeep. He had a huge moustache, smelt of tea and bidis, and wore a uniform made of coarse wool which tickled me and made me feel sleepy. When the surahi was lifted out of the jeep it overturned, and once again there was water everywhere. This incident reminded me so much of Baabu that, absent-mindedly, I trod hard on my younger sister's sandal, nearly tripping her up. 'You are the cause of all my problems!' Ma hissed at me through tightly clenched teeth so that no one could hear. She then grabbed hold of my arm as if to prevent me from falling over but actually pressed it so hard that my shoulder hurt.

I thought of Baabu because whenever we came to Naani's house, he never accompanied us. And as soon as we arrived, Ma would be lost in the company of maasis, maamis, Naani and old maidservants. If we tried going near her during the day, someone or other would say, 'Let the poor thing have some rest at least while she is here.' Ma too would put on a pathetic act as if we always harassed her at home. I felt disgusted at the thought of entering Naani's house, so I deliberately loitered behind near the bushes. A mongrel dog came near and sniffed at me. Then I heard someone mentioning my name inside the house and saying, 'Now where has she disappeared?'

I entered the house along with the dog and saw Naani sitting with Maama's son on her lap. As soon as she saw the dog, she shooed it away because to her all animals are as untouchables. The dog, used to being reprimanded, tucked its tail between its legs and went out. I was told to bend down and touch Naani's feet. Someone from the family said, 'Not like that . . . bend properly. You are born a girl and you will have to bend for the rest of your life, so you might as well learn.' Naani blessed me by waving her hand over my bowed back and said, 'This girl hasn't grown taller. Who would believe she is eight years old?'

Even though I pinched Maama's son, he kept following me around like an idiot. He was very fair, chubby and supposed to be cute. He was also tall for his age, and though only five years old could easily pass for seven. 'Will you tell me a story tonight?' he asked. I said no and pretended to read the newspaper.

'Oh what a nuisance this is,' Ma kept complaining. The old lady from the neighbourhood who had come to see Ma told Naani, 'This time Lali will definitely have a boy. Just look at her complexion – when she was expecting the girls it was pink, but now it has a tinge of yellow. I am sure it will be a boy this time.'

'Who knows, perhaps even this time . . .' moaned Ma as she put on a pathetic expression and began paring her nails.

'Is there anyone to cook for your husband?' asked the old lady. Her question set me thinking about Baabu, how good he smelt and the softness of his lap. And how when we came here Ma did not allow us to lie in her lap for too long and complained, 'Ugh! Oh! My bones are aching, my sari is all crushed. Get up now. I have such a lot of work to do, and to top it all there's this huge nuisance. Come on, get up.'

Naani folds her hands and prays: 'Oh goddess, protect my honour. At least this time let her take a son back from her parents' home.' At the end of the prayer she dries her tears with her pallav.

From the corner of my eyes I could see that my sisters were fast asleep. We were in a big room divided into two by a wooden partition. Right above my bed hung a big wall clock which was ticking away. Just before it struck the hour it made a hissing noise which was similar to my sister drawing in her breath just before howling. All the lights had been switched off and the room was flooded with moonlight. Tulsa dai was applying oil to the soles of Ma's feet and saying, 'If it's a boy this time, I will demand a sari with stainless steel zari.' Even in the bright moonlight I could not see Ma's face, but only her huge stomach which looked like a drum. Ma's sari had slipped down and Tulsa dai while feeling her stomach touched a painful spot which made Ma moan just like a cow does when returning home from the fields.

'If I have a boy this time, then I will be relieved of this burden forever,' she tells Tulsa dai, and then adds, 'You can go home now, your children must be waiting for you. Be sure you put the oil vessel under the bed, otherwise one of these kids will kick it over in the morning and . . .' Ah, a bad omen. Whenever Ma left a sentence unfinished it seemed to loom in the air, like the ticking of the clock. I wonder why grown-ups always complete their sentences when they are talking about pleasant things, but always leave them unfinished if it's something unpleasant. Like, 'Ah, a woman's fate . . .', or 'Oh, three girls . . .' There's always a silence after these half-statements.

There's a bright star in the sky. Is that the Dhruva star? Baabu used to say that if I worked hard I could become anything I wanted, just as Dhruva became a star. 'But I can't become a boy, can I?' I once asked obstinately. I was surprised at Baabu's reaction when he put on a serious look and said sternly, 'Don't argue with your elders now.' I find it difficult to understand them. My elder sister says one should never trust grown-ups because if they want to know something they will prise it out of you by hook or by crook, but they themselves will never tell you a thing.

It's true, nobody ever tells us anything. In this place, it's when we go to sleep that the world of the elders awakens, opening like a magic casket. I want to stay awake and listen; I don't know why I fall asleep half-way through. I wonder whose voice it is now; it sounds as if someone is crying in suppressed tones. Is it Chhoti Maasi? 'I don't even get as much respect as a dog does in that house,' she tells Ma. I wonder where she is treated worse than a dog, then I hear Ma telling her, 'All of us suffer like that, one just has to endure it.' My eyes shut and I fall asleep.

The next morning, when everyone is having breakfast I ask

Ma what 'endure' means. I remind her by asking, what does Chhoti Maasi have to endure? I get one light slap, then another, but before Ma strikes me again Maami saves me and says, 'Let it be. She's only a child, after all.' 'She's no child, she's a witch,' says Ma as her stomach wobbles in anger. 'She's always listening on the sly to elders talking. Heaven knows what will become of her.'

When I go into the garden, my elder sister shakes the flowers she has gathered at me. 'Oh . . . you! I have told you a hundred times not to question grown-ups. If you keep on like this, one day these people will beat you so hard you will die.' 'I will ask questions. I will. I will,' I answer crying. 'Then go and die,' says my elder sister, and continues to thread a garland for Naani's Gopalji.

Naani stands by her and says loudly, 'You are my precious Lakshmi,' with the intention that I should hear.

In the afternoons I tell the younger children horror stories of ghosts and demons who lived in the walnut tree. I tell them that if they should wake up at twelve o'clock on a full-moon night they would see children being bathed in blood. They would also hear the ghosts speaking through their noses which at first is difficult to follow. The children follow me all over the house like mice following the Pied Piper.

Bari Maami and Ma give us money to buy sweet-sour golis just to get rid of us in the afternoon. Their room has been darkened by sticking green paper on the windows, and it is full of women – Ma, Maami, Maasis and Naani. They eat all the time and have cushiony arms, fat half-naked legs and wrinkled stomachs. Then why do they keep telling us not to sit with our legs spread out? 'You all look like cows,' I tell the women, but no one seems to have heard me. Chhoti Maasi, who is lying on the floor with a pillow under her head takes a sour goli from us, starts sucking it and says, 'Jijaji is really the limit.' Suddenly laughter explodes in the room. Who? Why? How? I look all around the room for an answer, but no one is bothered about us here, they are too lost in their own conversation. I leave the room and bang hard on the door from outside, wondering if Ma will call me a nuisance. No one comes out to reprimand me, though.

'Move aside,' says Hari's mother who is carrying a tray laden with glasses of tea into the room. 'Move. This is not for you, it's for the grown-ups. Move out of my way.' Hari's mother's nose is like a frog's and her eyebrows meet above her nose. Whenever she laughs, her cheeks hang loose like dead bats. 'Do move aside,' she says to me again. 'I won't,' I say, and try to block her way. 'I'll move only if you say girls are nice.' 'All right, all right, I have said it, so now move out of the way,' says Hari's mother. 'No,' I persist, 'say it properly.'

'Oh, Hari's ma, what's happening?' asks Maasi irritably from the room. 'Are you going to bring the tea next year, or what?' Hari's mother knits her thick eyebrows together and says, 'This Lali's middle daughter won't let me . . .' She starts laughing, and as she does so her frog-like nose bobs up and down. I can hear Ma naming me and saying, 'That girl must be harassing her. She was born only to plague my life.' Someone in the room advises her that she should not get angry in her condition.

For a long time I sit outside the house watching the birds flying and wishing that I had been born a bird. 'Do mother birds too think their girl birds are inferior?' I wonder. Then I hear a voice calling, 'Where has she gone?' and I know someone is searching for me. I hide behind the wall where no one can ever find me. I wish, I wish that somewhere, anywhere, I could find that magic betel nut which would make me invisible as soon as I put it in my mouth. What wonderful fun that would be.

In the evening, when Naani finishes her story, she says, 'Now off you go to sleep, all of you.' My younger sister has already fallen asleep and Hari's mother carries her away into our room. I ask Naani if I can sleep next to her. Naani's body is soft and warm and her quilt smells of cardamom and cloves. Besides, Naani keeps a torch under her pillow. If you take it with you to the bathroom after the lights are off, you don't knock your toes against anything. But Naani says, 'No, as it is this boy doesn't leave me. Where is the space on this bed for the two of you? Go and sleep next to your mother. I'll tell you another story tomorrow. All right?' Naani's tone becomes sugary in the way of most grown-ups when they want to coax you into doing something. In the other room, my elder sister asks with her back turned to me, 'Did she let you sleep with her?' Her voice seems to be trembling with anger. Ma is snoring away. The clock ticks on. How can you sleep? Tick. Tick. Khrr. Khrr.

'Where are you? Girls?' calls Naani with a tray of crimson powder in her hands. In front of her there is a dish of halwa and a plate filled with puris. She has prepared those as offerings to the devi on Ashtami day. A mat has been spread in front of her for us to sit on. 'Come on girls, let me put the tikka on your foreheads.' She lights the camphor for aarti. 'Come now, let me do aarti to all of you.' My two sisters and Maama's beautiful daughters sit cross-legged in front of Naani. Naani puts a tikka on each forehead and then rings a bell. Exactly like the guard on the train. After the bell rings, she blows the conch. 'Poo-ooo.' I am suddenly transformed into a railway engine and race around the ledge of the courtyard. Inside, the room is filled with smells of camphor, halwa, ghee, and flowers. I shout, 'Come on, pay your fares to go to Calcutta. Poo-ooo.'

In the background I hear Naani saying, 'Come on dear, let me put the tikka on you. You are my kanyakumari, aren't you?'

'No,' I retort, 'I'm an engine.' Maama's son claps his hands with excitement and says, 'Oh, an engine, an engine.'

Suddenly I see Ma waddling towards me with a clenched fist and my stomach grows tight with fear. Her face is filled with rage. 'I'll make an engine out of you this very minute.'

The elderly neighbour intervenes, catches hold of Ma's hand and says, 'Have you gone mad, Lali?' She signals to me to obey, and adds, 'She is after all a child, a kanyakumari. Today is Ashtami, the devi's day; you mustn't hit a kanyakumari, it is a sin.'

I jump down from the ledge with a thud and see Naani serving the other girls halwa-puri with a tightly clenched mouth.

'Go on. Take the prasad from Naani. Why do you make your mother cry when she is in this condition?' Maasi asks me irritably.

'When you people don't love girls, why do you pretend to worship them?' My voice breaks into a sob and I feel so furious with myself that I want to swallow the burning camphor to choke my treacherous throat. I want to ask 'Why' again but don't risk it because I am afraid I will start to cry. I don't want to cry in front of them.

Hari's mother puts her hand up to her cheek and says in wonder, 'Ma-ri-ma, just listen to her. What a temper for a girl to show!'

Naani is distributing a rupee and a quarter to each girl. She addresses the wall, 'You can buy twenty sour golis with this money' and holds out a twenty-five paisa coin wrapped in a rupee note towards me. I notice the mark of the crimson powder on the tip of her thumb,' like a bloodstain.

I start moving back towards the wall and screaming 'I don't want all this halwa-puri, tikka or money. I don't want to be a goddess.' I scream so loudly that the pigeons pecking at the scattered grain in the courtyard take off in a flurry, as if a bullet had been fired somewhere.

Translated from the Hindi
by Rama Baru

LAKSHMI KANNAN

Lakshmi Kannan lives and works in New Delhi, and is a versatile and gifted bilingual writer. She writes her Tamil fiction under the name, Kaaveri. She has published one collection of short stories and a novel in Tamil. The collection *Rhythms* (1986) is her own translation of her short stories into English. Apart from other translations of leading Tamil writers, Lakshmi Kannan has published three collections of poems in English. She has also worked on the Tamil–English section of a lexicon in fourteen Indian languages, a project undertaken by the National Council of Education, Calcutta.

'Rhythms' is an intensely localised story, set in the Kapaleswar Temple complex of Mylapore, in one of the oldest parts of Madras, and it draws upon shared experiences of sound, smell and taste. The narrator follows the prescribed order of worship, making her offerings first to Ganesha, the elephant headed son of Shiva and Parvati, then to Muruga, eldest son of Shiva, then to Devi, the great goddess, finally entering Shiva's shrine.

The sculpture at the back of the temple, which the pious widows are anxious to explain, are of the Arubathimoovar – the sixty-three canonised saints – and the Navagriha, the nine planets of Hindu astronomy.

The musical scale that the author refers to, sa ri ga ma pa da ni sa, roughly equates to c d e f g a b c.

Rhythms

Having roasted people all through the day with its insane heat, Madras relented in the evening. It blew out cool gusts of sea breeze, soft as silk. The proverbial magic of dusk. In India, the moment can come stealing into your mind pervasively. And then, however much you try to hold on to the moment, it slips smoothly through the fingers to blend and vanish into the swiftly striding night. But it comes, the dusk, every day pressing on the skin of the eyelids like velvet, smoothing out the frayed edges of temper.

Kapaleswar Temple was preparing itself for the evening puja. Even as I walked towards the temple I could hear the distant chiming of its bells. Mingling in was the brassy timbre of the rickshaw bells. All along the way one walked, the air reverberated with sounds, all of them special to the evening hour. It tapped alive the subliminal, and generally lifted one away from a place, Madras or wherever. Evening must have set in other cities too, the hour of prayer with sounds brooding inward. Conch shells blown with a laboured heaving deep down from the stomach, the sounds amplified about three times as they rippled out, surging in waves and waves of resonance, wrapping you up like ribbons. From another corner, the long drawl of namaaz from faces looking up at the sky. Knifing through this by a strange contingency, the penetration of bhajans sung with practised ease. They made for a sudden loosening of the self which had stiffened with a day-long tension. This evening pressed down on all the senses, but my ears for some reason, pricked themselves up like highly sensitised antennae.

A solid gust of wind touched the face. It felt moist. It blew strongly through the leaves of the large peepul tree near the Kapaleswar Temple, the ruffled leaves letting off a chorus like a thousand hands, clapping. Soaking in these sounds, I slipped off my sandals outside the temple, and bought four packets of flowers and some coconut, when a piece of music floated in from somewhere. It sounded like part of a verse set to tune. Soon it was drowned by the noisy children scampering around the precincts of the temple. Groups of women talked in shrill tones and the flower-sellers screamed away their wares.

Going first into the altar of Ganesha, I offered the flowers to him. He was sitting short and squat. Puja over, I lifted my head to see the two monkeys perched on the canopy above. One of the monkeys had a big, inflated right cheek, filled with a guava. Or was it a mango? Despite the discomfort, the monkey was snarling at its companion. Cutting through these angry noises, the bells set off by the priest rang out loud and clear, arresting for a moment the two irate monkeys in mid-fight. The snarling stopped abruptly as they looked down at us with some surprise. In the pause it floated in again, that remote piece of verse, sung like a refrain. From an indefinite distance the measured rhythm was beaten out on a steady taal. If one were to distil the musical notes from the words, then the notes might easily run into a simple pattern of '*pa da ni sa . . . pa da ni*'.

Receiving the kumkum and sacred ash from the priest, I went over to the altar of Murugan. The priest here tried in vain to hide his irritation at having to take on so many orders for prayer. His arms and legs were expressive of his impatience as they went through the motions of the puja mechanically. The slokas he uttered escaped with the hissing sibilance of snakes through the chalky whiteness of his false dentures. The sounds had a certain cruel, metallic ring. The flaming camphor on a plate was whirled round and round the face of Murugan; an answering light leaping with a sparkle on the polished brass of his spear. The bells rang out, then faded, ushering in that remote refrain again, floating in the same taal – '*pa da ni sa . . . pa da ni . . .*' God, what a patiently repeated cadence, assiduously rendered . . .

I offered the third packet of flowers to the Devi. Here, the crowd pressed around on all sides. There were beggars in the garb of pious widows, furtive in approach. 'Yes child, what are you looking for? Do you know of Arubathimoovar lined up at the back of this alcove? Or the Navagrihas there? Now let me tell you all about them. Follow me . . . child, you have some change? I have to board this bus to Mambalam, can you give some . . . ?'

Pushing through the crowd I craned my neck to get a view of Devi. There she was, serene as ever. Then a strong smell of sweaty flesh wafted from the crowd and I crinkled my nose in disgust. But no! I shouldn't feel so repulsed by people who have come all the way to the temple. How sinful. Why, this is no crowd compared to Tirupathi. Now that's a place for you! From the foot of the hills to Tirumalai, there were crores of people, footing it all the way. Pulled upward by some inexplicable force, foot by foot on that hot earth, they carried the load of their own faith. Up on the hill was the Lord of the Seven Hills, receiving this frightful faith. Was he great or was it the faith of the surging people which made him so great? And strong? Which came first, the egg or the chicken? Let it be. This sticky crowd around me was a reality. Delicately blowing off the stench of human sweat was the fragrance from a garland of Tulsi leaves that someone had brought. There was a sudden wailing nearby, from a baby crushed in the crowd. And then there was the refrain again, now repeating itself in a stammering tone. But how? We were offered camphor water. Cupping the cool water in my palm, I tipped it into my mouth, the camphor-tulsi taste shooting into me like an arrow. It cleared my nose and ears. The refrain now came from a close proximity, the taal having taken on the sounds of oh, aah, au, ooh . . . Was that a canto at all? It seemed to be some distorted notes. Then what happened to the finely rendered 'pa da ni sa . . . pa da ni . . .'? Both had the same taal. Then why did this one strike with such a dissonance?

With the fourth and the last packet of flowers I went to Shiva's altar. Loudly, they pounded on my ears in a rhythmic assault. And there, inside the aisle to the left of the deity, was a man saying the 'oh, aah, au, ooh . . .' Eyes tightly shut, he swayed his head to and fro as he went on and on. He was probably thirty-five or forty years of age. His skin was a glowing copper-brown. Wearing no shirt, he had around him a damp silk dhoti laced with zari, over which he had wrapped a piece of red silk. One side of his face was tautly pulled back by paralysis, the distortion running along to his mouth and his limbs on the same side. Everything, the eye, the eyebrow and the tip of the nose was twisted. His arm dangled loose and lifeless, the leg on the same side limp as he leaned his weight against a pillar, supporting himself with the healthy leg. But he kept on swaying as he repeated the sounds, which loudly echoed in the vault. Eyes closed, his good arm raised towards the Shivalinga he continued his cry. So this was the distant verse set to tune! The sounds tumbled out of his coiled paralysed tongue, the words a stirring symphony of incoherence. I glanced in the direction of his good arm. There was the Shivalinga in gleaming black, its surface smooth as human skin after a million abhishekas in milk, sandalwood paste and rosewater.

'Give me your packet of flowers. Do you want a puja in your name?'

'Oh . . . ah . . . ooo . . . au . . .'

'Here, I'm asking you! What's your lineage?'

'Who, me? Bharadwaj.'

The priest took the packet of flowers from me and followed my eyes.

'You are looking at this man here? Actually, he's from a very good family. You know, the entire family is soaked in music. Poor man, he's so luckless. The stroke has not only paralysed his tongue, but wasted one side of his body too. Every day his people dress him up like this and send him here to pray . . . in the faith that he will be cured one day. Faith! That's the only thing that sustains us.'

The priest stepped inside with my packet of flowers. Now his slokas mingled oddly with the disjointed sounds of the paralysed man. An oddly cold feeling tightened at the pit of my stomach and sent a shiver through my body. I looked again at the man in the hope that he might open his eyes. But he had drawn the lids over his eyes like thick curtains. Within the darkness under the lids . . . did a blind hope germinate? His body swayed to the rhythm of his cadence.

I went around the sanctum in circumambulation and came out again through the main apse. I took a last look at the man and walked past him. The sounds chased me, the 'oh . . . ooo . . . au . . . ah . . .', wrapping themselves around me. Angry

intonations composed in some form of Nindastuti[1] – disappointment, rage and sadness beating out a taal on a recognisable
paradigm. Perhaps only a paralysed tongue could find the
nerve to castigate an erring god so freely, in such unambiguous
terms:

> 'How could you do this to me,
> Don't you have eyes?
> How could you be deaf to my cries?
> Don't you have ears?'

The sound tore the soft evening into tatters. A dawn salutation
to awaken a sleeping god.

Translated from the Tamil
by the author

[1] *Nindastuti*: A special genre of devotional verse in which the poet
intimately takes the liberty of berating a god for his failings.

AMBAI (C. S. LAKSHMI)

C. S. Lakshmi writes in Tamil under the name Ambai. She has published two collections of short stories as well as other stories which have appeared in various Tamil journals. She has also written a critical work in English, *The Face Behind the Mask* (1984), which examines the images of women presented by women writers in current popular fiction in Tamil. C. S. Lakshmi lives and works in Bombay. This story is from her second collection, published in 1988.

I have translated the Tamil title, 'Manjal Miin', literally as 'Yellow Fish'. Although the freshness of the image remains, I have lost the alliteration and the chiming of the 'soft' consonants of the Tamil. In Tamil the colour name *manjal* is inseparable from the turmeric root from which it takes its name. Turmeric is one of the most auspicious of all ritual objects and most closely associated with women, the main herb in ritual and daily baths, and the primary spice in cooking.

The story is set in the Maharashtra coast, hence the narrator – who is a migrant from the south – speaks Marathi to the fisher-boy.

Yellow Fish

H igh Summer. Already the sand feels hot. It will not hold its wetness. Away, to the left of the shrunken sea and spent waves, the sand spreads like a desert. Yet the eye is compelled by the sea alone. Now the white boat has arrived. This is the forerunner. Its appearance is the signal that the fishing boats are returning. It floats ashore like a swan, swaying from side to side. Far from the shore, bright spots begin to move. The fisherwomen make ready to welcome the boats ashore. Bright colours: blinding indigo, demonic red, profound green, assaulting blue. They stand vibrant against the white boat upon a faded blue and ash-grey sea.

Now it is possible to see the other boats. Walking further, quite close to the boats you may see the fish filling the nets. Bodies and hands darkened by the salt wind, the men will spread their nets and start sorting the fish the minute the boats come in. Now the fish splash into plastic troughs, round eyes wide open. The unwanted ones are thrown away. There is a general murmur of tired voices, rising for a split second, then falling.

Black hands. Brown wood of the boats. Between the meshes of the nets, white-bellied fish. Crowding near, the colours of the saris press upon the eyes gently but firmly. Painted troughs. Dry sand. An extraordinary collage of colours, on the shores of the wide-spread sea. A composition that imprints itself on the mind and memory.

A yellow fish is thrown away on the sand.

Of that palest yellow that comes before the withering and falling of leaves. It has black spots. As I stoop to watch, it begins to shudder and leap. The mouth gasps; gasps and closes. It shudders and tosses on the hot sand.

That mouth closes; closes and opens, desperate for water. Like Jalaja's mouth.

Too hasty infant Jalaja. She pushed and bumped her way out

into the world. Her name had already been decided. She who rises from the waters. Lotus. Jalaja. They had to put her in an incubator. I stood outside that room constantly, watching her. Her pale red mouth. Her round eyes. Sometimes she would open and close her mouth, as if sucking.

The ashes which Arun brought back from the electric crematorium were in a small urn, a miniature of those huge earthenware jars of Mohenjodaro and Harappa. Its narrow mouth was tied with a piece of cloth.

'Why is the mouth closed?'

'What mouth?'

'The mouth of the urn. Open it.'

'Anu. It contains only ashes.'

'I want to see. Open it.'

'Anu.'

'Open its mouth. That mouth . . .'

Loud racking sobs. The cloth was removed to reveal the urn's tiny mouth.

The ashes were in this very sea.

The sea is at some distance. The yellow fish leaps hopelessly towards it. Its mouth falls open, skyward. Lifted from the hot sand, it falls away from the fingers, heaving and tossing. It falls away again from a leaf with which I try to hold it.

A fisherboy is on his way back from splashing in the waves.

He comes when I summon him in Marathi,

'*Ikkade e*, come here.'

'Will you throw this yellow fish back into the sea?'

A quick snort of laughter. He grabs the fish firmly by its tail and starts running towards the sea. I run after him. He places it on the crest of an incoming wave. For a moment it splutters, helpless, like a drunk who cannot find the way home. Again it opens its mouth to the water, taking it in. Then a swish of the tail fin. An arrogant leap. Once again it swishes its tail and swims forward. You can see its clear yellow for a very long time. Then it merges into the blue-grey-white of the sea.

Translated from the Tamil
by Lakshmi Holmström

ISMAT CHUGTAI

Ismat Chugtai was born in 1915 and educated at Aligarh University. She was associated with the Progressive Writers Association started by the well-known Hindi writer Premchand and others during the Indian Independence movement. Since she started writing in the 1940s she has been a prolific writer of short stories and novels, and is considered one of the foremost of India's Urdu writers, widely admired for the outspokenness of her themes and the sharpness of her style.

Ismat Chugtai is extremely difficult to translate because of the vigour of the colloquial Lucknow Urdu in which she writes. Here she builds the story around a local custom, the chauthi ka jaura, the dress worn by the bride on the fourth day of the wedding celebrations, symbolising the consummation of the marriage, when the newly married bride and groom visited the bride's family for a special celebration. The dress was made of red cotton (*tool*) and sometimes lined in white. It was believed that during the preparation of the trousseau, if even one piece of the elaborate chauthi ka jaura was cut inexactly, then something would surely go wrong in the marriage negotiations. These negotiations would include the agreement of the mehr, an amount of money to be paid to the bride by the bridegroom.

In the story the women meet in the seh dari, literally 'three doored room', opening out into the courtyard, sometimes with folding doors so that it could be integrated into the verandah. It was essentially a women's space, an informal sitting room furnished modestly with a wooden divan, etc.

Bi-Amma and Bi-Aapa are the more respectful forms of the more usual Amma (mother) and Aapa (elder sister).

Chauthi
ka Jaura

O nce again a clean sheet was spread out over the wooden divan in the seh dari. Slivers of sunlight scattered all around the courtyard, pouring in through the cracks of the broken tiled roof which slanted above the verandah. The women of the neighbourhood sat silent, a little apprehensive, mothers clutching babies to their breasts, as if a grave incident was about to occur. Now and then a skinny irritable child would wail for want of its mother's milk.

'Now, now, my precious.'

The thin, emaciated mother would rock the child on her knees as if she were sifting husk from the rice. The children settled down to their crooning.

There were several hopeful eyes today staring at Kubra's mother's face. Two narrow widths of bridal red cotton had already been sewn together, but no one had yet ventured to mark the white lining. Kubra's mother was an expert when it came to laying out and cutting fabric. No one knew how many dowries had been dressed, how many layettes laid ready and how many shrouds measured out by those withered hands. Whenever someone in the neighbourhood ran short of fabric, or a million efforts to contrive a fabric failed, the problem would be brought to Kubra's mother. Kubra's mother would get rid of the bias and the starch, try out a triangle, then a square, apply the scissors in her imagination, measure and judge with her eyes and then break into a smile.

'The skirt and sleeves are no problem, the strip for the neckline you could have from my buqchi,' and the problem would be resolved. She would cut the material, make a bundle of the pieces and hand it over.

But today the piece of white lining material was really very small and everyone believed that her expertise would certainly fail. That was why they were looking at her, holding their breath. Her confident face showed no trace of worry though,

75

her eyes were quietly measuring the quarter yard or so of the lining material. The colour of the red cotton reflected off the bluish pallor of her face like the setting sun at twilight; the sad deep wrinkles brightened suddenly as if light were breaking through dark clouds, or as if a sudden fire had set a dense forest ablaze. Smiling she picked up her scissors.

A sigh of relief went up from the cluster of women. Infants were dumped on the floor. Unmarried girls with their arrow-sharp hawk-eyes threaded their needles quickly, the newly married ones donned their thimbles and Kubra's mother's scissors started their work.

In the farthest corner of the seh dari Hamida was sitting on the edge of a small string bed, her legs hanging down, chin resting on cupped hands, deep in her private thoughts.

Every afternoon, after the mid-day meal Bi-Amma would sit in the same seh dari, on the same wooden divan, just like this. She would open her buqchi and scatter a colourful criss-cross of fabrics about her. As Hamida's sister Kubra squatted next to the pail, scrubbing pots and pans, she would look at the shiny red cloth through the corners of her eyes. A flash of red would appear on her pale brown face, suddenly. Bi-Amma would unwrap the silvery sequined material lightly with careful hands and would spread it on her knees, and her withered face would seem to glow with a certain longing, a certain desire. The wrinkles on her face lit up to their very depths as if from torch light. The silver embroidery would tremble as if little lanterns flickered on every stitch. God knows how long it took for all that work to be done, and put away safely in the deep hearts of the coffin-like boxes. Those silvery sequins became dull with the passage of time and the glittering golden threads lost their sheen.

For Kubra's wedding procession never arrived. As each set of clothes became lack-lustre and dull it was put aside to be included in the main dowry and the special suit for the fourth day of marriage, the chauthi ka jaura, would be made again. With each new set of clothes new hopes were kindled. A clean white sheet was spread over the familiar divan and the women of the neighbourhood would arrive jingling their ankle-chains, their babies held under arm and betel-leaf in their hands.

'There will be enough for the band but not for the gusset . . .'

'Listen to her . . . are you going to use red cotton for the gusset, then?'

Then everyone's face would assume a worried expression. Kubra's mother would continue to measure the length and breadth of the cloth with her eyes, like an alchemist, in total silence. Then someone would whisper a remark about the brassiere and laugh loudly, and someone else would start singing wedding songs. One in a daredevil mood would make naughty remarks about the girl's in-laws-to-be and they would all start on ribald, bawdy jokes, teasing each other. On such occasions the unmarried girls were sent to sit in the verandah and to cover their heads. When a new round of laughter surfaced, these poor souls would heave a sigh and pray for the day when they too would be married and take their place amidst all that festivity. Away from this bustle, shy Kubra would hide herself in the storeroom which was always infested with swarms of mosquitoes. Meanwhile the cutting process would arrive at a very crucial stage. If even one piece were cut inexactly all the women would become very tense and Kubra would peep through the door terrified of the consequence.

That was the tragedy really: no single outfit was finished in peace, without worry. If any part of the trousers went wrong it was believed there would surely be repercussions. You could be sure that someone would sabotage the matchmaker's propositions. Either it would become common knowledge that the groom-to-be had a mistress, or his mother would demand a pair of solid gold bangles. If the trousers were even slightly awry then there would either be an argument about the amount of mehr or a demand for a dowry bed with solid silver legs. The omen of the chauthi ka jaura was very delicate, and extremely important. And yet, with all their mother's skill and flair, something always went wrong. Without fail, a minor mole of a problem, insignificant and small, gradually grew to mountainous proportions. She had begun collecting Kubra's dowry since the day of the child's 'Bismillah', when the little girl began her first lesson in the reading of the Koran. Every little piece of cloth was cleverly used and always made into something: either a sewing bag or a case for a mirror, decorated with silver-gold laces.

'These girls are like vines, they grow so fast, don't they?'

For Kubra to get married at all, the planning and design of the trousseau was crucial. This was what Bi-Amma believed. Since Father had died though, this task had become immensely difficult.

Hamida remembered her father.

He was so thin, every bone of his body sticking out, and as tall as a Muharram standard . . . Once he bent down it was difficult for him to stand up again. Early in the morning, every day he would get a fresh miswak, seat Hamida on his knees, and while cleaning his teeth he would be lost in his thoughts. God knows what he thought! And when a fibre of his miswak stuck in his throat, he would begin to cough. Hamida used to get very angry and jump off his knees. She hated the vibration her father's cough made. He would laugh at her show of anger, and it made his cough twist and tangle in his breast, as if there were slain pigeons fluttering there. Bi-Amma would always come and help him to regain his breath by patting and rubbing his back vigorously.

'In Heaven's name, what kind of laugh is that?'

He would laugh helplessly, all choked up and red-eyed. The cough would eventually subside and he would smile miserably as he managed to get his breath back.

'Why don't you do something about this cough, how many times have I told you?'

'The doctor at the hospital told me to have injections, and drink a pint of milk and eat half an ounce of butter a day.'

'To hell with those doctors. They tell you to eat butter when you have this cough, won't the fat make phlegm in your body? It is better to see a herbal doctor, I would say.'

Then he would start smoking his hookah, and start choking again.

'To hell with this hookah, it is this damn thing which gives you a cough. Do you ever think about your daughter who has now reached marriageable age?'

Now he would look at his young daughter Kubra, his eyes pleading for mercy. Kubra was young, but who could say when she had arrived at the age of puberty? It seemed as if she had become a young woman the day she started to read the first words of the Koran. What kind of youth was hers? She never ever had stars in her eyes nor let her hair fly loose over her cheeks. She had never given way to storms of emotions, never sought a lover, not even when the dark clouds gathered in the sky during the monsoons. She was always pensive, always looked harassed. That timid and huddled youth that had crept upon her, left her as stealthily as it came.

Father fell on the doorstep one day and no doctor's prescription helped him to recover from this fall. Now Hamida stopped crying for sweet bread, and no marriage proposals came for Kubra. Nobody knew that behind that canvas curtain there were two girls, one who was crossing the threshold of youth, the other whose youth was awakening dangerously, like a stirring cobra raising its head.

But Bi-Amma's daily routine did not change. Every afternoon she continued to sit in the seh dari, scattering the colourful bits of material about her and playing the wedding game. Once she managed to save some money and bought some crêpe material for seven-and-a-half rupees. The purchase was a must; there was a telegram from Kubra's uncle (from the mother's side) that his eldest son, Rahat, would be arriving by train the next day, in connection with his police training. Bi-Amma was in a fit of worry, as if her daughter's wedding procession had already arrived at her doorstep, and she hadn't even prepared the gold dust to sprinkle on the bride's hair. She had hysterics and in desperation she sent for her closest friend, her adoptive sister, Bundo's mother. 'You will only see my dead body if you don't come right away.'

The two of them had a meeting in whispered conspiratorial tones. Now and then they would throw cursory glances at Kubra who, as usual, was sitting out on the verandah, cleaning rice. Kubra knew very well what they were discussing. And there and then Bi-Amma took her tiny light weight gold ear-studs off and gave them to her adoptive sister to sell. Whatever it costs, she said, by this evening I must have an ounce of shiny gold tatting, a quarter of an ounce of sequins and fine gold trimming, and a quarter yard of red cotton for the belt. The room which was on the outer side of the house was cleaned thoroughly. Kubra had bought some lime and whitewashed the

79

room with her own hands. The room gleamed white but the skin of her hands began to peel off, and in the evening when she was grinding the spices for dinner, they hurt so badly she was bent with pain. She couldn't sleep all night and kept tossing and turning. First, because her hands hurt, and then, because Rahat was arriving by the morning train.

'Allah, my dear Allah, let this be my Aapa's lucky break. I offer my humblest prayers to you a hundred times over,' Hamida added to her morning prayers.

When Rahat arrived Kubra had already hidden herself in the mosquito-ridden storeroom. After he had eaten the sumptuous breakfast prepared for him and had retired to the sitting room, Kubra emerged from the storeroom, walking softly, like a bride, and started clearing the breakfast things away.

'Aapa, give them to me, I will wash them,' said Hamida mischievously.

'No, it's all right,' replied Kubra, her head bowed with shyness. Hamida teased her sister, while her mother smiled and continued to sew the silver lace with her swift hands. At first she had sold the ear-studs, then two pairs of ear-rings. Her heavy silver anklets were the next to be sold. Then her four bangles, given to her by her brother when she had been widowed, were sent to the goldsmith. Rahat was feasted on parathas and meatballs, pilaf rice and fine cuts of meat while they lived on bread and water.

'Things are bad these days, my dear child,' Bi-Amma said when she found Hamida sulking one day over the sacrifices they were making. Hamida would brood: we are feeding him rich foods while we ourselves go hungry. Aapa gets up early, starting the day like a machine. She herself has only a glass of cold water while she prepares his breakfast. This is usually parathas, made of layers upon layers of pastry brushed with butter and then fried. And also, he has milk and cream. If she could manage to take the fat out of her body, and layer his paratha with it she would do so gladly. And why not, he will be her man one day and then she will be the recipient of his earnings. Everyone waters the tree which is going to bear fruit for them. And one day when the tree blooms, and the branches are heavy with fruit, then all those people who have been ridiculing my big sister will be well and truly snubbed.

Even the thought of getting married and living happily made Kubra's face glow and shine, like a bride. She could hear the wedding music of the shehnai. She cleaned Rahat's room with great care, folded his clothes with loving hands, as if they were saying something to her. She washed his filthy socks, foul smelling vests and snotty handkerchiefs. She embroidered 'sweet dreams' on his pillow cases, which reeked of hair-oil. But none of this special treatment made any difference to his attitude. He would have his elaborate breakfast and then go to work, and in the evening eat his dinner, and go off to sleep in his room.

Bi-Amma's adoptive sister whispered to her, and Bi-Amma offered her own explanation:

'He is very shy.'

'Well, even so there should be some indication of his intentions. At least some little thing, the way he looks at her . . .'

'Heaven forbid, my daughter is not one of those girls . . . He hasn't even seen her,' Bi-Amma declared rather proudly.

'I am not saying that she ought to meet him, not at all. Oh, sister, you are silly. I am not suggesting anything like that. But what about this little sister of hers. When is she going to be of any use. Oh, naughty girl, why don't you speak to your brother-in-law-to-be. Make a joke, tease him, be friendly with him.'

'How am I to do that, auntie?'

'Why don't you just speak to him first, have a chat with him.'

'I feel shy, I just can't do it.'

'Silly girl, he is not going to eat you up, is he?' Bi-Amma sounded cross.

'Well no, but . . .' Hamida couldn't say anything. Then they had put their heads together, and after much deliberation decided that a practical joke should be played on Rahat. It made even Aapa smile and she murmured:

'Don't you laugh, you'll spoil it!'

'I won't,' Hamida had promised.

When he returned from work that evening, I took his dinner tray to him and placed it carefully on the table while he washed

81

his hands, examining me from tip to toe all the time. I was so embarrassed by him looking me up and down that I ran away, my heart beating fast. God, he had the eyes of a devil!

'Wretched girl, go and see if he eats the kebab. What's the use of a practical joke if no one is going to enjoy it or report it?'

Aapa looked at me, her eyes sad and full of hurt rejection, pleading. In her eyes I saw the dust of retreating wedding processions and the faded red of suits grown too dull for the chauthi ka jaura. I went back, my head hanging down. Rahat kept on eating quietly, he failed even to gaze at me. I saw him eating the kebab, and I should have laughed at him for being such a fool and not recognising what he was eating, but instead I felt as if someone had grabbed me by my throat. I was speechless. Bi-Amma was flabbergasted. She called me back. She swore at me under her breath, and was furious at me for not making the effort to be friendly. How could I tell her that the wretched man was busy eating those kebabs made of hay?

'Rahat bhai, did you like the meatballs?' I repeated the words Bi-Amma had told me to say. No answer. 'Please tell me if you enjoyed the kebabs,' Bi-Amma had pushed me to ask again.

'You brought the food and I ate it. Must have been tasty,' he replied, at last.

'You are a silly boy,' Bi-Amma couldn't contain herself any longer, 'you didn't notice that the kebabs were made of hay?'

'Made of hay? I have become so used to eating hay and husks that I can't tell the difference any more.'

Bi-Amma's face grew pale and Aapa could not look at me. Next day she did twice as much sewing as usual to earn enough money. Later that evening, when I, as usual, took him his dinner, he asked:

'So what have you brought me today? Is it sawdust today?'

'Don't you like our cooking?' I retorted acidly.

'It's not that. But it is a bit strange to be served kebabs made of hay and vegetables made of husk.'

I was furious. We live on bread and water, while he devours food enough for an elephant. He has rich and tasty dishes while my Aapa, my dear big sister, can't even afford to buy medicines for her colds and coughs. I came back angry.

Bi-Amma's adoptive sister's trick worked though, and Rahat

started spending more time at home. Aapa spent most of her time in the kitchen, and mother was always busy sewing the chauthi ka jaura. Rahat's eyes, full of insinuations, attacked me from all sides like sharp arrows. He found excuses to tease me when I took him his food, and always made heavy jokes to me. I was embarrassed and went to sit with Aapa. I felt like telling her: 'Aapa, he is your problem, you deal with him. I cannot put up with him any longer.' But I looked at her, and saw her dishevelled hair, a few greying as if ash had been sprinkled on her. I quickly pushed such thoughts away; this blasted cold, I thought, it is making her hair go grey. I heard Rahat call my name out loud. I ignored it, until Aapa turned around and looked at me like a wounded sparrow; I had to go.

'Are you cross with me?' he took the glass of water and then took hold of my hand. I twisted my wrist away and ran.

'What did he say?' Aapa's voice was soft and suppressed by shyness and modesty. I stared at her.

'He asked who cooked the dinner – it was so delicious, I couldn't stop eating, he said. I could have eaten the hand which cooked it – oh, no, I could have kissed it.' I babbled away, and held Aapa's hands tightly in mine. They were rough, and smelled of coriander and turmeric. I couldn't stop my tears. I said to myself: these hands which keep on working from dawn to dusk, they grind spices, fetch water, slice onions, make beds, clean shoes. They are like slaves, working from morning till night. God knows when their slavery is going to end. Will someone ever hold them tenderly, kiss them? Will they ever be decorated with henna? Will they ever smell of wedding scent? I wanted to scream.

'What did he say?' Her hands may have been coarse, but her voice was sweet, if only Rahat could listen. But Rahat had neither an ear, nor a nose, he only had a belly like a bottomless pit.

'And he was saying that I should ask my Aapa not to work so hard and to take medicine for her infections.'

'You liar!'

'He is a liar, not me!'

'Be quiet you silly thing,' she put her hands on my mouth. 'Look,' Aapa continued, 'this jumper is finished now, give it to him please. But don't tell him that I have knitted it.' I wanted to say, Aapa don't give him the jumper, your weak bones need it more, but I couldn't. I asked, 'Aapa, what will you wear?'

'Oh, I don't need anything, really. It is always so hot in the kitchen.'

When Rahat saw the jumper, he raised his eyebrows mischievously and asked, 'Did you knit this?'

'No.'

'Then I won't wear it.'

I felt like scratching his eyes out, the bastard. I wanted to say: this jumper was made by hands which are like unpaid servants and its every stitch carries the longings and dreams of an unlucky girl. It was knitted by hands made to rock a crib; why don't you hold those hands in yours, you fool, and they will carry you through the high and low seas of life. They don't play the sitar. They are neither trained to dance on the keyboard of a piano, nor have they had the opportunity to play with lovely fragrant flowers. They do the sewing all day long to earn enough money to feed you lavishly. They are dipped in and out of soap and soda, they put up with the heat of the kitchen, wash your filth, so that you can don clean clothes and pretend that you have a clear conscience. These hands are bruised by the work they do. Bangles never jingle on them, and nobody has ever held them with affection.

But I remained quiet. Bi-Amma always says that I have been brainwashed by my new friends who tell me strange and new things about hunger and death and famine and about the live pulsating heart suddenly going quiet.

'Why don't you wear this jumper? Look, your dress is so thin.'

Like a wild cat I scratched his face, pulled his hair and ran to my bed and flopped on top of it.

After Aapa finished making chapatis, she washed her hands quickly and came and sat by my side, drying her hands on her head-scarf.

'Did he say anything?' she couldn't help asking the question, her heart beating in anticipation.

'Aapa, Rahat is a wicked man.' I was going to tell her everything, I decided. 'He is very naughty,' she said, in a romantic tone, mingled with shyness. 'Aapa – listen Aapa, he is not a good man.' I was burning with hate. 'I am going to tell Bi-Amma today.'

'What happened?' Bi-Amma asked while spreading out her prayer-mat.

'See my bangles, Bi-Amma?'

'Did he break them?' Bi-Amma seemed delighted.

'Yes!'

'He was right to do that . . . You tease him so, why are you complaining so much? You aren't made of glass that will break if touched,' she coaxed. 'Anyway you can have your revenge when he comes for the chauthi. Make him remember it all his life,' she finished, and then started offering her prayers.

Again there was a conference between Bi-Amma and her sister and it was agreed that things were looking up. They smiled confidently . . . nodded their heads and said: 'Oh, she is so dull. We used to play so many practical jokes on our brothers-in-law.' And then Aunt started telling me the tricks of the trade and how because of her playfulness she had had her two cousins married off, even though both had been assumed to be on the shelf.

'One of the grooms was a hakim, he practised herbal medicines. He was very shy and when we teased him he would have palpitations. One day he just came out and asked my Uncle for his daughter's hand in marriage. The other one was a clerk in the Viceroy's office. Whenever he came to my Uncle's house and the girls realised he was there, they would start their tricks. Sometimes they would put red-hot chillis in his betel leaf or even salt in his sweet-dish. Of course he enjoyed it and started visiting daily. Whatever the weather, come hell or high water, he visited without fail. One day, he asked an acquaintance of his, to arrange his marriage in our family. When asked, "To whom?" he replied "To anyone". Heaven forbid I should tell a lie, but those girls were really ugly. The older sister looked like a peasant and the younger one had a squint. But their father gave them fifteen tolas of gold each and he got the boys jobs in the bara sahib's office.'

'Yes, well, if one has gold to give and can promise a good

job, one will certainly have no difficulty in finding a match for one's daughter,' Bi-Amma sighed.

'That is not the reason, dear sister, these boys need a little flattering these days. They will go any way you push them. They need to be pushed, that's all.'

But Rahat cannot be pushed. He is like a mountain. And, if I do try to push him, I may be crushed in the process, I thought, and looked at Aapa. She was sitting by the kitchen door, kneading the dough for chapatis. If she could have made the ground open up and hide her and her cursed state of not having a suitor, she would have done it there and then.

Did my sister need a man? No, but she was frightened at the thought of hunger. Her need was not for emotional fulfilment but for survival. She needed someone who could feed her, clothe her. She was a burden on her widowed mother, and had to be tidied away.

Even though Rahat was given plenty of inducements and reasons to be aware of our hopes and desires he uttered not a single word in acknowledgement, nor did his parents send any messages. Bi-Amma was tired of waiting, so she sold her heavy ankle-chain and arranged for an offering to be made to a special saint, one who would solve all her problems. The whole afternoon went by with the girls of the neighbourhood singing noisily in the inner courtyard. Aapa was so shy that she hid herself in the storeroom, allowing the ever-present mosquitoes to suck the last drops of blood running in her veins. Bi-Amma, her strength and energy drained away, sat on the divan, putting the final touches to the chauthi ka jaura. Her face manifested hope; hope that her worries were over; that her wish was going to be fulfilled; these were, she was convinced, the last moments before the realisation of her prayers. Once again there were torches shining from the deep wrinkles of her face. Aapa's friends were teasing her, trying to make her feel excited and happy, and her blood did flow red, at least the few drops left in her body. She had had a fever for a few days, now and then her face flushed momentarily, then darkness claimed it again. She beckoned to me, then produced a plate.

'It is the plate with the offering.'

Her breath touched my ears, hot and burning with the fever.

Holding the plate in my hand I thought, this sweet, this special sacred sweet will also find its way into Rahat's belly. That belly which has been filled by our sweat and blood for the last six months. But this sweet will make our dreams come true. I too could hear the wedding band, I could see myself running upstairs to watch the bridegroom arrive. His face is covered with large and heavy garlands, which fall all the way down to his horse's tail. My sister is wearing the red dress of the fourth day, her chauthi ka jaura. Adorned with red roses, shy and modest, she is walking gingerly, her dress glittering. Bi-Amma's face is bright and glowing with happiness . . . Aapa's eyelids are heavy with modesty, slowly she looks up at me once and a tear of gratitude drops and mingles in her silver lace and sequins. 'It all happened because of you,' Aapa says in her reticence.

'Go dear sister,' Aapa's voice woke me up from my reverie, and wiping my tears I went towards the sitting-room . . .

'This . . . this sweet is for you,' trying to control her throbbing heart, Hamida had tried to speak. Her legs were weak and trembling, as if she had put her feet down a snakepit. Then the mountain moved. Rahat opened his mouth. She stepped back frightened. But in the distance the shehnais wailed as if their wedding music was being strangled. She took a piece of the sweet in her hand and tried to reach Rahat's mouth. With a jerk her hand went deeper and deeper, inside the filth and darkness. A huge rock covered her and suffocated the cry which was trying to escape. The plate with its sacred sweet fell on the lantern, which in turn fell on the floor, flickered a few times and went out quietly. In the inner courtyard the girls were singing their songs of praises to the special saint who puts an end to sorrow.

Rahat, after expressing his eternal gratitude for the hospitality he had received, went home by the morning train. The departure was made in haste because his wedding date was fixed, and he was needed by his family.

After that no one ever fried eggs or cooked parathas in this house, or knitted sweaters. And the tuberculosis which had been stalking Bi-Aapa for some time now, caught up with her and seized her in one leap.

In the same verandah, on the same divan, a clean sheet was spread, and the women and girls of the neighbourhood sat around solemnly. White cotton lay in front of Bi-Amma like the wings of death. Her face quivered, weighed down by endurance. Her left eyebrow twitched. A wilderness of streams hissed down her cheeks. She smoothed and stretched the white cloth and laid it out four-fold while a million scissors sliced her heart to a million pieces. Unlike those other sets of clothes, this one would surely be worn.

Hamida shook off the past. The young girls sitting in the seh dari were chirping like minah birds. She went towards them. The red cotton was joined to its white lining. Red stood for the bright hopes of innocent brides; white for those dreams and desires that were never fulfilled.

And then, at once, everyone was silent. Kubra's mother sewed the last stitch and bit off the thread. Two large tears rolled slowly down her cheeks. Rays of light glowed from the wrinkles of her face, and she smiled as if it was Kubra's dress that was ready today, and any time now the shehnai would burst into song.

Translated from the Urdu
by Safiya Siddiqui

MAHASVETA DEVI

Mahasveta Devi was born in 1926 and has written many novels (*Amrita Sanchay* 1964, *Andharmanik* 1967, *Aranyer Adhikar* 1977 and *Chotti Munda o Tar Tir* 1979, among others) and short stories in Bengali. Her work is powerful, moving and infused with a sense of the movement of history. She is also a prolific journalist; besides editing a Bengali journal, *Bortika*, she has written several articles and reports in English on peasant labour in West Bengal. Currently, most of her time is given to her work among the tribal communities in the border areas of the states of West Bengal, Bihar and Orissa.

'Draupadi' is one of three stories from the collection *Agnigarbha* (womb of fire) published as a collection in 1978, and set against the Naxalite activities of 1967–72. In May 1972, a peasant uprising in protest against the oppression of the landless peasantry and tribal cultivators took place at Naxalbari, in the northern tip of West Bengal. This was supported by Communist revolutionaries who were later to form a separate party, the Communist Party of India, Marxist-Leninist. During the five years that followed, there were several such 'Naxalite' uprisings elsewhere in India, notably Andhra, Punjab, Bihar and Kerala as well as in other parts of West Bengal. By 1970, several students from the cities had joined the peasant movement, while urban guerrilla activities were also taking place within the city of Calcutta itself. The West Bengal State government retaliated sharply, and with help from the Centre, the police and the military forces brutally put an end to both urban and peasant action.

In Mahasveta's story, the main character's name, Draupadi, (the tribal version is Dopdi) is also that of the heroine of the Indian epic, the *Mahabharata*. In the epic, Draupadi is married to the five Pandava brothers. The eldest, Yudhistira, at one point loses his kingdom and all his possessions to his cousins, the Kauravas, in a game of dice. He then stakes and loses Draupadi. Then follows one of the best known episodes of the epic. Draupadi is violently dragged by the hair in front of the assembly of men, and one of the Kauravas, Dussasana, attempts to strip her. Draupadi, however, prays to Lord Krishna, who works a miracle: the more the sari is pulled, the more it grows. Draupadi can never be disrobed.

This translation by Gayatri Chakravorty Spivak was first published, with a critical foreword, by the University of Chicago Press in *Critical Inquiry* (1981) and later in Elizabeth Abel (ed.), *Writing and Sexual Difference* (pp. 261–82; Harvester Press, Brighton, 1982) and in Gayatri Chakravorty Spivak, *In Other Worlds* (pp. 179–96: Methuen, New York, 1987).

In her foreword, Gayatri Spivak writes 'the italicised words in the translation are in English in the original . . . Rather than encumber the story with footnotes, in conclusion I shall list a few items of information.' These notes appear at the end of the story.

Draupadi

Name, Dopdi Mejhen; age, twenty-seven; husband, Dulna Majhi (deceased); domicile, Cherakhan; Bankrajharh, information whether dead or alive and/or assistance in arrest, one hundred rupees . . .

An exchange between two liveried *uniforms*.

FIRST LIVERY: What's this, a tribal called Dopdi? The list of names I brought has nothing like it! How can anyone have an unlisted name?

SECOND: DRAUPADI Mejhen. Born the year her mother threshed rice at Surja Sahu (killed)'s at Bakuli. Surja Sahu's wife gave her the name.

FIRST: These officers like nothing better than to write as much as they can in English. What's all this stuff about her?

SECOND: *Most notorious* female. *Long wanted in many* . . .

Dossier: Dulna and Dopdi worked at harvests, *rotating* between Birbhum, Burdwan, Murshidabad, and Bankura. In 1971, in the famous *Operation* Bakuli, when three villages were *cordoned* off and *machine gunned*, they too lay on the ground, faking dead. In fact, they were the main culprits. Murdering Surja Sahu and his son, occupying upper-caste wells and tubewells during the drought, not surrendering those three young men to the police. In all this they were the chief instigators. In the morning, at the time of the body count, the couple could not be found. The blood-sugar level of Captain Arjan Singh, the *architect* of Bakuli, rose at once and proved yet again that diabetes can be a result of anxiety and depression. Diabetes has twelve husbands – among them anxiety.

Dulna and Dopdi went underground for a long time in a *Neanderthal* darkness. The Special Forces, attempting to pierce that dark by an armed search, compelled quite a few Santals in the various districts of West Bengal to meet their Maker against their will. By the Indian Constitution, all human beings, regardless of caste or creed, are sacred. Still, accidents like this do happen. Two sorts of reasons: (1), the underground couple's skill in self-concealment; (2), not merely the Santals but all tribals of the Austro-Asiatic Munda tribes appear the same to the Special Forces.

In fact, all around the ill-famed forest of Jharkhani, which is under the jurisdiction of the police station at Bankrajharh (in this India of ours, even a worm is under a certain police station), even in the southeast and southwest corners, one comes across hair-raising details in the eyewitness records put together on the people who are suspected of attacking police stations, stealing guns (since the snatchers are not invariably well educated, they sometimes say 'give up your *chambers*' rather than give up your gun), killing grain brokers, landlords, moneylenders, law officers, and bureaucrats. A black-skinned couple ululated like police *sirens* before the episode. They sang jubilantly in a savage tongue, incomprehensible even to the Santals. Such as:

    Samaray hijulenako mar goekope

and,

    Hende rambra keche keche
    Pundi rambra keche keche

This proves conclusively that they are the cause of Captain Arjan Singh's diabetes.

Government procedure being as incomprehensible as the Male Principle in Sankhya philosophy or Antonioni's early films, it was Arjan Singh who was sent once again on *Operation Forest* Jharkhani. Learning from Intelligence that the above-mentioned ululating and dancing couple were the escaped corpses, Arjan Singh fell for a bit into a *zombie* like state and finally acquired so irrational a dread of black-skinned people that whenever he saw a black person in a ballbag, he swooned, saying 'They're killing me,' and drank and passed a lot of water. Neither uniform nor Scriptures could relieve that depression. At long last, under the shadow of a *premature and forced retirement*, it was possible to present him at the desk of Mr

Senanayak, the elderly Bengali specialist in combat and extreme-Left politics.

Senanayak knows the activities and capacities of the opposition better than they themselves do. First, therefore, he presents an encomium on the military genius of the Sikhs. Then he explains further: Is it only the opposition that should find power at the end of the barrel of a gun? Arjan Singh's power also explodes out of the *male organ* of a gun. Without a gun even the 'five Ks'[1] come to nothing in this day and age. These speeches he delivers to all and sundry. As a result, the fighting forces regain their confidence in the *Army Handbook*. It is not a book for everyone. It says that the most despicable and repulsive style of fighting is guerrilla warfare with primitive weapons. Annihilation at sight of any and all practitioners of such warfare is the sacred duty of every soldier. Dopdi and Dulna belong to the *category* of such fighters, for they too kill by means of hatchet and scythe, bow and arrow, etc. In fact, their fighting power is greater than the gentlemen's. Not all gentlemen become experts in the explosion of 'chambers'; they think the power will come out on its own if the gun is held. But since Dulna and Dopdi are illiterate, their kind have practised the use of weapons generation after generation.

I should mention here that, although the other side make little of him, Senanayak is not to be trifled with. Whatever his *practice*, in *theory* he respects the opposition. Respects them because they could be neither understood nor demolished if they were treated with the attitude, 'It's nothing but a bit of impertinent game-playing with guns.' *In order to destroy the enemy, become one.* Thus he understood them by (*theoretically*) becoming one of them. He hopes to write on all this in the future. He has also decided that in his written work he will demolish the gentlemen and *highlight* the message of the harvest workers. These mental processes might seem complicated, but actually he is a simple man and is as pleased as his third great-uncle after a meal of turtle meat. In fact, he knows that, as in the old popular song, turn by turn the world will change. And in every world he must have the credentials to survive with honour. If necessary he will show the future to what extent he alone understands the matter in its proper perspective. He knows very well that what he is doing today the future will forget, but he also knows that if he can change colour from world to world, he can represent the particular world in question. Today he is getting rid of the young by means of *'apprehension and elimination'*, but he knows people will soon forget the memory and lesson of blood. And at the same time, he, like Shakespeare, believes in delivering the world's *legacy* into youth's hands. He is Prospero as well.

At any rate, information is received that many young men and women, *batch by batch* and on jeeps, have attacked police station after police station, terrified and elated the region, and disappeared into the forest of Jharkhani. Since after escaping from Bakuli, Dopdi and Dulna have worked at the house of virtually every landowner, they can efficiently inform the killers about their targets and announce proudly that they too are soldiers, *rank and file*. Finally the impenetrable forest of Jharkhani is surrounded by real soldiers, the *army* enters and splits the battlefield. Soldiers in hiding guard the falls and springs that are the only source of drinking water; they are still guarding, still looking. On one such search, army informant Dukhiram Gharari saw a young Santal man lying on his stomach on a flat stone, dipping his face to drink water. The soldiers shot him as he lay. As the .303 threw him off spread-eagled and brought a bloody foam to his mouth, he roared 'Ma–ho' and then went limp. They realized later that it was the redoubtable Dulna Majhi.

What does 'Ma–ho' mean? Is this a violent slogan in the tribal language? Even after much thought, the Department of Defence could not be sure. Two tribal-specialist types are flown in from Calcutta, and they sweat over the dictionaries put together by worthies such as Hoffman-Jeffer and Golden-Palmer. Finally the omniscient Senanayak summons Chamru, the water carrier of the *camp*. He giggles when he sees the two specialists, scratches his ear with his 'bidi', and says, The Santals of Maldah did say that when they began fighting at the time of King Gandhi! It's a battle cry. Who said 'Ma–ho' here? Did someone come from Maldah?

The problem is thus solved. Then, leaving Dulna's body on the stone, the soldiers climb the trees in green camouflage.

They embrace the leafy boughs like so many great god Pans and wait as the large red ants bite their private parts. To see if anyone comes to take away the body. This is the hunter's way, not the soldier's. But Senanayak knows that these brutes cannot be dispatched by the approved method. So he asks his men to draw the prey with a corpse as bait. All will come clear, he says. I have almost deciphered Dopdi's song.

The soldiers get going at his command. But no one comes to claim Dulna's corpse. At night the soldiers shoot at a scuffle and, descending, discover that they have killed two hedgehogs copulating on dry leaves. Improvidently enough, the soldiers' jungle scout Dukhiram gets a knife in the neck before he can claim the reward for Dulna's capture. Bearing Dulna's corpse, the soldiers suffer shooting pains as the ants, interrupted in their feast, begin to bite them. When Senanayak hears that no one has come to take the corpse, he slaps his *anti-Fascist paperback* copy of *The Deputy* and shouts, '*What*?' Immediately one of the tribal specialists runs in with a joy as naked and transparent as Archimedes' and says, 'Get up, *sir*! I have discovered the meaning of that 'hende rambra' stuff. It's Mundari *language*.'

Thus the search for Dopdi continues. In the forest *belt* of Jharkhani, the *Operation* continues – will continue. It is a carbuncle on the government's backside. Not to be cured by the tested ointment, not to burst with the appropriate herb. In the first phase, the fugitives, ignorant of the forest's topography, are caught easily, and by the law of confrontation they are shot at the taxpayer's expense. By the law of confrontation, their eyeballs, intestines, stomachs, hearts, genitals, and so on become the food of fox, vulture, hyena, wildcat, ant, and worm, and the untouchables go off happily to sell their bare skeletons.

They do not allow themselves to be captured in open combat in the next phase. Now it seems that they have found a trustworthy courier. Ten to one it's Dopdi. Dopdi loved Dulna more than her blood. No doubt it is she who is saving the fugitives now.

'They' is also a *hypothesis*.

Why?

How many went *originally*?

The answer is silence. About that there are many tales, many books in press. Best not to believe everything.

How many killed in six years' confrontation?

The answer is silence.

Why after confrontations are the skeletons discovered with arms broken or severed? Could armless men have fought? Why do the collar-bones shake, why are legs and ribs crushed?

Two kinds of answer. Silence. Hurt rebuke in the eyes. Shame on you! Why bring this up? What will be will be . . .

How many left in the forest? The answer is silence.

A *legion*? Is it *justifiable* to maintain a large battalion in that wild area at the taxpayer's expense?

Answer: *Objection*. 'Wild area' is incorrect. The battalion is provided with supervised nutrition, arrangements to worship according to religion, opportunity to listen to 'Bibhida Bharati'[2] and to see Sanjeev Kumar and the Lord Krishna face-to-face in the movie *This Is Life*. No. The area is not wild.

How many are left?

The answer is silence.

How many are left? Is there anyone *at all*?

The answer is long.

Item: *Well*, *action* still goes on. Moneylenders, landlords, grain brokers, anonymous brothel keepers, ex-informants are still terrified. The hungry and naked are still defiant and irrepressible. In some *pockets* the harvest workers are getting a *better wage*. Villages sympathetic to the fugitives are still silent and hostile. These events cause one to think . . .

Where in this picture does Dopdi Mejhen fit?

She must have connections with the fugitives. The cause for fear is elsewhere. The ones who remain have lived a long time in the primitive world of the forest. They keep company with the poor harvest workers and the tribals. They must have forgotten book learning. Perhaps they are *orienting* their book learning to the soil they live on and learning new combat and survival techniques. One can shoot and get rid of the ones whose only recourse is extrinsic book learning and sincere intrinsic enthusiasm. Those who are working practically will not be exterminated so easily.

Therefore *Operation* Jharkhani *Forest* cannot stop. Reason: the words of warning in the *Army Handbook*.

2

Catch Dopdi Mejhen. She will lead us to the others.

Dopdi was proceeding slowly, with some rice knotted into her belt. Mushai Tudu's wife had cooked her some. She does so occasionally. When the rice is cold, Dopdi knots it into her waistcloth and walks slowly. As she walked, she picked out and killed the lice in her hair. If she had some *kerosene*, she'd rub it into her scalp and get rid of the lice. Then she could wash her hair with baking *soda*. But the bastards put traps at every bend of the falls. If they smell *kerosene* in the water, they will follow the scent.

Dopdi!

She doesn't respond. She never responds when she hears her own name. She has seen in the Panchayat office [3] just today the notice for the reward in her name. Mushai Tudu's wife had said, 'What are you looking at? Who is Dopdi Mejhen! Money if you give her up!'

'How much?'

'Two – hundred!'

Oh God!

Mushai's wife said outside the office: 'A lot of preparation this time. A-11 new policemen.'

Hm.

Don't come again.

Why?

Mushai's wife looked down. Tudu says that Sahib has come again. If they catch you, the village, our huts . . .

They'll burn again.

Yes. And about Dukhiram . . .

The Sahib knows?

Shomai and Budhna betrayed us.

Where are they?

Ran away by train.

Dopdi thought of something. Then said, Go home. I don't know what will happen, if they catch me don't know me.

Can't you run away?

No. Tell me, how many times can I run away? What will they do if they catch me? They will *counter* me. Let them.

Mushai's wife said, We have nowhere else to go.

Dopdi said softly, I won't tell anyone's name.

Dopdi knows, has learned by hearing so often and so long how one can come to terms with torture. If mind and body give way under torture, Dopdi will bite off her tongue. That boy did it. They countered him. When they counter you, your hands are tied behind you. All your bones are crushed, your sex is a terrible wound. *Killed by police in an encounter . . . unknown male . . . age twenty-two . . .*

As she walked thinking these thoughts, Dopdi heard someone calling, Dopdi!

She didn't respond. She doesn't respond if called by her own name. Here her name is Upi Mejhen. But who calls?

Spines of suspicion are always furled in her mind. Hearing 'Dopdi' they stiffen like a hedgehog's. Walking, she *unrolls the film* of known faces in her mind. Who? Not Shomra, Shomra is on the run. Shomai and Budhna are also on the run, for other reasons. Not Golok, he is in Bakuli. Is it someone from Bakuli? After Bakuli, her and Dulna's names were Upi Mejhen, Matang Majhi. Here no one but Mushai and his wife knows their real names. Among the young gentlemen, not all of the previous *batches* knew.

That was a troubled time. Dopdi is confused when she thinks about it. *Operation* Bakuli in Bakuli. Surja Sahu arranged with Biddibabu to dig two tubewells and three wells within the compound of his two houses. No water anywhere, drought in Birbhum. Unlimited water at Surja Sahu's house, as clear as a crow's eye.

Get your water with canal tax, everything is burning.

What's my profit in increasing cultivation with tax money?

Everything's on fire.

Get out of here. I don't accept your Panchayat nonsense. Increase cultivation with water. You want half the paddy for sharecropping. Everyone is happy with free paddy. Then give me paddy at home, give me money, I've learned my lesson trying to do you good.

What good did you do?

Have I not given water to the village?

You've given it to your kin Bhagunal.

Don't you get water?

No. The untouchables don't get water.

The quarrel began there. In the drought, human patience catches easily. Satish and Jugal from the village and that young gentleman, was Rana his name?, said a landowning moneylender won't give a thing, put him down.

Surja Sahu's house was surrounded at night. Surja Sahu had brought out his gun. Surja was tied up with cow rope. His whitish eyeballs turned and turned, he was incontinent again and again. Dulna had said, I'll have the first blow, brothers. My greatgrandfather took a bit of paddy from him, and I still give him free labour to repay that debt.

Dopdi had said, His mouth watered when he looked at me. I'll pull out his eyes.

Surja Sahu. Then a *telegraphic message* from Shiuri. *Special train. Army.* The *jeep* didn't come up to Bakuli. *March-march-march.* The *crunch-crunch-crunch* of gravel under hobnailed boots. *Cordon up. Commands* on the *mike.* Jugal Mandal; Satish Mandal, Rana *alias* Prabir *alias* Dipak, Dulna Majhi-Dopdi Mejhen *surrender surrender surrender. No surrender surrender. Mow-mow-mow down the village.* Putt-putt putt-putt – *cordite* in the air – puttputt – *round the clock* – putt-putt. *Flame thrower.* Bakuli is burning. *More men and women, children . . . fire – fire. Close canal approach. Over-over-over by nightfall.* Dopdi and Dulna had crawled on their stomachs to safety.

They could not have reached Paltakuri after Bakuli. Bhupati and Tapa took them. Then it was decided that Dopdi and Dulna would work around the Jharkhani *belt.* Dulna had explained to Dopdi, Dear, this is best! We won't get family and children this way. But who knows? Landowner and moneylender and policemen might one day be wiped out!

Who called her from the back today?

Dopdi kept walking. Villages and fields, bush and rock – *Public Works Department* markers – sound of running steps in

99

back. Only one person running. Jharkhani *Forest* still about two miles away. Now she thinks of nothing but entering the forest. She must let them know that the *police* have set up *notices* for her again. Must tell them that that bastard Sahib has appeared again. Must change *hideouts*. Also, the *plan* to do to Lakkhi Bera and Naran Bera what they did to Surja Sahu on account of the trouble over paying the field hands in Sandara must be cancelled. Shomai and Budhna knew everything. There was the *urgency* of great danger under Dopdi's ribs. Now she thought there was no shame as a Santal in Shomai and Budhna's treachery. Dopdi's blood was the pure unadulterated black blood of Champabhumi. From Champa to Bakuli the rise and set of a million moons. Their blood could have been contaminated; Dopdi felt proud of her forefathers. They stood guard over their women's blood in black armour. Shomai and Budhna are halfbreeds. The fruits of the war. Contributions to Radhabhumi[4] by the American soldiers stationed at Shiandanga. Otherwise, crow would eat crow's flesh before Santal would betray Santal.

Footsteps at her back. The steps keep a distance. Rice in her belt, tobacco leaves tucked at her waist. Arijit, Malini, Shamu, Mantu – none of them smokes or even drinks tea. Tobacco leaves and limestone powder. Best medicine for scorpion bite. Nothing must be given away.

Dopdi turned left. This way is the *camp*. Two miles. This is not the way to the forest. But Dopdi will not enter the forest with a cop at her back.

I swear by my life. By my life Dulna, by my life. Nothing must be told.

The footsteps turn left. Dopdi touches her waist. In her palm the comfort of a half-moon. A baby scythe. The smiths at Jharkhani are fine artisans. Such an edge we'll put on it Upi, a hundred Dukhirams – Thank God Dopdi is not a gentleman. Actually, perhaps they have understood scythe, hatchet, and knife best. They do their work in silence. The lights of the *camp* at a distance. Why is Dopdi going this way? Stop a bit, it turns again. Huh! I can tell where I am if I wander all night with my eyes shut. I won't go in the forest, I won't lose him that way. I won't outrun him. You fucking jackal of a cop, deadly afraid of death, you can't run around in the forest. I'd run you out of breath, throw you in a ditch, and finish you off.[5]

Not a word must be said. Dopdi has seen the new *camp*, she has sat in the *bus station*, passed the time of day, smoked a 'bidi' and found out how many *police convoys* had arrived, how many *radio vans*. Squash four, onions seven, peppers fifty, a straight-forward account. This information cannot now be passed on. They will understand Dopdi Mejhen has been countered. Then they'll run. Arijit's voice. If anyone is caught, the others must catch the *timing* and *change* their *hideout*. If *Comrade* Dopdi arrives late, we will not remain. There will be a sign of where we've gone. No *comrade* will let the others be destroyed for her own sake.[6]

Arijit's voice. The gurgle of water. The direction of the next *hideout* will be indicated by the tip of the wooden arrowhead under the stone.

Dopdi likes and understands this. Dulna died, but, let me tell you, he didn't lose anyone else's life. Because this was not in our heads to begin with, one was countered for the other's trouble. Now a much harsher rule, easy and clear. Dopdi returns – good; doesn't return – *bad. Change hideout*. The clue will be such that the opposition won't see it, won't understand even if they do.

Footsteps at her back. Dopdi turns again. These three-and-a-half miles of land and rocky ground are the best way to enter the forest. Dopdi has left that way behind. A little level ground ahead. Then rocks again. The *army* could not have struck *camp* on such rocky terrain. This area is quiet enough. It's like a maze, every hump looks like every other. That's fine. Dopdi will lead the cop to the burning 'ghat'. Patitpaban of Saranda had been sacrificed in the name of Kali of the Burning Ghats.

Apprehend!

A lump of rock stands up. Another. Yet another. The elderly Senanayak was at once triumphant and despondent. *If you want to destroy the enemy, become one*. He had done so. As long as six years ago he could anticipate their every move. He still can. Therefore he is elated. Since he has kept up with the literature, he has read *First Blood* and seen approval of his thought and work.

101

Dopdi couldn't trick him, he is unhappy about that. Two sorts of reasons. Six years ago he published an article about information storage in brain cells. He demonstrated in that piece that he supported this struggle from the point of view of the field hands. Dopdi is a field hand. *Veteran fighter. Search and destroy.* Dopdi Mejhen is about to be *apprehended.* Will be *destroyed.* Regret.

Halt!

Dopdi stops short. The steps behind come around to the front. Under Dopdi's ribs the *canal* dam breaks. No hope. Surja Sahu's brother Rotoni Sahu. The two lumps of rock come forward. Shomai and Budhna. They had not escaped by train.

Arijit's voice. Just as you must know when you've won, you must also acknowledge defeat and start the activities of the next *stage.*

Now Dopdi spreads her arms, raises her face to the sky, turns towards the forest, and ululates with the force of her entire being. Once, twice, three times. At the third burst the birds in the trees at the outskirts of the forest awake and flap their wings. The echo of the call travels far.

3

Draupadi Mejhen was apprehended at 6.53 p.m. It took an hour to get her to *camp.* Questioning took another hour exactly. No one touched her, and she was allowed to sit on a canvas camp stool. At 8.57 Senanayak's dinner hour approached, and saying, 'Make her. *Do the needful*,' he disappeared.

Then a billion moons pass. A billion lunar years. Opening her eyes after a million light years, Draupadi, strangely enough, sees sky and moon. Slowly the bloodied nailheads shift from her brain. Trying to move, she feels her arms and legs still tied to four posts. Something sticky under her arse and waist. Her own blood. Only the gag has been removed. Incredible thirst. In case she says 'water' she catches her lower lip in her teeth. She senses that her vagina is bleeding. How many came to make her?

Shaming her, a tear trickles out of the corner of her eye. In the muddy moonlight she lowers her lightless eye, sees her breasts, and understands that, indeed, she's been made up right. Her breasts are bitten raw, the nipples torn. How many? Four – five – six – seven – then Draupadi had passed out.

She turns her eyes and sees something white. Her own cloth.[7] Nothing else. Suddenly she hopes against hope. Perhaps they have abandoned her. For the foxes to devour. But she hears the scrape of feet. She turns her head, the guard leans on his bayonet and leers at her. Draupadi closes her eyes. She doesn't have to wait long. Again the process of making her begins. Goes on. The moon vomits a bit of light and goes to sleep. Only the dark remains. A compelled spread-eagled still body. Active *pistons* of flesh rise and fall, rise and fall over it.

Then morning comes.

Then Draupadi Mejhen is brought to the tent and thrown on the straw. Her piece of cloth is thrown over her body.

Then, after *breakfast*, after reading the newspaper and sending the radio message 'Draupadi Mejhen apprehended', etc., Draupadi Mejhen is ordered brought in.

Suddenly there is trouble.

Draupadi sits up as soon as she hears 'Move!' and asks, Where do you want me to go?

To the Burra Sahib's tent.

Where is the tent?

Over there.

Draupadi fixes her red eyes on the tent. Says, Come, I'll go.

The guard pushes the water pot forward.

Draupadi stands up. She pours the water down on the ground. Tears her piece of cloth with her teeth. Seeing such strange behaviour, the guard says, She's gone crazy, and runs for orders. He can lead the prisoner out but doesn't know what to do if the prisoner behaves incomprehensibly. So he goes to ask his superior.

The commotion is as if the alarm had sounded in a prison. Senanayak walks out surprised and sees Draupadi, naked, walking towards him in the bright sunlight with her head high. The nervous guards trail behind.

What is this? He is about to cry, but stops.

103

Draupadi stands before him, naked. Thigh and pubic hair matted with dry blood. Two breasts, two wounds.

What is this? He is about to bark.

Draupadi comes closer. Stands with her hand on her hip, laughs and says, The object of your search, Dopdi Mejhen. You asked them to make me up, don't you want to see how they made me?

Where are her clothes?

Won't put them on, *sir*. Tearing them.

Draupadi's black body comes even closer. Draupadi shakes with an indomitable laughter that Senanayak simply cannot understand. Her ravaged lips bleed as she begins laughing. Draupadi wipes the blood on her palm and says in a voice that is as terrifying, sky splitting, and sharp as her ululation, What's the use of clothes? You can strip me, but how can you clothe me again? Are you a man?

She looks around and chooses the front of Senanayak's white bush shirt to spit a bloody gob at and says, There isn't a man here that I should be ashamed. I will not let you put my cloth on me. What more can you do? Come on, *counter* me – come on, *counter* me – ?

Draupadi pushes Senanayak with her two mangled breasts, and for the first time Senanayak is afraid to stand before an unarmed *target*, terribly afraid.

Translated from the Bengali
by Gayatri Chakravorty Spivak

Translator's notes

1. The 'five Ks' are *Kes* (unshorn hair); *kachh* (drawers down to the knee); *karha* (iron bangle); *kirpan* (dagger); *kanga* (comb; to be worn by every Sikh, hence a mark of identity).

2. 'Bibhida Bharati' is a popular radio programme, on which listeners can hear music of their choice. The Hindi film industry is prolific in producing pulp movies for consumption in India and in all parts of the world where there is an Indian, Pakistani, and West Indian labour force. Many of the films are adaptations from the epics. Sanjeev Kumar is an idolised actor. Since it was Krishna who rescued Draupadi from her predicament in the epic, and, in the film the soldiers watch, Sanjeev Kumar encounters Krishna, there might be a touch of textual irony here.

3. 'Panchayat' is a supposedly elected body of village self-government.

4. 'Champabhumi' and 'Radhabhumi' are archaic names for certain areas of Bengal. 'Bhumi' is simply 'land'. All of Bengal is thus 'Bangabhumi'.

5. The jackal following the tiger is a common image.

6. Modern Bengali does not distinguish between 'her' and 'his'. The 'her' in the sentence beginning 'No comrade will . . .' can therefore be considered an interpretation.

7. A sari conjures up the long, many-pleated piece of cloth, complete with blouse and underclothes, that 'proper' Indian women wear. Dopdi wears a much-abbreviated version without blouse or underclothes. It is referred to simply as 'the cloth'.

ATTIA HOSAIN

Attia Hosain was born in Lucknow, India in 1912, and belonged to an aristocratic Taluqdari or landowning family. Her education combined English liberal schooling at La Martinière and Isabella Thoburn College in Lucknow, with traditional lessons in Urdu, Persian and Arabic at home. Influenced in the 1930s by the nationalist movement and the Progressive Writers Group in India, she became a journalist, broadcaster and writer of short stories. She came to England in 1947. She presented programmes for the BBC Eastern Service and appeared on television and the West End stage.

Attia Hosain is best known for her collection of short stories *Phoenix Fled* (1953), in which 'The First Party' appeared, and the novel *Sunlight on a Broken Column* (1961). Both books essentially draw upon a pre-Partition, pre-Independence India, in the middle of huge political and social change.

The First Party

After the dimness of the verandah, the bewildering brightness of the room made her stumble against the unseen doorstep. Her nervousness edged towards panic, and the darkness seemed a forsaken friend, but her husband was already steadying her into the room.

'My wife,' he said in English, and the alien sounds softened the awareness of this new relationship.

The smiling, tall woman came towards them with outstretched hands and she put her own limply into the other's firm grasp.

'How d'you do?' said the woman.

'How d'you do?' said the fat man beside her.

'I am very well, thank you,' she said in the low voice of an uncertain child repeating a lesson. Her shy glance avoided their eyes.

They turned to her husband, and in the warm current of their friendly ease she stood coldly self-conscious.

'I hope we are not too early,' her husband said.

'Of course not; the others are late. Do sit down.'

She sat on the edge of the big chair, her shoulders drooping, nervously pulling her sari over her head as the weight of its heavy gold embroidery pulled it back.

'What will you drink?' the fat man asked her.

'Nothing, thank you.'

'Cigarette?'

'No, thank you.'

Her husband and the tall woman were talking about her, she felt sure. Pinpoints of discomfort pricked her and she smiled to hide them.

The woman held a wineglass in one hand and a cigarette in the other. She wondered how it felt to hold a cigarette with such self-confidence; to flick the ash with such assurance. The woman had long nails, pointed and scarlet. She looked at her

107

own – unpainted, cut carefully short – wondering how anyone could eat, work, wash with those claws dipped in blood. She drew her sari over her hands, covering her rings and bracelets, noticing the other's bare wrists, like a widow's.

'Shy little thing, isn't she, but charming,' said the woman as if soothing a frightened child.

'She'll get over it soon. Give me time,' her husband laughed. She heard him and blushed, wishing to be left unobserved and grateful for the diversion when other guests came in.

She did not know whether she was meant to stand up when they were being introduced, and shifted uneasily in the chair, half rising; but her husband came and stood by her, and by the pressure of his hand on her shoulder she knew she must remain sitting.

She was glad when polite formality ended and they forgot her for their drinks, their cigarettes, their talk and laughter. She shrank into her chair, lonely in her strangeness yet dreading approach. She felt curious eyes on her and her discomfort multiplied them. When anyone came and sat by her she smiled in cold defence, uncertainty seeking refuge in silence, and her brief answers crippled conversation. She found the bi-lingual patchwork distracting, and its pattern, familiar to others, with allusions and references unrelated to her own experiences, was distressingly obscure. Overheard light chatter appealing to her woman's mind brought no relief of understanding. Their different stresses made even talk of dress and appearance sound unfamiliar. She could not understand the importance of relating clothes to time and place and not just occasion; nor their preoccupation with limbs and bodies, which should be covered, and not face and features alone. They made problems about things she took for granted.

Her bright rich clothes and heavy jewellery oppressed her when she saw the simplicity of their clothes. She wished she had not dressed so, even if it was the custom, because no one seemed to care for customs, or even know them, and looked at her as if she were an object on display. Her discomfort changed to uneasy defiance, and she stared at the strange creatures around her. But her swift eyes slipped away in timid shyness if they met another's.

Her husband came at intervals that grew longer with a few gay words, or a friend to whom he proudly presented 'My wife'. She noticed the never-empty glass in his hand, and the smell of his breath, and from shock and distress she turned to disgust and anger. It was wicked, it was sinful to drink, and she could not forgive him.

She could not make herself smile any more but no one noticed and their unconcern soured her anger. She did not want to be disturbed and was tired of the persistent 'Will you have a drink?', 'What will you drink?', 'Sure you won't drink?' It seemed they objected to her not drinking, and she was confused by this reversal of values. She asked for a glass of orange juice and used it as protection, putting it to her lips when anyone came near.

They were eating now, helping themselves from the table by the wall. She did not want to leave her chair, and wondered if it was wrong and they would notice she was not eating. In her confusion she saw a girl coming towards her, carrying a small tray. She sat up stiffly and took the proffered plate with a smile. 'Do help yourself,' the girl said and bent forward. Her light sari slipped from her shoulder and the tight red silk blouse outlined each high breast. She pulled her own sari closer round her, blushing. The girl, unaware, said, 'Try this sandwich, and the olives are good.'

She had never seen an olive before but did not want to admit it, and when she put it in her mouth she wanted to spit it out. When no one was looking, she slipped it under her chair, then felt sure someone had seen her and would find it.

The room closed in on her with its noise and smoke. There was now the added harsh clamour of music from the radiogram. She watched, fascinated, the movement of the machine as it changed records; but she hated the shrieking and moaning and discordant noises it hurled at her. A girl walked up to it and started singing, swaying her hips. The bare flesh of her body showed through the thin net of her drapery below the high line of her short tight bodice.

She felt angry again. The disgusting, shameless hussies, bold and free with men, their clothes adorning nakedness not hiding it, with their painted false mouths, that short hair that looked

109

like the mad woman's whose hair was cropped to stop her pulling it out.

She fed her resentment with every possible fault her mind could seize on, and she tried to deny her lonely unhappiness with contempt and moral passion. These women who were her own kind, yet not so, were wicked, contemptible, grotesque mimics of the foreign ones among them for whom she felt no hatred because from them she expected nothing better.

She wanted to break those records, the noise which they called music.

A few couples began to dance when they had rolled aside the carpet. She felt a sick horror at the way the men held the women, at the closeness of their bodies, their vulgar suggestive movements. That surely was the extreme limit of what was possible in the presence of others. Her mother had nearly died in childbirth and not moaned lest the men outside hear her voice, and she, her child, had to see this exhibition of . . . her outraged modesty put a leash on her thoughts.

This was an assault on the basic precept by which her convictions were shaped, her life was controlled. Not against touch alone, but sound and sight, had barriers been raised against man's desire.

A man came and asked her to dance and she shrank back in horror, shaking her head. Her husband saw her and called out as he danced, 'Come on, don't be shy; you'll soon learn.'

She felt a flame of anger as she looked at him, and kept on shaking her head until the man left her, surprised by the violence of her refusal. She saw him dancing with another girl and knew they must be talking about her, because they looked towards her and smiled.

She was trembling with the violent complexity of her feelings, of anger, hatred, jealousy and bewilderment, when her husband walked up to her and pulled her affectionately by the hand.

'Get up. I'll teach you myself.'

She gripped her chair as she struggled, and the violence of her voice through clenched teeth, 'Leave me alone', made him drop her hand with shocked surprise as the laughter left his face. She noticed his quick embarrassed glance round the room, then the hard anger of his eyes as he left her without a word. He laughed more gaily when he joined the others, to drown that moment's silence, but it enclosed her in dreary emptiness.

She had been so sure of herself in her contempt and her anger, confident of the righteousness of her beliefs, deep-based on generations-old foundations. When she had seen them being attacked, in her mind they remained indestructible, and her anger had been a sign of faith; but now she saw her husband was one of the destroyers; and yet she knew that above all others was the belief that her life must be one with his. In confusion and despair she was surrounded by ruins.

She longed for the sanctuary of the walled home from which marriage had promised an adventurous escape. Each restricting rule became a guiding stone marking a safe path through unknown dangers.

The tall woman came and sat beside her and with affection put her hand on her head.

'Tired, child?' The compassion of her voice and eyes was unbearable.

She got up and ran to the verandah, put her head against a pillar and wet it with her tears.

ANITA DESAI

Anita Desai was born in 1937 of a Bengali father and a German mother. She has written several novels, of which the best known in England are *The Village by the Sea* (1982), *Clear Light of Day* (1980), *Fire on the Mountain* (1987), *In Custody* (1984) and *Baumgartner's Bombay* (1988).

'The Farewell Party' comes from the collection *Games at Twilight* (1978). Anita Desai's stories are of contemporary urban India, in this case a middle-class 'company' world which could easily be duplicated elsewhere in Indian towns. Against this shifting world she places the intensely private lives of Bina and Raman.

The
Farewell Party

B efore the party she had made a list, faintheartedly, and marked off the items as they were dealt with, inexorably – cigarettes, soft drinks, ice, *kebabs* and so on. But she had forgotten to provide lights. The party was to be held on the lawn: on these dry summer nights one could plan a lawn party weeks in advance and be certain of fine weather, and she had thought happily of how the roses would be in bloom and of the stars and perhaps even fireflies, so decorative and discreet, all gracefully underlining her unsuspected talent as a hostess. But she had not realised that there would be no moon and therefore it would be very dark on the lawn. All the lights on the verandah, in the portico and indoors were on, like so many lanterns, richly copper and glowing with extraordinary beauty as though aware that the house would soon be empty and these were the last few days of illumination and family life, but they did very little to light the lawn which was vast, a still lake of inky grass.

Wandering about with a glass in one hand and a plate of cheese biscuits in another, she gave a start now and then to see an acquaintance emerge from the darkness, which had the gloss, the sheen, the coolness but not the weight of water, and present her with a face, vague and without outlines but eventually recognisable. 'Oh,' she cried several times that evening, 'I didn't know you had arrived. I've been looking for you,' she would add with unaccustomed intimacy (was it because of the gin and lime, her second, or because such warmth could safely be held to lead to nothing now that they were leaving town?). The guest, also having had several drinks between beds of flowering balsam and torenias before launching out onto the lawn, responded with an equal vivacity. Sometimes she had her arm squeezed or a hand slid down the bareness of her back – which was athletic: she had once played tennis, rather well – and once someone said, 'I've been hiding in this corner, watching you,' while another went so far as to say, 'Is it true you are leaving us, Bina? How can you be so cruel?' And if it were a woman guest, the words were that much more effusive. It was all heady, astonishing.

It was astonishing because Bina was a frigid and friendless woman. She was thirty-five. For fifteen years she had been bringing up her children and, in particular, nursing the eldest who was severely spastic. This had involved her deeply in the workings of the local hospital and with its many departments and doctors, but her care for this child was so intense and so desperate that her relationship with them was purely professional. Outside this circle of family and hospital – ringed, as it were, with barbed wire and lit with one single floodlight – Bina had no life. The town had scarcely come to know her for its life turned in the more jovial circles of mah-jong, bridge, coffee parties, club evenings and, occasionally, a charity show in aid of the Red Cross. For these Bina had a kind of sad contempt and certainly no time. A tall, pale woman, heavy-boned and sallow, she had a certain presence, a certain dignity, and people, having heard of the spastic child, liked and admired her, but she had not thought she had friends. Yet tonight they were coming forth from the darkness in waves that quite overwhelmed.

Now here was Mrs Ray, the Commissioner's wife, chirping inside a nest of rustling embroidered organza. 'Why are you leaving us so soon, Mrs Raman? You've only been here – two years, is it?'

'Five,' exclaimed Bina, widening her eyes, herself surprised at such a length of time. Although time dragged heavily in their household, agonisingly slow, and the five years had been so hard that sometimes, at night, she did not know how she had crawled through the day and if she would crawl through another, her back almost literally broken by the weight of the totally dependent child and of the three smaller ones who seemed perpetually to clamour for their share of attention, which they felt they never got. Yet now these five years had telescoped. They were over. The Raman family was moving and their time here was spent. There had been the hospital, the girls' school, the boys' school, picnics, monsoons, birthday parties and measles. Crushed together into a handful. She gazed down at her hands, tightened around glass and plate. 'Time has flown,' she murmured incredulously.

'Oh, I wish you were staying, Mrs Raman,' cried the Commissioner's wife and, as she squeezed Bina's arm, her fragrant talcum powder seemed to lift off her chalky shoulders and some of it settled on Bina who sneezed. 'It's been so nice to have a family like yours here. It's a small town, so little to do, at least one must have good friends . . .'

Bina blinked at such words of affection from a woman she had met twice, perhaps thrice before. Bina and her husband did not go in for society. The shock of their first child's birth had made them both fanatic parents. But she knew that not everyone considered this vital factor in their lives, and spoke of 'social duties' in a somehow reproving tone. The Commissioner's wife had been annoyed, she always felt, by her refusal to help out at the Red Cross fair. The hurt silence with which her refusal had been accepted had implied the importance of these 'social duties' of which Bina remained so stubbornly unaware.

However, this one evening, this last party, was certainly given over to their recognition and celebration. 'Oh, everyone, everyone is here,' rejoiced the Commissioner's wife, her eyes snapping from face to face in that crowded aquarium, and, at a higher pitch, cried 'Renu, why weren't you at the mah-jong party this morning?' and moved off into another powdery organza embrace that rose to meet her from the night like a moth and then was submerged again in the shadows of the lawn. Bina gave one of those smiles that easily-frightened people found mocking, a shade too superior, somewhat scornful. Looking down into her glass of gin and lime, she moved on and in a minute found herself brought up short against the quite regal although overweight figure, in raw silk and homespun and the somewhat saturnine air of underpaid culture, of Bose, an employee of the local museum whom she had met once or twice at the art competitions and exhibitions to which she was fond of hauling her children, whether reluctant or enthusiastic, because 'it made a change', she said.

'Mrs Raman,' he said in the fruity tones of the culture-bent

Bengali, 'how we'll miss you at the next children's art competitions. You used to be my chief inspiration – '

'Inspiration?' she laughed, incredulously, spilling some of her drink and proffering the plate of cheese biscuits from which he helped himself, half-bowing as though it were gold she offered, gems.

'Yes, yes, inspiration,' he went on, even more fruitily now that his mouth was full. 'Think of me – alone, the hapless organiser – surrounded by mammas, by primary school teachers, by three, four, five hundred children. And the judges – they are always the most trouble, those judges. And then I look at you – so cool, controlling your children, handling them so wonderfully and with such superb results – my inspiration!'

She was flustered by this unaccustomed vision of herself and half-turned her face away from Bose the better to contemplate it, but could find no reflection of it in the ghostly white bush of the Queen of the Night, and listened to him murmur on about her unkindness in deserting him in this cultural backwater to that darkest of dooms – guardian of a provincial museum – where he saw no one but school teachers herding children through his halls or, worse, Government officials who periodically and inexplicably stirred to create trouble for him and made their official presences felt amongst the copies of the Ajanta frescoes (in which even the mouldy and peeled-off portions were carefully reproduced) and the cupboards of Indus Valley seals. Murmuring commiseration, she left him to a gloomy young professor of history who was languishing at another of the institutions of provincial backwaters that they so deplored and whose wife was always having a baby, and slipped away, still feeling an unease at Bose's unexpected vision of her which did not tally with the cruder reality, into the less equivocal company provided by a ring of twittering 'company wives'.

These women she had always encountered in just such a ring as they formed now, the kind that garden babblers form under a hedge where they sit gabbling and whirring with social bitchiness, and she had always stood outside it, smiling stiffly, not wanting to join and refusing their effusively nodded invitation. They were the wives of men who represented various mercantile companies in the town – Imperial Tobacco, Brooke

Bond, Esso and so on – and although they might seem exactly alike to one who did not belong to this circle, inside it were subtle gradations of importance according to the particular company for which each one's husband worked and of these only they themselves were initiates. Bina was, however unwillingly, an initiate. Her husband worked for one of these companies but she had always stiffly refused to recognise these gradations, or consider them. They noted the rather set sulkiness of her silence when amongst them and privately labelled her queer, proud, boring and difficult. Also, they felt she belonged to their circle whether she liked it or not.

Now she entered this circle with diffidence, wishing she had stayed with the more congenial Bose (why hadn't she? What was it in her that made her retreat from anything like a friendly approach?) and was taken aback to find their circle parting to admit her and hear their cries of welcome and affection that did not, however, lose the stridency and harshness of garden babblers' voices.

'Bina, how do you like the idea of going back to Bombay?'

'Have you started packing, Bina? Poor you. Oh, are you having packers over from Delhi? Oh well, then it's not so bad.'

Never had they been so vociferous in her company, so easy, so warm. They were women to whom the most awful thing that had ever happened was the screw of a golden earring disappearing down the bathroom sink or a mother-in-law's visit or an ayah deserting just before the arrival of guests: what could they know of Bina's life, Bina's ordeal? She cast her glance at the drinks they held – but they were mostly of orange squash. Only the Esso wife, who participated in amateur dramatics and ran a boutique and was rather taller and bolder than the rest, held a whisky and soda. So much affection generated by just orange squash? Impossible. Rather tentatively, she offered them the remains of the cheese biscuits, found herself chirping replies, deploring the nuisance of having packing crates all over the house, talking of the flat they would move into in Bombay, and then, sweating unobtrusively with the strain, saw another recognisable fish swim towards her from the edge of the liquescent lawn, and swung away in relief, saying, 'Mrs

D'Souza! How late you are, but I'm so glad—' for she really was.

Mrs D'Souza was her daughter's teacher at the convent school and had clearly never been to a cocktail party before so that all Bina's compassion was aroused by those school-scuffed shoes and her tea-party best – quite apart from the simple truth that she found in her an honest individuality that all those beautifully dressed and poised babblers lacked, being stamped all over by the plain rubber stamps of their husbands' companies – and she hurried off to find Mrs D'Souza something suitable to drink. 'Sherry? Why yes, I think I'll be able to find you some,' she said, a bit flabbergasted at such an unexpected fancy of the pepper-haired school teacher, 'and I'll see if Tara's around – she'll want to see you,' she added, vaguely and fraudulently, wondering why she had asked Mrs D'Souza to a cocktail party, only to see, as she skirted the rose bed, the admirable Bose appear at her side and envelop her in this strange intimacy that marked the whole evening, and went off, light-hearted, towards the table where her husband was trying, with the help of some hired waiters in soggy white uniforms with the name of the restaurant from which they were hired embroidered in red across their pockets, to cope with the flood of drinks this party atmosphere had called for and released.

Harassed, perspiring, his feet burning, Raman was nevertheless pleased to be so obviously employed and be saved the strain of having to converse with his motley assembly of guests: he had no more gift for society than his wife had. Ice cubes were melting on the tablecloth in sopping puddles and he had trouble in keeping track of his bottles: they were, besides the newly bought dozens of beer bottles and Black Knight whisky, the remains of their five years in this town that he now wished to bring to their end – bottles brought by friends from trips abroad, bottles bought cheap through 'contacts' in the army or air force, some gems, extravaganzas bought for anniversaries such as a nearly full bottle of Vat 69, a bottle with a bit of *crème de menthe* growing sticky at the bottom, some brown sherry with a great deal of rusty sediment, a red Golconda wine from Hyderabad, and a bottle of Remy Martin that he was keeping guiltily to himself, pouring small quantities into a whisky glass at his elbow and gulping it down in between mixing some very weird cocktails for his guests. There was no one at the party he liked well enough to share it with. Oh, one of the doctors perhaps, but where were they? Submerged in grass, in dark, in night and chatter, clatter of ice in glass, teeth on biscuit, teeth on teeth. Enamel and gold. Crumbs and dregs. All awash, all soaked in night. Watery sound of speech, liquid sound of drink. Water and ice and night. It occurred to him that everyone had forgotten him, the host, that it was a mistake to have stationed himself amongst the waiters, that he ought to move out, mingle with the guests. But he felt himself drowned, helplessly and quite delightfully, in Remy Martin, in grass, in a border of purple torenias.

Then he was discovered by his son who galloped through the ranks of guests and waiters to fling himself at his father and ask if he could play the new Beatles record, his friends had asked to hear it.

Raman considered, taking the opportunity to pour out and gulp down some more of the precious Remy Martin. 'All right,' he said, after a judicious minute or two, 'but keep it low, everyone won't want to hear it,' not adding that he himself didn't, for his taste in music ran to slow and melancholy, folk at its most frivolous. Still, he glanced into the lighted room where his children and the children of neighbours and guests had collected, making themselves tipsy on Fanta and Coca-Cola, the girls giggling in a multi-coloured huddle and the boys swaggering around the record-player with a kind of lounging strut, holding bottles in their hands with a sophisticated ease, exactly like experienced cocktail party guests, so that he smiled and wished he had a ticket, a passport that would make it possible to break into that party within a party. It was chillingly obvious to him that he hadn't one. He also saw that a good deal of their riotousness was due to the fact that they were raiding the snack trays that the waiters carried through the room to the lawn, and that they were seeing to it that the trays emerged half-empty. He knew he ought to go in and see about it but he hadn't the heart, or the nerve. He couldn't join that party but he wouldn't wreck it either so he only caught hold of one of the waiters and suggested that the snack trays be carried out from the kitchen straight onto the lawn, not by way of the drawing-room, and led him towards a group that seemed to be without snacks and saw too late that it was a group of the company executives that he loathed most. He half-groaned, then hiccuped at his mistake, but it was too late to alter course now. He told himself that he ought to see to it that the snacks were offered around without snag or error.

Poor Raman was placed in one of the lower ranks of the companies' hierarchy. That is, he did not belong to a British concern, or even to an American-collaboration one, but merely to an Indian one. Oh, a long-established, prosperous and solid one but, still, only Indian. Those cigarettes that he passed around were made by his own company. Somehow it struck a note of bad taste amongst these fastidious men who played golf, danced at the club on Independence Eve and New Year's Eve, invited at least one foreign couple to every party and called their decorative wives 'darling' when in public. Poor Raman never had belonged. It was so obvious to everyone, even to himself, as he passed around those awful cigarettes that sold so well in the market. It had been obvious since their first disastrous dinner party for this very ring of jocular gentlemen, five years ago. Nono had cried right through the party, Bina had spent the evening racing upstairs to see to the babies' baths and bed-time and then crawling reluctantly down, the hired cook had got drunk and stolen two of the chickens so that there was not enough on the table, no one had relaxed for a minute or enjoyed a second – it had been too sad and harrowing even to make a good story or a funny anecdote. They had all let it sink by mutual consent and the invitations to play a round of golf on Saturday afternoon or a rubber of bridge on Sunday morning had been issued and refused with conspiratorial smoothness. Then there was that distressing hobby of Raman's: his impossibly long walks on which he picked up bits of wood and took them home to sandpaper and chisel and then call wood sculpture. What could one do with a chap who did that? He himself wasn't sure if he pursued such odd tastes because he was a social pariah or if he was one on account of this oddity. Not to speak of the spastic child. Now that didn't even bear thinking of, and so it was no wonder that Raman swayed towards them so hesitantly, as though he were wading through water instead of over clipped grass, and handed his cigarettes around with such an apologetic air.

But, after all, hesitation and apology proved unnecessary. One of them – was he Polson's Coffee or Brooke Bond Tea? – clasped Raman about the shoulders as proper men do on meeting, and hearty voices rose together, congratulating him on his promotion (it wasn't one, merely a transfer, and they knew it), envying him his move to the metropolis. They talked as if they had known each other for years, shared all kinds of public schoolboy fun. One – was he Voltas or Ciba? – talked of golf matches at the Willingdon as though he had often played there with Raman, another spoke of *kebabs* eaten on the roadside after a party as though Raman had been one of the gang. Amazed and grateful as a schoolboy admitted to a closed society, Raman nodded and put in a few cautious words, put away his cigarettes, called a waiter to refill their glasses and broke away before the clock struck twelve and the golden carriage turned into a pumpkin, he himself into a mouse. He hated mice.

Walking backwards, he walked straight into the soft barrier of Miss Dutta's ample back wrapped and bound in rich Madras silk.

'Sorry, sorry, Miss Dutta, I'm clumsy as a bear,' he apologised, but here, too, there was no call for apology for Miss Dutta was obviously delighted at having been bumped into.

'My dear Mr Raman, what can you expect if you invite the whole town to your party?' she asked in that piercing voice that invariably made her companions drop theirs self-consciously. 'You and Bina have been so popular – what are we going to do without you?'

He stood pressing his glass with white-tipped fingers and tried to think what he or Bina had provided her with that she could possibly miss. In any case, Miss Dutta could always manage, and did manage, everything single-handedly. She was the town busy-body, secretary and chairman of more committees than he could count: they ranged from the Film Society to the Blood Bank, from the Red Cross to the Friends of the Museum, for Miss Dutta was nothing if not versatile. 'We hardly ever saw you at our film shows of course,' her voice rang out, making him glance furtively over his shoulder to see if anyone were listening, 'but it was so nice *knowing* you were in town and that I could count on you. So few people here *care*, you know,' she went on, and affectionately bumped her comfortable middle-aged body into his as someone squeezed by, making him remember that he had once heard her called a man-eater, and wonder which man she had eaten and even consider, for a moment, if there were not, after all, some charm in those powdered creases of her creamy arms, equalling if not surpassing that of his worn and harassed wife's bony angles. Why did suffering make for angularity? he even asked himself with uncharacteristic unkindness. But when Miss Dutta laid an arm on top of his glass-holding one and raised herself on her toes to bray something into his ear, he loyally decided that he was too accustomed to sharp angles to change them for such unashamed luxuriance, and, contriving to remove her arm by grasping her elbow – how one's fingers sank into the stuff! – he steered her towards his wife who was standing at the table and inefficiently pouring herself another gin and lime.

'This is my third,' she confessed hurriedly, 'and I can't tell you how gay it makes me feel. I giggle at everything everyone says.'

'Good,' he pronounced, feeling inside a warm expansion of relief at seeing her lose, for the moment, her tension and anxiety. 'Let's hear you giggle,' he said, sloshing some more gin into her glass.

'Look at those children,' she exclaimed, and they stood in a bed of balsam, irredeemably crushed, and looked into the lighted drawing room where their daughter was at the moment the cynosure of all juvenile eyes, having thrown herself with abandon into a dance of monkey-like movements. 'What is it, Miss Dutta?' the awed mother enquired. 'You're more up in the latest fashions than I am – is it the twist, the rock or the jungle?' and all three watched, enthralled, till Tara began to totter and, losing her simian grace, collapsed against some wildly shrieking girl friends.

A bit embarrassed by their daughter's reckless abandon, the parents discussed with Miss Dutta whose finger by her own

admission, was placed squarely on the pulse of youth, the latest
trends in juvenile culture on which Miss Dutta gave a neat
sociological discourse (all the neater for having been given
earlier that day at the convocation of the Home Science College)
and Raman wondered uneasily at this opening of flood-gates in
his own family – his wife grown giggly with gin, his daughter
performing wildly to a Chubby Checker's record – how had it
all come about? Was it the darkness all about them, dense as
the heavy curtains about a stage, that made them act, for an
hour or so, on the tiny lighted stage of brief intimacy with such
a lack of inhibition? Was it the drink, so freely sloshing from
end to end of the house and lawn on account of his determina-
tion to clear out his 'cellar' (actually one-half of the sideboard
and the top shelf of the wardrobe in his dressing-room) and his
muddling and mixing them, making up untried and experimen-
tal cocktails and lavishly pouring out the whisky without a
measure? But these were solid and everyday explanations and
there was about this party something out of the ordinary and
everyday – at least to the Ramans, normally so austere and
unpopular. He knew the real reason too – it was all because the
party had been labelled a 'farewell party', everyone knew it was
the last one, that the Ramans were leaving and they would not
meet up again. There was about it exactly that kind of sentimen-
tal euphoria that is generated at a ship-board party, the one
given on the last night before the end of the voyage. Everyone
draws together with an intimacy, a lack of inhibition not
displayed or guessed at before, knowing this is the last time,
tomorrow they will be dispersed, it will be over. They will not
meet, be reminded of it or be required to repeat it.

As if to underline this new and Cinderella's ball-like atmosphere of friendliness and gaiety, three pairs of neighbours now
swept in (and three kochias lay down and died under their feet,
to the gardener's rage and sorrow): the couple who lived to the
Ramans' left, the couple who lived to their right, and the couple
from across the road, all crying, 'So sorry to be late, but you
know what a long way we had to come,' making everyone
laugh identically at the identical joke. Despite the disparity in
their looks and ages – one couple was very young, another
middle-aged, the third grandparents – they were, in a sense, as

123

alike as the company executives and their wives, for they too bore a label if a less alarming one: neighbours, it said. Because they were neighbours, and although they had never been more than nodded to over the hedge, waved to in passing cars or spoken to about anything other than their children, dogs, flowers and gardens, their talk had a vivid immediacy that went straight to the heart.

'Diamond's going to miss you so – he'll be heartbroken,' moaned the grandparents who lived alone in their spotless house with a black labrador who had made a habit of visiting the Ramans whenever he wanted young company, a romp on the lawn or an illicit biscuit.

'I don't know what my son will do without Diamond,' reciprocated Bina with her new and sympathetic warmth. 'He'll force me to get a dog of his own, I know, and how will I ever keep one in a flat in Bombay?'

'When are you going to throw out those rascals?' a father demanded of Raman, pointing at the juvenile revellers indoors. 'My boy has an exam tomorrow, you know, but he said he couldn't be bothered about it – he had to go to the Ramans' farewell party.'

One mother confided to Bina, winning her heart forever, 'Now that you are leaving, I can talk to you about it at last: did you know my Vinod is sweet on your Tara? Last night when I was putting him to bed, he said, "Mama, when I grow up I will marry Tara. I will sit on a white horse and wear a turban and carry a sword in my belt and I will go and marry Tara." What shall we do about that, eh? Only a ten year difference in age, isn't there – or twelve?' and both women rocked with laughter.

The party had reached its crest, like a festive ship, loud and illuminated for that last party before the journey's end, perched on the dizzy top of the dark wave. It could do nothing now but descend and dissolve. As if by simultaneous and unanimous consent, the guests began to leave (in the wake of the Commissioner and his wife who left first, like royalty) streaming towards the drive where cars stood bumper to bumper – more than had visited the Ramans' house in the previous five years put together. The light in the portico fell on Bina's pride and joy, a Chinese orange tree, lighting its miniature globes of fruit like golden lanterns. There was a babble, an uproar of leave-taking (the smaller children, already in pyjamas, watched open-mouthed from a dark window upstairs). Esso and Caltex left together, arms about each other and smoking cigars, like figures in a comic act. Miss Dutta held firmly to Bose's arm as they dipped, bowed, swayed and tripped on their way out. Bina was clasped, kissed – ear-rings grazed her cheek, talcum powder tickled her nose. Raman had his back slapped till he thrummed and vibrated like a beaten gong.

It seemed as if Bina and Raman were to be left alone at last, left to pack up and leave – now the good-byes had been said, there was nothing else they could possibly do – but no, out popped the good doctors from the hospital who had held themselves back in the darkest corners and made themselves inconspicuous throughout the party, and now, in the manner in which they clasped the host by the shoulders and the hostess by her hands, and said 'Ah, *now* we have a chance to be with you at last, now we can begin *our* party,' revealed that although this was the first time they had come to the Ramans' house on any but professional visits, they were not merely friends – they were almost a part of that self-defensive family, the closest to them in sympathy. Raman and Bina felt a warm, moist expansion of tenderness inside themselves, the tenderness they had till today restricted to the limits of their family, no farther, as though they feared it had not an unlimited capacity. Now its close horizons stepped backwards, with some surprise.

And it was as the doctors said – the party now truly began. Cane chairs were dragged out of the verandah onto the lawn, placed in a ring next to the flowering Queen of the Night which shook out flounces and frills of white scent with every rustle of night breeze. Bina could give in now to her two most urgent needs and dash indoors to smear her mosquito-bitten arms and feet with Citronella and fetch Nono to sit on her lap, to let Nono have a share, too, in the party. The good doctors and their wives leant forward and gave Nono the attention that made the parents' throats tighten with gratitude. Raman insisted on their each having a glass of Remy Martin – they must finish it tonight, he said, and would not let the waiters clear away the ice or glasses yet. So they sat on the verandah steps, smoking and yawning.

Now it turned out that Dr Bannerji's wife, the lady in the Dacca sari and the steel-rimmed spectacles, had studied in Shantiniketan, and she sang, at her husband's and his colleagues' urging, Tagore's sweetest, saddest songs. When she sang, in heartbroken tones that seemed to come from some distance away, from the damp corners of the darkness where the fireflies flitted,

> Father, the boat is carrying me away,
> Father, it is carrying me away from home,

the eyes of her listeners, sitting tensely in that grassy, inky dark, glazed with tears that were compounded equally of drink, relief and regret.

SHASHI DESHPANDE

Shashi Deshpande was born in Dharwar, India, and educated in Bombay. She now lives in Bangalore. Her short stories were first published in various English periodicals in India, and have now appeared in four collections: *The Legacy* (1971), *The Miracle* (1986), *It Was the Nightingale* (1986) and *It Was Dark* (1986), all published by Writers Workshop, Calcutta. She has also written five novels of which the last, *That Long Silence* (1988), was published by Virago.

'My Beloved Charioteer' comes from the collection *It Was Dark*. The title refers to Lord Krishna who, in the epic *Mahabharata*, is charioteer to Arjuna, urging him not to falter in the great battle of Kurukshetra.

My Beloved Charioteer

I smile as I hear them at last, the sounds I am waiting for. A rush of footsteps, the slam of the bathroom door . . . I wince as the sound whams through the silent house . . . and, a minute later, another bang. And then, bare feet running towards me.

'You shouldn't bang the doors that way,' I say reproachfully. 'You might wake Mummy.'

She sits opposite me, cross-legged on the low wooden stool, hair tousled, cheeks flushed. 'Oh, she won't wake up for hours yet,' she says cheerfully. 'Have you had your tea, ajji?' Our daily routine. I can never confess to her that I have had a cup an hour earlier. This is her joy, that I wait for her.

'No, I've been waiting for you. Have you brushed your teeth?'

She makes a face. 'I'll do it later,' she says, trying to be brusque and casual.

'You'll do no such thing. Go and brush them at once.'

'Only today, ajji. From tomorrow, I promise, I'll brush them first,' she cajoles.

'Nothing doing.' I try hard to be firm. But I can't fool her. She knows I am on her side. She lowers her voice to a conspiratorial whisper. 'Mummy won't know. She's sleeping.'

Now, of course, she leaves me no choice. I have to be firm. She goes reluctantly. And is back so fast, I have to ask, 'Did you really brush? Properly? Show me.'

'Look.'

I have to grin back at the grinning, impish face. 'Now tea for me.'

'No,' I say, 'tea for me. Milk for you.'

Ultimately, as always, we compromise and her tea is a pale brown. I switch off the Primus and, without the hissing sound, our voices sound loud and clear. We look at each other guiltily, thinking of the sleeper, and try to speak in lowered tones. Happiness can mean so many things to so many people. For me, it is this. The beginning of a new day with this child. We talk of so many things. But too soon it is time for her to go to school. Bathed and fresh, she sets off.

When she is gone, silence settles on the house. A silence that will not lift till she returns. I had got used to this silence in the last seven years. It had never seemed terrible to me. It was a friendly silence, filled with the ghosts of so many voices in my life. They came back to keep me company when I was alone . . . my younger brother, my aunt who loved me when I was a child, my two infant sons who never grew up, and even the child Aarti, who seems to have no connection with this thin, bitter woman who now shares the silence with me. But since she came, the friendly ghosts have all gone.

It is late before she wakes. I have had my bath, finished my puja, and am half-way through cooking lunch, when I hear her stirring. I take down the dal from the fire and put on the tea. By the time tea is ready, she comes into the kitchen. Wordlessly she takes a cup from me. She drinks it in hungry gulps as if she has been thirsting for hours, then thrusts the cup back at me. I pour out some more. I, too, say nothing. Earlier, I used to ask, 'Slept well?' And one day, she had put down the cup with a trembling hand and said, 'Slept well? No, I never do that. I haven't slept well since Madhav died. I'll never sleep well again all my life. I have to take something every night so that I can close my eyes for a few hours. Now, never ask me again if I slept well.' Nine months I carried this daughter of mine in my body. I had felt within me every beat of her heart, every movement of her limbs. But . . . and this my doctor had told me then . . . my pains and shocks could never penetrate to her, she was so well protected. Even now, she is protected from my pains. Even now, I have no protection against her pains. I suffer with her, but like all my other emotions, it is a futile suffering. For I cannot help her. I can only fumble and blunder and make things worse.

'Why didn't you let me know earlier?' she had asked me angrily when she had come home after her father's death. 'Why didn't you send for me earlier?'

'Don't tell Aarti yet,' he had said, 'I don't want to frighten her. Not now specially.'

Habits of obedience die harder than any other. I had not

dared to inform Aarti. And the next day he had had another attack and died instantly. Three months later Priti had been born. She never saw her grandfather.

'Who is that, ajji?' she had asked me once, seeing his photo.

'Your grandfather, Priti.'

'My grandfather,' she had pondered. 'And what was he of yours?'

What was he of mine? The innocent question had released a flood of feelings within me. 'My husband,' I had said bluntly, at last.

As I settle down to cooking lunch, I wonder whether Aarti will today like what I am cooking. Whether she will enjoy her food and eat well. I know she will not, but the hope is always in me. Just as I hope that one day she will talk and laugh again. But that day, one day, when she had laughed, she had frightened me. She had burst into loud laughter, shattering the tenuous peace of the house. 'What is it?' I had asked her, wondering whether to smile, to laugh, to respond in some way to her.

'Isn't it gloomy here? The right atmosphere for a pair of desolate widows. That's what we are, aren't we?'

Widows . . . I remember my mother who was one. She had had a shaven head, worn only coarse red saris, and been shorn of all ornaments all her life after my father's death. And I think of Aarti, who for days neglects herself. And then, one day dresses up, makes up her face and wears flowers in her hair. And yet Aarti it is whose face has the arid look of a desert.

Life has been cruel to her. It was her father whom she had loved; and he died, while I live. It was her husband whom she had loved even more than the child; and it was he who died, while Priti is left to her. Children are more sensitive than we think. They understand so many things we think they don't. Otherwise why would she have said one day to me, 'Ajji, can I sleep in your room at night?'

I am old and grey and have lost all that I have loved in life but these two persons . . . but at her words, my heart had leapt in happiness. Yet, I had restrained my joy and asked her, 'Why, Priti?'

'I'd like to. You can tell me stories at night. And there are so many things I suddenly remember at night and want to tell you. And . . .'

'But Mummy is with you.'

The child's face had fallen. 'But, ajji, if I try to talk to her, she says, "Go to sleep, Priti, and don't bother me." And she never sleeps at all, but just reads and smokes. And I don't like that smell.'

The child has a high and clear voice and I had hushed her in a sudden fear that she might be overheard. Yes, she smokes incessantly now. Earlier, she had tried to hide it from me. But not for long. When I was a child, in my father's house, it had been considered wrong even for a man to smoke. But today, I would of my own accord let my daughter smoke if I thought it brought her happiness. But it doesn't. She puffs out smoke as if she is emitting bitterness. There is an infinity of bitterness in her now. And I cannot help her. I can only try to look after her body. Such a small thing, but even in that I fail. She is thin and brittle. Most of the time she never dresses up. Just goes round in an old gown, her hair tied up with a rubber band. Priti, looking at an old photograph one day, had wistfully said, 'My Mummy was so pretty, wasn't she, ajji?'

The child's pride in her mother had roused in me a rage against Aarti. She seems to me like a child sulking because she does not have what she wants, wilfully ignoring the things she has. Has anyone promised us happiness for a lifetime, I want to ask her?

'Why don't you go out?' I had asked her once.

'Where?'

I had mumbled something she had not heard. She had gone on instead.

'There is nowhere I want to go. Everywhere, I see couples. I can't bear to see them. I could murder them when I see them talking and laughing.'

This talk amazes me. I cannot understand her. My niece had once told me of something she had read in an American magazine. About children of eleven, twelve, thirteen and fourteen who stab and throttle and rape and gouge out eyes . . . often for no reason at all. And I had wondered . . . what kind of parents can they be who give birth to such monsters? Now, I know better. The accident of birth can be cruelly deceiving. We fool ourselves that our children are our own, that we know them. But often, they are as alien to us as baby cuckoos born in a crow's nest. And yet we cannot escape the burden of parentage. If my daughter is so empty that she can hate people who are happy, the fault is, to some extent, mine.

These bitter thoughts do not often occupy me. I have my work. The quiet routine of my day is like balm to my soul. Daily chores are not monotonous but soothing. Now that the child is with me, the day is full of meaning. I wait, as eager as a child myself, for her to return from school. When she has a holiday, I don't know who is happier, she or I. If there is an unexpected holiday, we are equally full of glee. But when she, *my* daughter and *her* mother, comes to us, we feel guilty and hide our happiness.

'Do you remember your Papa?' Aarti had asked her one day with a sudden harshness.

'Papa?' There had been a moment's hesitation. 'Of course, I remember.'

'I can't imagine you do. You never speak of him.'

The child had stared at her with a frightened face, feeling guilty for she knew not what; and when Aarti had left us, she had burst into sobs, clinging to me. And I had been full of pity, not for her, but for Aarti, who could turn happiness into a wrong. But I can say nothing to her. She has never shared anything with me and now she hides her sorrow like a dog its bone. She guards it jealously and will not let me approach. And I have kept my distance. It was only in my imagination that I cuddled her as a child, only in my imagination that I shared her happiness and confidences as a young girl. And now I assuage her grief in the same way. 'Look,' I tell myself I will say to her, pouring some water into my cupped palms. 'Look,' I will say as the water seeps through, leaving nothing. 'You cannot hold on. You will have to let it go.'

But I know I'm fooling myself. I have no courage to speak. I am only a foolish, middle-aged woman who has never known how to win anyone's love. Priti's affection . . . that is a gift of Heaven, that ray of sunshine God sends even to the darkest corners. For Aarti, it was always her father. Even now, she spends the whole afternoon prowling in what was his room. It is seven years since he died, but the room is unchanged. I have kept everything as it was. I dust and sweep it meticulously myself. But strangely, in spite of this, it has a neglected look like Priti has sometimes. Priti is well-fed and well-dressed; she has her tonics and vitamins and all the other things they give children these days. Still, a neglected child peeps out of her eyes at times, filling me with pity and guilt.

Now I can hear Aarti moving round in his room. Even after his death, he can give her something I can't. The thought hurts. Hurts? It's like having salt rubbed into a raw wound. Suddenly it is unbearable and I go and open the door of his room. She is sitting on his chair, her feet on his table, smoking and staring at nothing. As she hears me, she turns round startled . . . I have never disturbed her till now . . . and with the movement of her feet she knocks down his photograph which stands on the table. Now it lies on the floor, face down. She rushes to pick it up. The glass has cracked. Long splinters of glass lie on the floor and the photograph looks somehow naked. She looks up at me, something showing through the deliberate blankness. 'I'm sorry, mother. I'm sorry.' I stare down at the photograph and say nothing. 'I'm sorry,' she repeats. 'Don't look like that.' She passes her hand over the photograph. 'I'll get it fixed tomorrow. I promise I'll do it.'

'No, don't!' My words are harsh and abrupt and she looks at me in surprise. 'I don't care if it's broken. I don't want to see it here. I never want to see it again.'

She looks up at me, stunned, frightened. 'What's wrong with you? What's happened to you?'

'Nothing. I'm all right. But I don't want it. Let it go.'

'What are you saying? What is it?'

'Let it go, let it go,' I repeat. We are speaking in sibilant, strangled whispers. Can he hear us? Can he hear me?

'I don't understand you. Let what go? He is my father.' She is still crouching there on the floor, holding the photograph in her two hands.

'Yes, your father. But what was he to me? The day he died, I let him go. Like that.' Now I make the gesture I had imagined . . . cupping my palms together and then separating them. She stares at my hands with fascinated eyes. 'And there was nothing left. Nothing.'

'But I . . . I am his daughter. And yours. Am I nothing? Am I?' She is panting, her eyes hot and angry.

'What are you then?' I ask her. 'You are just smoke and a bit of ash . . . like those cigarettes you smoke. Like my married life.' Pain lays its talons on her face. Her eyes are anguished. But I force myself to go on. What have I to lose? Nothing. Only the child's love. And this cannot destroy that. On the contrary, I have a feeling that she is with me now, giving me strength for the battle, urging me on to it. My beloved charioteer. 'He was your father . . . but what was he of mine? I lived with him for twenty-five years. I know he didn't like unstringed beans and stones in his rice. I know he liked his tea boiling hot and his bath water lukewarm. I know he didn't like tears. And so, when your baby brothers died, I wept alone and in secret. I combed my hair before he woke up because he didn't like to see women with loosened hair. And I went into the backyard even then, because he hated to find stray hairs anywhere. And once a year he bought me two saris; always colours that I hated. But he never asked me and I never told him. And at night . . .'

She is still crouching there, her hair falling about her face.

She whimpers like a puppy. 'Don't,' she says. 'Don't tell me. Don't.' With each negative she bangs the photograph she still holds in her hands and the glass splinters again and again. Now, he is totally exposed to both of us. But there is no pity in me. It is not the dead who need your compassion . . . it is the living. Not the dead who crave for loyalty, but the living.

'I don't want to hear,' she says.

How innocent she is in spite of her age, her education, her books, her marriage and child that knowledge can still hurt. It reminds me of the day she had grown up and I had tried to explain. And she had cried out in the same way, 'Don't tell me. Don't!' This is another kind of growing up, when you see your parents as people.

'At night,' I go on relentlessly, 'I scarcely dared to breathe, I was so terrified of disturbing him. And once, when I asked whether I could sleep in another room . . . I don't know how I had the courage . . . he said nothing. But the next day, his mother, your grandmother, told me bluntly about a wife's duties. I must always be available. So, I slept there, afraid to get up for a glass of water, scared even to cough. When he wanted me, he said, "Come here." And I went. And when he finished, if I didn't get out of his bed fast enough, he said, "You can go." And I went.' I know these things should not be said to her, his daughter and mine. But I am like a river in the monsoon. I have no control over myself.

'And one day when you were here . . . you and Madhav . . . I heard you both talking and laughing in your room. And I stood outside and wondered . . . what could you be talking about? I felt like I did when I was a child unable to read, looking at a book. Until then, I had hoped that one day he would say he was pleased with me. That day I knew it would never happen. I would always be outside the room. I would never know what goes on inside. And that day, I envied you, my own daughter. You hear me, Aarti? I envied you. And when he died, I felt like Priti does when school is over and the bell rings. You understand, Aarti? You understand?'

Why am I also crying? We look at each other. She looks at me as if she has never seen me before. Then, with a sudden movement, she springs up and glares at me. Whose is the victory? Whose? I have made her look at me. But what, my heart shrivels at the thought, if she does not like what she sees? And as she moves backwards and starts running away from the room, from me, I realise what I have done. And then I hear the cry, 'Ajji, I'm home. Where are you?'

'Here,' I call back loudly. 'I'm here.'

SHAMA FUTEHALLY

Shama Futehally was born in Bombay in 1952 and studied English at the Universities of Bombay and Leeds. She was a Lecturer in English and Cultural History for eight years at Bombay and Ahmedabad. Her articles, reviews and short stories have appeared in various Indian journals. She is currently writing a novel.

'The Meeting' first appeared in *The Indian P.E.N.* in 1987.

The Meeting

Sakina arranged the two thick blue cups, the sugar-bowl, and the large grey tea-pot on the tray. Every day, at this time, she found herself trying unsuccessfully to overlook the tea-pot's slightly chipped handle. The tray was Kashmiri and had been beautiful, but now dust filled the spaces between the carving and there were the usual circular stains left by sticky cups. She was getting up to make the tea later every day, and at the back of her mind there was the slight fear that Abba would finally say something about it. But these days the afternoon heat was almost solid, it weighed you down till you passed out in sleep, surfacing in desperation to brush away a fly crawling over the eyelid, or the throat, or the forehead. So you were never really rested. Although her bed dipped uncomfortably in the middle and she lay on a khadi bedspread which was too thick, still Sakina was always reluctant to emerge from her little bed.

She had slowly bathed, dressed, and stood for a quarter of an hour in front of the mirror in the cupboard door, applying lipstick from a small stub. The listlessness remained. And as always, she felt not quite equal to encountering her father, after a gap of so many hours.

He would be waiting for her, she knew, sitting up grim and eager in bed. And as she came in he would look at her with a mocking half-gleam. He would address her in English. 'All dressed up? And for which knight in shining armour, may I ask?' Abba was a great one for English.

She went heavily into the sitting-room to get a tea-cosy from the chest of drawers. Since Amma's death the sitting-room had become darker. It was dark even in the morning, and by the evening it looked like a prison. When Amma was alive the room always looked effortlessly clean and light. Even the tea-tray looked different, with Amma pouring the tea graciously. She tried, secretly, to achieve the same effect. Especially on the very rare occasions when there were guests, she would hunt frantically for lace doilies and clean napkins, and she would do her best to pour the tea like Amma.

She picked up the tray and began to climb the stairs. A shaft of light was coming through the small window on the landing, making a zig-zag of light on the steps. They were of grey stone, small and uneven as in most Rampur houses. She had often come to grief while climbing them and dreaming away, but when carrying her father's tray she was particularly careful.

The stairs were almost spiral. Perhaps that was why, whenever she took up the tray, she felt she was chained to a huge dark wheel which went slowly – so slowly! round and round. It consisted of Abba's room, kitchen, tea-tray, and climbing the circular stairs. Round and round and round.

Was that the doorbell? For all her experience she could never help a faint jump of the heart at the sound of the doorbell. Because it was so unexpected. A sound that came so suddenly could also, there was a chance in a thousand, supply a sudden miracle. But now she had learnt to maintain her dignity before the doorbell. She never rushed to it, telling herself carefully that it would only be the cleaning woman come to ask for some dry pickle, or the dhobi who would unrelentingly put down his large pile of clothes. And she always felt a sad triumph when proved right. For another moment she listened, deliberately without interest, and went on.

And now she was at Abba's door. The tightness in her chest was unbearable, as if she knew today was going to be worse than usual. She knocked. There was a quick, eager response and she went in looking only at the tea-tray. She dragged forward the cane stool and put the tray down. She knew he wanted to smile ferociously at her, eyes gleaming in anticipation of something. But she was conscious of the lipstick she had worn, and now she would have to be nonchalant about it till it was no longer possible for him to comment. She knew, without looking, that his false teeth were in a glass by his side and that he would soon reach out and fit them on, feeling carefully around his jaw.

'Salaam Abba,' she said quietly, pouring the tea.

Immediately he smiled at her with would-be humorous anticipation, and she turned back to the tea.

Their silence began to buzz in the room like a trapped fly. Sakina looked helplessly at the mosquito net, which was grey with dust, and black at the edges. From time to time Abba glanced at her. Finally his glance pulled her irresistibly, and she was looking at him with the usual feeling of slight fright. Something was coming. The mocking gleam became more intent; Abba had some advantage which he didn't want to waste. Sakina looked. 'If I could have a minute of your time . . .' with mock solemnity. Abba was always desperately humorous when he was nervous. 'I have something to say which may not be deemed quite unworthy of your attention.'

For the hundredth time she wished he wouldn't insist on speaking to her in English. She sat in her chair, legs splayed, unable to start her tea, helplessly listening to this English.

Abba, still eyeing her, took a sip of tea. Then with an elaborate click he put down his cup. 'Suppose,' he shot at her, 'I told you that there is a proposal for you?'

Sakina lifting her eyes to his, wondered what he was doing. There could be no proposal for her. There had never been any question of it. Not for a girl so fat, so dark, whose shalwars hung elephantine from the waist. She looks like an ayah, a cousin had said once. And the remark had fixed itself in her mind like a nail, casting a long thin shadow on all she thought and felt and did.

'Well? You don't want to know who it is?'

'*Who it is*?' A real man? Sakina's lips moved, but she could say nothing. To say anything, to speak about this seriously, was presumptuous. She looked uneasily away. To be talking about these things! In English!

Abba's disgust was beginning. With the desperate gesture that he was so often driven to he pushed his cup away. No one knew what he suffered. No one pitied him for this daughter of his, who looked like a servant, who was unmarried at twenty-nine, who would never wear smart churidars or high heels (for he was fond of all this, Abba, in spite of living in Rampur) and walk with a little flick as he had seen during his six weeks in the US. Talk to her of marriage and she behaved like this. There she sat, large and shapeless in her shalwar-kameez.

Abba spoke in the voice of one who has given up. 'All right. You don't care. You are, of course, too superior, but it is my duty to tell you and be done with it.'

(So Abba must have lectured, when he was at the University. Small, bristly, stentorian, he must have boomed thus to his perpetually half-empty class.)

'There happens, in this town of ours, to be a Mr Jamal. He is not a nobody. He was a Revenue Officer before retirement. He has a son. And he has sent me a message to ask if my exalted daughter would spare a glance for this son.'

Sakina's lips began to move with the beginnings of incredulity. She gathered her legs uncertainly together and made a slight movement with her dupatta. Looking at the floor, she felt she was unable to speak. The words, 'He has a son, he has a son' were going round and round in her mind.

Abba appeared a little more satisfied. 'Well?' he said, in Urdu at last, 'Shall we arrange a meeting?'

Sakina's face moved further down. She gave a barely perceptible nod and glanced at Abba to see if he had seen it. Then she pulled her dupatta over her face, picked up the tea-tray and hurried from the room.

Never had she thought it would be for her to behave like this. During her brother's marriage, the bride had looked at the floor throughout the three days, her dupatta veiling her face. She had burst into tears of legitimate shyness when someone teased the dupatta away. Sakina, bumbling among the refreshments in an ill-fitting gharara, had watched her ceaselessly and had thought of nothing else. And now the time may come . . . !

Downstairs she poured herself another cup of tea which she could enjoy in private. For once she put in as much sugar as she wanted. She savoured every sip, sitting carefully on the bed with the dupatta adjusted around her shoulders. And she had the new feeling, embarrassingly, of looking forward to dinner with Abba. But at dinner Abba kept turning a satirical gaze towards her, so she was on edge in case she should slip unawares into her own thought, the unspeakable thought which today imprisoned her more than usual. Suddenly Abba barked, 'The boy is not a film star, you know. Don't get all sorts of romantic ideas.'

Sakina's face burned. She wished she could retort, 'Who said I had romantic ideas?' But it would not have helped. It was as if Abba knew that, try as she might, 'the son' was acquiring in her mind exactly the figure, the shadowy chest and neck, of her cousin H. Seven years ago H. had gone out of his way to be kind to her, and since then his figure in outline, his strong fair arms, his handsome quizzical lips, moved with her like a parallel body wherever she went. And his figure always became suddenly visible, like a ghost, at the sound of the doorbell.

Just now, staring in paralysis at her plate, she reminded herself anxiously that 'the son' would be very different. But she was discovering that in some unexpected way it hardly mattered. He is probably quite plain, she thought, with a new poise and contentment.

The next few days passed in a strange state. Something sweet-smelling seemed to be floating in and around her, swirling in great curves as she rounded the staircase or moved about the kitchen. She enjoyed setting out the tea-tray with gently curving movements, or lingering on the terrace after lunch. She no longer sought the refuge of her little bed. Even Abba stopped mocking her and speaking in English. Sakina tried not to think about the fifteenth, the date when 'the son' and his family were to come, as if the calendar event would somehow mean the end of this unaccustomed sweetness.

But it was coming. One morning Abba said abruptly, 'Your aunt Naseem will come here and act as hostess – on the fifteenth.' Sakina said nothing and stayed perfectly still, like someone who waits hidden against a wall for an unwanted person to pass.

On the fourteenth, immediately after breakfast, she escaped into the bathroom to wash her hair, which she had oiled the night before. It wouldn't do to be caught washing her hair on the fifteenth. She rubbed her feet with pumice and cleaned the cuticles of her nails. By the evening she was feeling sick. During the night she got out of bed every so often to see the time, and in the morning she was so full of dread that it seemed to her time had stood still.

But the morning wore on. There was some sort of silent jerky lunch with Abba. Naseema Khala arrived wearing a new smile, laden with parcels of sweets wrapped in magenta tissue-paper. Sakina saw with dismay that she had also brought her two excited schoolgirl daughters. They were set to work arranging sweets and samosas and namkeen in silver dishes. Sakina had done nothing. Naseema Khala, fussy and indulgent, took charge of her toilette. Sakina did not dare to press for the rose-pink sari she wanted to wear but fortunately Naseema Khala said nothing against it. The sari was pleated and re-pleated, matching bangles were found, a perfume was chosen. Her hair was coiled in a knot at the back and Sakina saw with secret gratitude that her aunt had brought some flowers for her hair and was taking them out of a packet of leaves. When Sakina looked in the mirror for the last time she had a feeling she had very rarely had before. It was as if Life, having decided to give her a change, had determined to do so properly. Because, on this day when it was most needed, colour and shape and mood had come together in the right way, and she was almost pretty.

She heard the shrilling of the doorbell. For once it would live up to its sudden promise. A bustle, a chair pushed back, Abba's voice, loud but deferential. Solemnly Naseema Khala put her hand on her niece's arm to lead her downstairs. Still feeling strangely confident, strangely in tune, as if she were moving to music, Sakina descended the stairs. She entered the sitting-room with her head bowed and sat quietly down on the sofa to which she was led.

When she looked up, Sakina felt gentle and blank. What she saw was difficult to take in. 'Slowly, slowly,' her mind said. 'Let us go slowly.' She had a confused impression of a crowd of women in filmy saris, smiling and silent. Apart from Abba there were two men in the room. One was an old man. The other was a shrunken man of about forty, partly bald, with paan-stained teeth. What made her completely still, what she was not sure of having really seen, was his expression. He was glinting at her with obvious enjoyment, like a stranger at the cinema. When he caught her eye he gave a little, practised, evil smile.

Stillness, said her mind, stillness. In the stillness a stone was gathering itself to descend slowly through her, but it was far away still. Without knowing what she was doing she looked towards him again and saw his fingers, over-eager, slightly dirty, clasping and unclasping themselves. It was too much of an effort to move her eyes. All around her lay the too numerous dishes of sweets, absurd pointless food. Her bangles were glinting purposelessly in her lap. Somewhere deep down she was even conscious of relief. Nothing had changed after all, life was still the life she had always known.

For the next half-hour Sakina's mind was reduced to a small throbbing point – a dot which existed only till it could stumble away, rush out of all this. If this would end, if this would end. She waited for the end like a bow drawn on a string. She would rush to Abba and, ungainly as usual, ask for escape. He would bark terribly, but surely he would, surely, surely – with rising panic – allow her to stumble away.

When the chairs finally began to scrape back she was almost unconscious of the sound. Everyone rose, moved to the door, and now she was alone in the room. All at once she felt sweat along her thighs, her back, staining her armpits. She would move. She would get out. She would go to her room to her small bed. She thought of her little bed with defeated guilt, as of a friend who has been neglected for days but is now needed again.

From the window came the sound of chatter, faintly self-congratulatory talk which they seemed to want to prolong. She was conscious of relief that they were staying away so long. She would move soon. She would go up to her bed. She was trying to force her legs to move when the curtain – Amma's bead-work curtain – parted and Naseema Khala came in. Her expression was tender, fussy, delighted. (She looked so much like Amma.) When she looked up at her aunt, Sakina felt the tears starting at last. They were so familiar, such gentle old friends. Now she had them again. Naseema Khala came straight to her and clasped her tightly.

'Now our Sakina will leave us and go away!' she said.

143

VISHWAPRIYA L. IYENGAR

Vishwapriya Iyengar was born in 1958 and now lives in Delhi. Since 1978 she has been a journalist and writer of plays, poems and short stories. Many of her articles have come out of research into the social and economic conditions of the fisherfolk of Kerala and children's working conditions in Tamil Nadu. Her short stories have been published in magazines and journals: she is now working on a collection. 'The Library Girl' was published by *Imprint*, Bombay, in 1985.

The story is set in a Muslim neighbourhood or basti, where everybody is addressed using kinship terms (like *Baba* 'father', *Beti* 'daughter') even when they are not related.

The
Library Girl

T ripping on the torn seam of her ghagra she ran quickly
through narrow paths that turned into corners at every few
steps. Quickly, before the corrugated ripples came down and
the eye shut. 'The eye of the basti,' Talat thought fancifully.

A sore or a showpiece, but the eye? Ridiculous. The library
was the most incongruous place in the basti. The basti was
many centuries old; the grave of an honoured poet and famous
saint gave it historical authenticity. No, they would rather the
eye was in the tomb.

Asad Baba removed the tin tray from the oven. The soft smell
of freshly baked rusks spilt out into the open road. Va'al-e-qum,
Baba. Asad Baba shook his head: No, not even the rusks would
tempt Talat to pause for a conversation. The fire in his oven and
the hot tray – black with years of baking – made him feel lonely
. . . He would have liked to share the evening batch.

Zahir and Ali called Talat the 'library girl' just as many others
in the basti did. They flocked to secret corners watching her go
and return.

'Quickly, quickly, before the library closes and my book is
lost inside . . .' Va'al-e-qum, Baba. Va'al-e-qum, Baji. Va'al-e-
qum, little brother. Va'al-e-qum, little goat. Tomorrow they will
dress you in chillies. A tiny rat lay dead on the circular iron lid
of the sewer. The powerful smack of a broom. Talat laughed.
Va'al-e-qum, pest.

Aziza Baji was not just a librarian, thought Talat, she was a
social worker. She was important. What she liked best about
Aziza Baji was that she never smelt of cooked food. The library
was like a palace with so many beautiful books. She liked to sit
on the cold white steel chairs and open the pages. She liked to
become a tiny ant that moved between the letters of the words.

Karim Baba sat in his closet-like shop surrounded by a dozen
century-old clocks encased in rosewood coffins. Only one
worked but it did not have an enamel dial. On the white paper

disc it said a quarter to six. His hands had shaken when he wrote, 'Made in England'. He could sell it for two hundred rupees if the paper disc was not discovered. Va'al-e-qum, Baba. Va'al-e-qum, Beti. His temples throbbed against the stiff skull-cap. She ran like a bolt of sunshine, little library girl with her book clutched to her bosom. He watched her disappear around the corner with immense sadness: some buds would never blossom in this basti. Eventually there was never enough sunshine and the soil was too cold. She would have reached the library now. He closed the door and fixed the padlock. He pressed the cold, tarnished brass key to his lips and put it in his pocket.

Talat was sixteen or seventeen years old, she did not know for sure. When she was younger, she used to go to school and then one day it had stopped abruptly. Maybe Father had quarrelled with Mother about money for school fees or Mother had quarrelled with the school teachers about money.

Only two days after she had left school, Ammi had taken her to the bazaar in a cycle-rickshaw with the promise of a wonderful expedition. Ammi wanted yellow satin, the colour of the noonday sun. The shopkeepers had laughed at this ghost-woman in a burqa who spoke so intensely about yellow. But they had found the exact shade that Ammi sought and along with it they had bought silver star-shaped sequins. Sun and stars, thought Talat, feeling a mixture of exhilaration and despondency as she sat watching an azure twilight and listened to the cycle bells of the rickshaws.

For many days Talat prayed desperately for a wedding in the family so that she could wear her new ghagra, but there had been none.

Ammi sat up all night sewing the ghagra-kameez for Talat. The kerosene lamp had become black and smoky but Ammijaan had sewn like a possessed woman. Towards dawn she began fixing the stars and Talat fell asleep reciting her numbers. It did not matter if she awoke late for there would be no school for her the next morning.

Another day she had heard Ammi and Abba quarrelling bitterly and it had frightened her. Ammi was asking how, if there was money for Tahir's education, there was none for

Talat's. Her father had laughed and then shouted. She stood at the edge of the ditch outside their house and overheard, 'Buy her silk, satin, velvet, silver – but, fool woman, don't compare her with Tahir.' Even now when she remembered the low husky voice of her father droning those words, Talat shuddered. When he left the house, she had slipped in with the shadows.

Ammijaan's eyes were red and her face covered with tears. Her hands were shaking as she slashed the meat with her long iron knife. Kheema, thought Talat, will she put peas in it? Ammi had screamed when she saw Talat creeping in. 'Go wear your new ghagra and go out and play.' Talat felt bewildered; she wanted to ask, 'When will the kheema be ready?' She had worn the ghagra-kameez and stood for a long time before the mirror. She could see Ammi in the kitchen and knew that Ammi too could see her. Ammi's long thick fingers were a little bloodstained and she stroked her cheeks. Mother and child gazed at each other through the mirror. But her mother had frightened her. Her eyes were like crows trapped in the cage of her face.

Talat had gone out to play. In the giant-wheel of mirth she had forgotten what she had played and where. But someone had been jealous of her yellow satin suit because many sequins had been torn and ugly hand prints of grease had been smudged on it instead.

Whenever she thought about school there came before her a picture of her grease-stained suit.

The library was opposite a hide shop. Hides hung in neat rows from the beams. Brown, dry hides in the exact shape of a goat. The neck and the four legs all sewn up. They made good water-bags. But the library had a curtain that was always drawn. It was the only place in the basti that did not have to exhibit its wares. A red curtain like the skirt of Anarkali.

Talat parted the curtain with restrained excitement. 'Salaam al-e-qum Aziza Baji,' she smiled in triumph. She looked shyly at Aziza and then went to the book-shelf. Her arms filled with books, she sat down on the steel chair. There were pictures in the library that she loved to see: aeroplanes, trucks, and women working in the fields. The walls in her house were bare. There were many marks on the walls and when Ammi's lamp moved its flames to the wind's music, these marks would become pictures, but she did not like the stories they told.

Today she read a story about a dancer who tried to escape death. She told death to dance in her shadow and sang to the sun, asking him to kill all shadows. But the sun said, 'How can I kill death if there is no death?' So the dancer told the sun to give her night and the sun agreed. In the night the dancer lost her shadow and danced forever. The attenuated cries of 'Allah ho Akbar' froze her fantasy. The tick of the library clock became the pricking of a sewing needle upon her flesh. Abba would soon be returning from the Azan and it was time for her to be back. Tomorrow Aziza Baji would give her a book about a famous doctor who had helped the poor people of China. Aziza Baji had told Talat many stories about this man. Talat liked to read about people who change things that seemed unchangeable. 'Until tomorrow, khuda hafiz.' Talat ran through the narrow road that twisted and slipped into a darkness called home. The book about the dancer was well hidden in the folds of her kameez. Little lights burned on the road as the library girl returned. Old eyes, young eyes, men's and women's eyes: in curiosity, in envy and in desire these lights burnt, unseen by the library girl who ran in trepidation as the name of Allah rose and fell on the ear-caves of a bleak evening.

And then it was a month of festivities.

Talat sat on a low divan, her arms propped against a blue velvet bolster and she read about the doctor in China. The velvet too, smelt of curry and her fingers curled around the fabric with hesitant sensuality.

They heard the crunch of gravel beneath thick boat-like leather soles, and the rubbing of the soles on a mat. Ammi wiped the moisture from her upper lip with a cloth kept for cleaning the kitchen. Abba lifted the curtain and stepped in. Above the doorway was some ornate Persian lettering, in praise of God, Talat presumed. She did not understand Persian. Abba had a bulky brown-paper packet underneath his black coat. Today he had been to Jamma Masjid and he must have shopped. Talat gave him a glass of sweetened water. Rose petals floated in the water. He stared at the child with mock seriousness. He drank hastily and little droplets clung to the hair of his beard. Talat gave him a towel but he did not wipe the water away. Instead, he sat down on the divan, exactly on the spot where she had hidden her book. It was safe underneath the mattress, but she was still afraid. 'It's Persian,' he said, pointing at the mysterious package with a dark, dry finger with a long nail. 'Open it, it is a gift for you, child.'

Ammi watched through the mirror. Grandmother, who was crocheting a white skull-cap on her knee, jutted out her neck as Talat delicately eased the jute twine out. She put her hands into the paper packet and shuddered with delight: 'Ooh, it's as soft as a new-born kitten.' 'It's Persian,' her father repeated. He would never say 'Iran'. She pulled out a long black cloth of silk. It slipped from her hands and fell. A black cat slept on the grey cement floor. Grandmother's old fingers knotted the white thread. Ammi rubbed rock-salt on the goat's leg.

Talat picked up the black fabric and she exclaimed with delight, 'Why! It is the most perfect burqa ever!' She lifted it up against her for all to see. The face mask was a fine net mesh. 'See, the net is as fine as the lattice-work in Fatehpur Sikri.' Her mother rubbed salt into the goat's breast and did not know if glass crystals were not being rubbed into her own. The old woman dropped her eyes onto a crocheted flower.

Only her father's eyes shone with pride and pleasure. Talat wore the burqa for him and smiled. She turned to the mirror. A wooden eagle held the mirror between its claws. Talat laughed. Ammi took out her long black iron knife and began to rub salt into the rust spots at the tip. She saw her beautiful sun and star child become night in the mirror. In haste she cut the meat that had not yet softened, in haste she cut her thumb.

Talat saw her own veiled face in the mirror and felt afraid. She had also seen her mother's face. In the cage the crows had died. Her father said, 'I have business to attend to,' and left. The old woman let out a scream of exasperation. The skull-cap had disintegrated into a confusion of knots. Grandmother slapped Tahir hard on his cheeks. He distracted her, she said, asking for star-sweets. There was the mark of her bony fingers on his plump cheeks. Tahir ran out crying disconsolate sobs.

Still wearing her Persian burqa Talat took her book from under the mattress and ran behind Tahir. She lost him around a corner and when she found him again he was with a group of boys. In his hands he held a stick like a gun and was pointing at a horse. Bang . . . bang . . . boom. Talat smiled at him. Play with your sticks, little brother, but I will cut the meat.

Talat ran quickly, quickly before the library closed. Va'al-e-qum, Baba. Va'al-e-qum, Baji. Now she would go to the library and exchange her book. Aziza Baji had promised her a truly wonderful book. Va'al-e-qum, little sister. She ran trailing her black Persian robe down the dirty streets. Today she would pause and speak, she thought, as she gathered up her robe. Asad Baba was putting a tray of buns into the oven. Talat smiled. Va'al-e-qum, Baba. He thought his old eyes were playing tricks on him and he burnt his fingers as he placed the tray a little too deep inside the oven. The library girl had not come today and he watched instead a burqa-ed woman turn the corner. In the little attic room above the bakery, Ali and Zahir played chess. Between moves they glanced at the street through the little window. It was turning dark and the library girl had not come.

Inside the veil Talat felt sick and cold. Today no one had smiled back at her and no one had said her Persian robe was beautiful. Karim Baba stood outside his clock shop. He clutched the key in his pocket. He had waited a long time. He wanted to tell Talat that he had sold the round clock with the paper dial for one hundred and seventy-five rupees. He would have liked to have given her a few rupees for an orange dupatta, or, he smiled distractedly, for a book. Tomorrow would be too late, his begum would have appropriated the money. Why hadn't the child gone to the library? Had the bud already begun to wither?

When Talat smiled at him through the black net he had turned his back. Neither the mad dog nor the enchanted child had stalked the streets today.

Within the veil, a darkness seized Talat. It bandaged her mouth, her eyes, and sealed her voice. Today her smiles had lit nothing. Blank faces had become ash in her gaze. She wanted to . . . she wanted to lift the veil and say, 'Look . . . it's me. Only me in a Persian robe. It's a joke.' But the robe had hands that clasped her mouth.

Quickly, quickly, before the library closes and the eye shuts forever. But the eye was in the tomb and had shut a long time ago. Two more corners to turn and she would be there. That wonderful book. What was it about? She had already forgotten. One more corner and she heard the corrugated shutter being pulled down. The clink-clink-clink of Aziza Baji's glass bangles. Turquoise blue? She ran, shouting, 'For the love of God wait for me. Do not close the library yet, give me my book.' She ran, tripping on her black robe.

She could not see the red curtains. Grey metal shone dully, very dully, in the moonlight. Aziza had seen a woman in a burqa waving her hands, falling down and weeping. Inside, evening had stretched the emptiness taut; she was very exhausted. Aziza had to catch a bus, she lived a long way from the basti.

Talat cried and Talat screamed inside her black veil. But they did not hear and did not see. Long after the name of Allah had turned evening into night she walked home slowly, very slowly.

PADMA HEJMADI

Padma Hejmadi was born in Madras, and educated in India and at the University of Michigan, Ann Arbor. She has given readings and seminars at several universities in the United States and has published three collections of short stories.

'Birthday Deathday' is the title story from the collection published by the Women's Press in 1985, under the name Padma Perera. Her essays and articles have appeared in various journals, including the *New Yorker* and the *Saturday Evening Post*.

Birthday
Deathday

For a long time the train circles the town, defining it, as a
dog will circle a patch of ground to mark his sleeping place.
As other journeys have circled their destination – Innsbruck,
two years ago; the bus from Venice reaching a cup of hills and
then slowly rounding its rim in the darkness, descending tier
by smaller tier to a handful of jewels glimmering at the bottom
of the valley. 'Innsbruck!' the driver cried when the jewels
became street lights: a destination reached. 'Innsbruck—!'
springing out on Austrian soil and at once becoming aggress-
ively Italian, pushing the blue cap to the back of his head, tired
but tirelessly male and appreciative, eyeing each woman pass-
enger as she stepped out pale and blinking a little, dizzy from
circling the hills.

As I have circled decisions, hesitating on the brink of commit-
ment: what is this, before I embrace it? But I cannot know until
I've embraced it. As I could not identify the jewels until they
turned into Innsbruck, nor can really assimilate this dusty
Deccan town, last seen five years ago, until I return again today.
Is this the measure of age then? – not chronology but layers of
awareness: the remembering, the likening, the overlap of
experience. I am not twenty-five but two similar journeys to be
encompassed and understood.

'Excuse me, shall I pull down that window for you?' The man
across. Unctuous. Fatly solicitous.

'No, thank you.' Take notes to share with your sister: a
profiteer, what else? Bet he bribed the booking clerk to get a
lower berth. Will she say that or will you? Being with her is a
perpetual *déjà vu*: everything felt is repeated; everything known
is deepened and returned by her quality as by time.

'But you are facing the engine, aren't you? You may be
getting coal in your eye.'

'No, no. I'm all right. Really. Don't bother. It's very kind of

153

you.' Kind indeed, when scarcely half an hour has elapsed since he bullied his secretary so unmercifully at the last station! Such misplaced and heavy-handed chivalry. Probably beats his wife. Look studiedly out at the dark earth slipping past: black-cotton-soil-of-the-Central-Indian-plateau . . . At what point did that cease being a textbook phrase and become landscape seen from moving windows? Why, when a trip grows from ambition to actuality, does it at once change its shape? Poring over atlases as a child, tracing routes with a grubby forefinger: I want to go there and there and there. See that and that and that. When first did 'there' and 'that' get tinged with 'them' – a place endued with persons met, an alien landscape made unalterably yours because you caught a cold there or ran into a friend at the corner or were so desperately unhappy that in acknowledging your misery you accepted its surroundings as well?

Neither colds nor griefs nor friendships in Innsbruck, yet a journey out as jewelled as the journey in: to my tropical eyes the very first glimpse of springtime in a temperate climate – such new and tender green light everywhere, everywhere, everywhere, until the whole world had turned to emerald. Here the ground is black and baked; the sun beats down. No, the journeys are not similar after all. There in Europe the circles were described in depth, feasting the eyes and the senses. Here in India these train tracks draw horizontal rings around the town while the town itself stands deep with age and implication, casually shuffling the centuries together as if they were a well-thumbed pack of cards.

Remember writing about that to my husband last time, five years ago, when he was still merely a friend and a foreigner, adding: 'You must come here, you simply must.' And now he will . . . and now he will . . . Train wheels take up the rhythm, toss it irrepressibly along. I dare not smile, the man across may smile back and start making overtures again. With a violent lurch the tempo slows down: . . . and . . . now . . . he . . . will. Why are they stopping? Have we arrived already?

'No signal probably,' the man says.

Nothing outside but the hot blue immensity of sky; fields lying fallow; a single bullock-cart propped forward on its shafts, the bull disengaged and tethered to a stump close by, the driver snoozing in the shade of a scraggly babul tree. Clusters of huts in the distance: dried thatch, mud walls, black earth. Suddenly out of nowhere a beggar woman comes – thin, of no age at all, hair pulled back into a peasant knot, protruding teeth, a baby asleep on her shoulder. She has covered its head with the tattered end of her sari; beneath it escape stick-like arms and legs. I open my purse and find a coin.

'You should wait until we are about to start and *then* give,' says the man. 'Now, see, they'll all come running.'

In place of the woman a boy of less than three. Faded blue shirt barely covering his belly; around his hips a thin black cord against the evil eye; his sex, spindly thighs and feet stained with dust and urine; one eye a running sore on which flies settle and do not fly away. He doesn't raise his hand to ward them off, he just extends it, palm upward: 'Amma . . .'

'You are simply encouraging them. This is how even able-bodied fellows become beggars.' (Echoes of a cartoon in a Madras newspaper: one wayside beggar informing another: 'I have decided to open a branch office.') An old man now, a girl, a cripple, two more men – 'See what I told you? Able-bodied chaps.'

No more coins left, no change to pay the porter when I get off. Suddenly I am afraid: of vultures gathering, of the fattest vulture of them all in front of me, drawing up a bulging dhoti-clad leg to lean back more comfortably against the buttoned upholstery. The train gives a warning lurch. Calmly he feels in his pocket, opens a shiny wallet and, shaking out a few coins, flings them from the window just as we begin to move. The beggars scatter and then avidly converge, getting down on their hands and knees, scrounging in the dust; left behind. Wheels rattle louder, spin faster, devouring every hunger and shame and platitude: *If you give to one, they all come running. Whatever you do is a drop in the ocean* . . . The man belches, complacent. His point has been proven, his vanity fed.

Abroad, in Europe and America, I've chafed against the stuffy impersonality of trains: hermetically sealed off from outside smells and sounds, neatly dispensing with even their own thudding clatter as they glide in and out of dumb-show stations. Here one is thrown open with every window to every scrap and

155

pain of life. To shut out, to soft-pedal, is to be lessened: not so lacerated, not so responsible, that much less alive. Profiteers are part of the bargain then – will this trip never end?

All of a sudden it does. Against the sliding blur of people and noise – red turbans of the coolies, cries of the platform vendors, bookstalls, piles of luggage, cavernous waiting rooms – a vivid delicate face springs into focus, eagerly scanning each compartment as it rumbles by. My sister. Thin hand, replica of my own, clasps mine. We have never looked alike, only hands to show the comforting kinship.

'How was it?'

'All right.' Tell her later.

Jostling of people, manoeuvring of luggage. 'Suitcase, bedding, water-jug. Nothing else? Sure?'

'Sure. Oh, and I've no change.'

'What did you do, eat it? Never mind, I have enough.'

Incredible how anyone so exquisite can be so efficient. To avoid the last-minute scramble she has engaged a porter well ahead of time. Number 83 on his brass badge; but by now, especially with the train so late, she must have divined not only his name but that of his wife, his children, his village and his sure-fire remedy for whooping cough. He coils his turban into a cushion padding the crown of his head, places the suitcase on top of it, swings up the bed-roll in a single gesture and strides off towards the exit. Holding the heavy earthen water-jug between us, we try to follow, only to be blocked off at every second step by what seems to be a welcoming committee of sorts thronging my fellow traveller. Flashbulbs pop and sizzle against an overpowering odour of roses and human sweat. Can't point him out to my sister, he is hidden by the crowds, unseen but well imagined: laden with garlands and the lard of his own importance. In a sudden access of distaste I lose my bearings. 'Hey, where did our porter go?'

'Jeevanlal? He said he'd wait for us at the gate – what are you giggling at?'

Your knowing his name. Reaffirmation of faith and familiarity. Sheer giddy relief that, for once, those whom I most cherish will be safe within the bounds of a single country, not scattered haphazard across the globe to turn travel from a luxury to a life-line.

Answering my thoughts, she tells me the moment we escape the clamour of the platform: 'Guess whose cable we got today?'

My turn to beg. 'He's coming soon?'

'Day after tomorrow. The visa has come through. He wired to say he'd grab the earliest available flight out.'

Never has this town been more layered with time, personal time now, three layers on every dust mote: the future of his arrival day after tomorrow; the actuality of our presence here today; and over it all the remnants of the past, five years ago: a sense of reading over my own forgotten shoulder, therefore, able to wander in the garden or write letters while the elders talked, shown the town as now I can show my sister.

'We haven't been together on a trip like this since high school, do you realise that?'

But she doesn't hear me, busy settling accounts with Jeevanlal and wearing her absorbed, practical face so absurdly resembling her three-year-old son's that I in turn am distracted and do not hear when she speaks.

'Psst! Snap out of it. I said taxi or tonga?'

'Tonga, of course.' Remember to tell him this when he arrives: as children, out in the districts, down endless country roads edged with rice fields, we went to elementary school in a tonga painted bright blue, the horse stepping smartly along in feathered crest and jingling harness, the driver whistling film songs to its beat.

Today our driver is mournful, with drooping moustaches and a dispirited horse called Raja. When he says 'Ai, Raja, ai!' and flourishes his whip, it livens tentatively up to a trot, only to lapse back soon enough to its habitual shuffle.

'Leave him be,' my sister says. 'We are in no hurry. Is he an old horse?'

'Old? *Raja*? Why, I got him scarcely a month ago at the very best age a horse can be – ' Moustaches bristle; he is lying and they both know it, a companionable feeling.

She asks him where he lives, he tells her; talks of his brother, a tenant farmer; the monsoons; the crops; a new dam being built upriver . . . See it again: her inheritance, as firstborn, of our parents' gift: of giving themselves so simply to the substance of things while never losing their own complexity, so that every human encounter is allowed to fill its limits, whether rounded and complete or probing jagged corners; in accord or in argument, always that sense of a touchstone.

Easy to think, away from them: 'It couldn't be. Distance does it. I'm idealising,' only to come home and be witness again, watching her now, wondering: When did envy of her as a sister stop and delight in her as a person begin? Past how many childhood resentments, absences, miles, years, growing up parallel though separate to reach this spacious closeness – a ripening result of time, once more, as only this dusty town can evoke it.

'When did you arrive?'

'Yesterday.'

'How are our host and hostess?'

Eyes solemnly wide. 'They are away today, but you can imagine.'

'Yes, I can.' I start giggling again. Between us they are a private joke with all the probable improbability of a cartoon: Highly respected literati from a wealthy business clan who have set themselves up as patrons of the arts and the sciences alike, benignly engrossed in charities, ideally engrossed in each other – perfect couple, share and share alike: he takes on the sciences while she appropriates the arts. Regularly over the years they have also brought up innumerable nieces and nephews, sheltered destitute cousins and widowed great-aunts, finally becoming, though childless themselves, titular heads of a huge and constantly accruing household. Why then should their laudable lives give off such a tinny sound?

'Perhaps,' my sister suggests thoughtfully, 'because they seem to stake such proprietary claim on all compassion and conjugal bliss . . . Nobody can expect to get away with that, now can they?' Chin in hand, as we jog up and down, she watches the road unrolling like a broad grey ribbon beneath the tonga wheels, skirting bazaar and cantonment area to take us to the oldest quarter of the town beyond the university campus. 'I was thinking about it when I woke up today. Lay in bed waggling my foot and listening to all the early-morning sounds

158

around their place – cook yelling, taps running, old lady brushing her teeth with a neem-twig and making such alarming noises in the process that—'

'Good God!' At my groan, so loud and unexpected, the tonga driver turns around to glance speculatively at us above his moustaches. 'Don't tell me *she's* there now.'

'Where else would she be, poor thing? And they've never harboured an international marriage in the house before, so you might as well prepare yourself for an inquisition.'

Dismaying prospect. The old lady, our hostess's aunt, is like no other old lady we know: possessed and personified by a curiosity so all-consuming that she has passed into a proverb in our dialect – eternally she lifts lids to peek beneath, opens doors to hear within, tweaks the curtains in every bedroom to flush out some possibly lurking lover . . . Yet now in the old house she stands like a painting under the high shadowy arches of the verandah: deep red sari offsetting white walls, grey stone floors; a waiting, parched-ivory face, deceptively bland and fine-boned.

'Why are you so late? How much did you pay the tonga? How many hours did you spend on the train? Were you alone in the compartment? Did anyone try to molest you? Why hasn't your husband come with you, have you quarrelled? Oh, will the visa be ready by the time he leaves? Is this why you and he and your sister are coming from three different directions on three different days instead of travelling together like sensible people? Where will you go next? Where are your parents now? How long . . . ?'

Age. This too, ceaseless reckoning of people and places and times, usually dismissed in formula: Curiosity Keeps Her Alive. Or could it perhaps have been congenital in her case? Once to be deplored, now accepted and even indulged. With so little of it left, she is entitled to leaven her life as she chooses. ('Crowded as our conditions are, we can have room and respect for our old people.' Who said that, so righteous and resonant? Politician? Poet? Someone in a dream?) So now she welcomes visitors, fusses over the younger generation— 'The boys are in Darjeeling, the girls are down south.'

Can't get a word in edgewise to ask what boys? Which girls?

No matter. For the moment, a house blessedly empty and beautiful. Curtains from Orissa, handwoven and the colour of wet earth. Kashmiri rugs on the floor – mountain and cloud, kingfisher and chenar leaf, against the cool grey stone. A Tibetan prayer wheel. Tanjore bronzes. On one entire wall a great carved lintel from a South Indian temple. Objects disparate yet coherent like the landscapes they represent, blown together by the wind through open doors, held together by the spaces in the old house, intact as when a spendthrift Nawab built it fifteen generations ago.

'Lovely,' I admit *sotto voce* under the continuing barrage of questions. 'And no air conditioning or closed doors, thank God.'

'If it salves your conscience any,' my sister murmurs back, 'that lintel was neither bought nor yanked off. Presented-in-appreciation-of-charitable-services-rendered. She told me.'

Abruptly the barrage stops. 'What are you talking about? . . . Go and wash up, children. We've put you in what used to be the harem.'

Three rooms to the side of the house open out on to a courtyard completely enclosed by high stone walls, shaded by a mango tree at one end and a jackfruit at the other. 'And no doubt a eunuch standing guard in between,' my sister mutters. 'So much for the good old days.'

'What eunuch?' at once the old voice demands eagerly behind us. 'Where, where?'

Day after tomorrow, driving home from the airport, my sister will probably warn him: 'Listen, your bugging devices are nothing compared to our old lady, so just you watch out.' Sitting between them, I shall be able to look from one profile to the other, maybe against a wet darkness blurring past the windows, light rain falling. As a child, remember being most still when most happy, unable to move lest the brimming moment spill. 'It's all right,' he will say, unperturbed. 'I've got used to you scrutable Orientals by now.' But we forget: the old lady speaks no English, except for one word. Might otherwise leave him alone, aside from a constant unwinking scrutiny when he is in sight, meanwhile pelting us with questions, plying him with food and uttering her one English word. 'Eat,' she will say benevolently. 'Eat, eat . . .' 'Just like my mother,' he will groan. Even so she will not perpetually smile like her niece, our hostess, and make small talk, mouth flattening sweet and smug across pretty white teeth; nor, like our host, introduce him to officials: military officials, government officials, business officials – an avalanche of bureaucratic handshaking from which he may never recover.

Even to conjecture the scene, here on this first day of my visit, makes me quail. 'Sightseeing,' my sister whispers. 'That's the answer. We'll take him out sightseeing morning, noon and night until we leave.' By evening we have already become conspirators, truly contemporaries as we escape the house to pitch our moment's presence against the entrancing centuried town. Walking down the narrow bazaar lanes, we practise translating the names of things into English, all for his delectation when he should arrive day after tomorrow. ('Look, the green gourd in the basket. That's *dil pasand*, Heart's Choice. And that knobbly one over there – that's called *kala kand*, the Root of Art. It's true, I swear it!')

But how to translate the untranslatable: exactly what it means to hear these languages sounding together again, plosive to fricative like clapper to bell: liquid Hindi phrases decorating a vegetable; harsh clatter of Marathi haggling in a market; pure classical Urdu spoken by the old retainers at the tombs of the Muslim saints, and by the caretaker declaiming to us at the Chakki, an ancient flour mill with its creaking water-wheel still in use—

'The water comes in underground tunnels from an unknown source in the hills seven miles away,' the caretaker enunciates slowly and deeply and beautifully into pale gold evening light, as if he were reciting a poem. Day after tomorrow perhaps a question to be translated: How can it be unknown if you know it is seven miles away? Are you sure no one ever found it – neither engineer nor sanitary inspector, not even the urchins playing in the hills or a cowherd grazing his flock? Today we listen, my sister and I: belief is sustenance, like the water itself.

'Mian Mohur.' The name resounds majestically on the care-taker's tongue, his delivery rising in grandeur from ode to epic. 'Mian Mohur, the hunchback slave who became our prime minister in 1600. It was he who installed this water supply and we can still use it safely, all our townspeople, all these centuries later.'

It churns over the wheel, splashes down exquisitely carved and inlaid channels, past formal gardens (sunlight, grass, croton leaves) to a place of pure white minarets and petalled arches, fluted pillars and marble floors. 'Sshh, listen—' A mosque. Within, the chanting sounds and stops and sounds again. We move away, not to disturb.

'You know,' I tell her, 'this is one of the things I've most missed, being away from home.' How can I explain it? Only hands can gesture together, showing her everything coalesced – not just sunlight, grass, croton leaves, but a total opposite of what it was like abroad where I have lived since my marriage. 'Life was somehow so compartmentalised there. One language at a time. One era at a time. One religion at a time. Except for the cities, which were another problem entirely, everything else was pruned down to stay in its place, very tidy. No bursting of boundaries, of things spilling over into your life willynilly, like this jumble of languages and religions and the past and the present that we are smitten with here. Yes, that was perhaps the most cramping of all: the business of being caught perpetu- ally and irretrievably within your own time-span; clutching the present, being clutched by the present . . .'

'Inevitable, though, isn't it?' Thoughtfully my sister traces the outline of a leaf with her forefinger. 'After all, theirs is a different idiom of existence, so they are bound to possess a different sense of time. Don't you see? For us it is an underpin- ning, such a constant dimension that without it we are well and truly lost. Meaning, if the past can cripple us, it can also provide our crutches. For whatever that's worth.' Yes, we've both learned that, culturally as well as personally, our respective marriages having taken us towards the same insight from opposite ends – I in rebelling against tradition, she in accepting it. After a pause, she adds: 'Did you know that the language in some of the Vedic texts has no present tense? Because the moment a word is uttered, it is past.'

Typically, while I am still mulling over that, she has a practical prescription to offer. 'Tell you what, let's to go the caves tomorrow.'

'Marabar?' I laugh. No, not the mythical Marabar; just Buddhist caves here in the bare northern hills overlooking the town: dark, unpretentious, a little smudged by time.

'Carved between the fifth century BC and the second century AD,' our guide Abdulla waves a reckless hand the next day. What's a couple of centuries more or less? Our hosts have insisted he accompany us on the expedition (impossible to contemplate two young women going off unescorted to that lonely hillside), but we like the young rascal: the way he stood shock-headed, solemnly at attention while being interviewed in the big house; the way he now goes whistling, chattering, throwing out casual snippets of information – mostly inaccurate – as he picks his way over thorn and pebble and scrub to reach the easternmost cave.

Last time I was here, it was a friend who took us around: a meticulous, erudite man; dates and trends and theories holding their shape in his mind as palpably as the shapes of chaitya and vihara around us. This time we have no need of annotations – enough to know, outside, the feel of sunwarmed stone at fingertips; inside, the musty smell of bats and centuries; and from far away the sound of a child's voice floating faintly into the dimness. We turn to each other, struck by the same thought.

'Listen to that, Abdulla. More people coming up the hill. Why don't you go and show them around, that way you have two groups of clients at one trip? We can wait for you here.'

'Here' is a boulder perched on the hillside, slightly askew but with the huge and solid certainty of Krishna's butter-ball. Abdulla wavers, his feet turned towards the exit, his face half-turned towards us in doubt. 'Yesterday there were goondas here, such hooligans! Don't know where they came from. Luckily they didn't deface anything but they threw stones at tourists and tried to dislodge rocks and hack at the roots of trees to bring them down. I don't know if I should—'

'Don't worry, it's all right. Really. Look, if we sit on this boulder we'll be within your view all the time, so you can keep an eye on us as you promised.' She smiles reassuringly at him;

163

succumbing, he grins back – a broad delighted gleam of teeth in the darkness – and disappears.

'Devious, aren't you?'

'Certainly.' Unabashed, she scrambles up after me. Not since our teens have we felt such a gleeful sense of playing truant, flouting censure ('Graceless, two grown women climbing rocks like monkeys!'), sitting there with our saris billowing around us. It was she who draped a sari on me, when I first wore it to school, admonishing sternly: No pins. No long strides.

'Remember that?'

We don't talk together so much as simply be together, using not sentences so much as spaces shared – for those we both love; for filling in blanks; for pooling the discoveries of our separate lives (how in my foreign flat privacy can change to loneliness, how in her bustling joint-family home companionship can turn to chaos); catapulting back and forth from the past to the possible; ranging at random over books read, pictures seen, people met, clothes worn; moving from experience to insight; from language to dialect to the kinship of silence.

Especially here, the reason for our pilgrimage. 'It's not only the stone, even the stillness here is sculptured. Have you noticed?'

I notice: Abdulla's whistle can't penetrate it, nor the chattering family he escorts. (Father sporting dark glasses, mother a wad of betel leaf in her cheek; twin sons with breaking voices and downy upperlips; a small girl in a vivid red skirt.) Silence is what the Buddhist monks have left behind in this place, carved as carefully as their caves: the accumulated peace of their years of discipline and meditation. Met with thrice before, recognised again, this quiet that is not disturbed by noise – once in a Thai temple; once in a synagogue in Cochin; once, unforgettably, in that mountain village in Japan, tucked away behind the hills, so remote you could fool yourself into believing fate couldn't touch you there.

Shrilly the family troops out of one cave and into another. Teeth gleaming, Abdulla follows. Above us the sky turns hazy with heat; a kite circles, lazily watchful. In front, the hill falls away in a series of bumpy slopes to the plateau below: at one end of it, a potters' village (narrow streets, women carrying brass pitchers balanced on their heads) and at the other, almost directly beneath us, the ruined splendour of the Empress's Golden Palace, very seventeenth-century Moghul, gaudy and sombre at once.

On cold nights the wind must whistle eerily through those broken arches; today it blends faint noises from the town. Small deliberate creak of the Chakki's water-wheel, clang of cycle bells, human hum of the bazaar, mechanical sounds from a crew of men laying a new road just around the bend of the hill and out of sight: a dull banging, whirring, drilling, pause; banging, whirring, drilling, pause – suddenly a deafening explosion.

Everything moves. Dizzy, I turn to my sister, find her staring back at me equally startled, one rueful eyebrow climbing her forehead. 'Don't tell me I'm pregnant again.'

'You couldn't be. I felt it too.'

'Oh, it's the dynamite, silly. From the road.'

She has scarcely finished speaking when there is another explosion, louder than the first. With it, a rumbling, a sliding. Our rock pitches forward and we are thrown off balance, scrabbling frantically at its surface for a handhold. 'Let's get out of here.' But we can't. Try to move, and the boulder teeters again, rolling forward another few inches before coming precariously to rest just short of a small rocky ledge.

'Don't move!' Abdulla has come running out; his terrified face sets the seal on our danger.

Then this must be one of the rocks that the hooligans tried to dislodge yesterday for the pleasure of seeing it hurtle downhill. What they began anything can complete at any moment – another reverberation, our slightest movement, a sneeze. The ledge might break our fall; it might not. The entire family surrounds Abdulla now, circle of frozen upturned faces staring at us, we staring back, petrified until made part of the boulder in a desperate travesty of stillness. My heart thudding or hers? So loud, so violent, it might shake the boulder, send us crashing down, ending . . .

'Buttress it—' Again caught by the same thought, we can

scarcely whisper. Somehow the father understands and fore-stalls us, suddenly galvanised into authority. 'Stones. Pick up the heaviest you can find and lay them against the base of the boulder. We can try to keep it from moving. You, Amol—' A quick stream of Bengali to one of the twins and the boy takes off, running zigzag down the steps of the hill followed by his mother's anxious cry. Perhaps 'Be careful, you might fall!' Again the father interrupts, brusque. 'Sshh, no noise. Come on, Abdulla. Hurry.'

Time topples . . . slowed down to their every movement: a nightmare choreography, their bending down, picking up each stone, staggering over with it, carefully lowering and easing it into place against our rock. May not work. Against the whole height of the hill, one small boy, now a dwindling brown streak still zigzagging down the bottom steps. Things happen in threes. Two blasts already. One more, and the end. No one speaks. The child says shrilly 'Ma?—' on a high note of fear. With a hand on her shoulder the mother turns her away, glancing briefly back at us, implacable, one-mother-to-another: *If anything should happen to you, I want to spare her the sight.*

Notice it all. Take in every detail to keep from shaking. Three dried grasses waving on the ledge. Black and ochre dust. My sister's blue sari on the rock, rock the colour of a water buffalo's back. Child's red skirt vanishing around a tree trunk. Remember the mother's look to recognise it afterwards if there is an afterwards. Now, childless, I must let my sister accept that look: having children she has more value. We are not only ourselves but what others have invested in us. – One more day. Please let me have one more day until he arrives tomorrow. Vertigo; falling; down into terror; no tomorrow. But cling. Cling to the thought of it; *until he comes tomorrow. Please.* Flesh has never been so sweet, to look, to touch, to be with one another, laugh over the names of vegetables – oh God, if prayer is so easy it couldn't be prayer.

As the fourth stone settles into place there is a slight bump, the rock begins to teeter. Watching Abdulla jump out of the way, we daren't move, breathe, clutch each other; but nothing happens. One more stone may do it, hold back the rock. If there isn't another blast, if the twin reaches in time to warn the road crew. Time. Not layers or tenses now but time itself. Runnels of sweat down back, down legs. Palms clammy; thighs damp against the rock. No need to ask what she is thinking. Never so close, never so separate; separate investments. Like joined twins being relentlessly torn apart, morsel by morsel of flesh and memory. Always complaining you didn't look alike in life, now perhaps in death you will, no more complaints, equally mangled – Stop it.

From the road a confused noise but no report. Amnesty once more. With it, a sudden ineradicable rage. Why, why, if this is to be the end, were these last vouchsafed days frittered away in hypocrisy, mouthing politenesses to our host and hostess; why not my husband here; her family; our parents – our lives are those we love.

JUMP. Have I said it aloud? Turn to her at last, unable to focus or see her face; only the eyes, familiar, loved, hazel-flecked; my older sister, my touchstone self commanding NO. SIT STILL. BE STILL. BE, become . . . Not dynamite exploding but all my separate selves, from the centre outwards, from him, from what we have built between us, to become beggar's hunger, profiteer's greed, old woman's curiosity, embrace them each and die, stop the waiting; not half in love with easeful death but totally, totally, cool caved dark – Tomorrow. Think. Concentrate. Tomorrow. Without him, death may be impossible as life. *Tomorrow*.

If no explosion yet, probably never. The twin has reached. 'They're coming!' Shrill, it's the child again, resilient, red skirt bobbing up and down. She has come all the way from fear to excitement: A spectacle! Men with ropes, pulleys, axes on their shoulders; climbing slowly, tortuously up the jagged steps. In abeyance now, the chaos, the anger, the unbearable love – And for her? Next to me, a still, beautiful blur, what is she thinking, what am I thinking, going off at tangents, always talking to him in my head: 'Stupid, isn't it, having to stave off terror by watching yourself stave off terror?'

With help on the way we can force ourselves to look down now, concede the worst: rock, hillside, gravity, pulling you down into death. Infinitesimal too, our deaths like our lives, mere scratches on Mian Mohur's water system, just two more

167

dead for the Golden Palace. Now, saved from it, it is possible to entertain the idea, entertaining idea, death.

Pulleys; men; noise. Ropes flung tight around the belly of our rock and fastened to a tree trunk at either end. Barricade of stones built higher. Brown, sinewy arms streaked with sweat; hot heavy breathing in the sun; palms flattened, braced against the boulder. Peremptory order: 'Now jump.'

We jump. Saris billow behind; absurd parachutes. Alive, alive. Safe. At least for the moment. Tell them, thank them. Mouth dry, hand at last clutching her, as if never to let go. 'You saved our lives—' Invitations to dinner; baksheesh; gratitude; recompense absurd as parachutes, all the way down the steps of the hill to the potters' village below (through narrow dusty streets, past women balancing pitchers on their heads); pebbles underfoot; reek of drains and cowdung; to where our hosts' car awaits, handing time back to us – stolid anachronism, parked next to the Golden Palace.

Stepping in, I hear her pause and turn to Abdulla. All this time, noticing and noticing, I haven't noticed his face: waxen, still terrified, skin pulled perilously taut across high cheekbones. 'Of course it wasn't your fault,' she is saying crisply. 'After all, we suggested it ourselves. Didn't we? How on earth were *you* supposed to know the boulder was pried loose? I'll tell them that. Don't worry. We'll sign a paper, if you like.'

As a guide, his reputation would have died with us. Still very well might. But suddenly, nerves frayed endlessly beneath the endlessly burning sun, I turn on her in exasperation, protesting in our dialect – blessed obscure dialect that nobody here understands – 'Will you stop being so impossibly good? You're too much, worrying about him after what we've been through.'

She glares at me, annoyed in return, not saintly in the least. 'Damn it, it's his livelihood, isn't it? We are safe now, it's all over. What about *him*?' Again that parental heritage: no vehement claims on virtue, merely this willingness to take each moment wholly and then leave it as wholly behind: receive and relinquish with open hands. Theirs after all is the same wisdom that sang the Vedas in the past tense.

She has always possessed that. It is I who need to go on

innumerable journeys, almost die, to learn; meanwhile slowly counting my age by birthdays of knowledge.

Above us the caves are pitted dark and high in the hillside; here the broken archways of the Golden Palace wear the sky proudly, like an immense blue crown.

RUKHSANA AHMAD

Rukhsana Ahmad taught English language and literature at the University of Karachi, Pakistan, before coming to live in the United Kingdom in 1973. She has worked as a freelance journalist and has written several plays for Tara Arts Company, the most recent of which is *Black Shalwar*. Some of her short stories appear in *Right of Way* (Women's Press, 1988), an anthology of prose and poetry written by Asian women in the Asian Women Writers' Collective based in London.

The Gate-Keeper's Wife

Annette's short sun-bleached hair spiked wispily away from her face as her weary fingers pushed through it. She felt wizened and faded as she rubbed the sides of her cotton skirt down with the palms of her hands in a vain attempt to push out the creases. Time to go. It was nearly five o'clock. But the sun, not seeming to notice this, still blazed down vengefully on the breathless, parched scene below.

She dropped back the corner of the heavy curtains flinching from the glare, cherishing the last few moments of the cool darkness left to her before she had to face its white hostility. Two people had died of heat stroke the day before. It was a record summer for sweltering temperatures. She felt irritated by the mindless cruelty of the sun, remembering how hushed and still all the birds in the aviary had been the day before, how listless all the magnificent cats had seemed. Surely it had to stop. 120 degrees fahrenheit was a ridiculous peak to maintain . . . enough to turn the most dedicated of sun worshippers into apostates. At the best of times Lahore Zoo was not a perfect place for animals; these temperatures were putting their lives at serious risk. Surely it must stop soon.

'*Sahib aa gaya*?' she asked in her heavily accented Urdu as the lime juice with soda appeared from behind the curtain magically. Kammu's timing was always perfect.

'No, Memsahib,' his tone was mildly apologetic as he answered, eyes averted respectfully, holding the tray out before her.

'Thank you, tell driver, five minutes,' she sought the aid of her hands to gesticulate her meaning this time.

Not back yet. Won't see him now till dinner time. He was supposed to go for golf at five-thirty. Maybe he's changing at the club again. He could have telephoned. Nine years of this and it still hurts. She tried to block the hurt from her mind as she got her things together. A little navy parasol, beige straw

171

bag, sunglasses and the vet's handbook permanently borrowed from the British Council Library. The heat outside lashed her face as she hastened into the cool protection of the blue Toyota.

The zoo was not far from their house on the G.O.R. estate. Thirty-seven years after the British had left it was still the most privileged address in Lahore with its awesome Government Officers' Residences, faded but desperately holding on to the aloofness of their old masters, as they stood in their vast lawns behind exclusive boundary walls.

It was past locking-up time at the zoo, five o'clock; but in the absence of the threatening finality of a bell it took the efforts of the entire staff to persuade people to believe that the gates would shut at five and that they must head for the way out or be locked in. Reluctant children sucking ice lollies which dribbled down their fingers in the intense heat faster than they could gulp them down dragged their feet accompanied by relieved adults, ready for the shade, hurrying for whatever transport (or the lack of it) awaited them outside the gate.

The gate-keeper interrupted his role of town crier to open the gates for Annette's car. They drove past the last few stragglers towards the depot and the superintendent's residence located at the far end. Hussain was all prepared for her arrival, books and registers, buckets and pans laid out in the verandah where he sat on what looked like a dried-out chair, his feet, dry and dusty, sticking out of his thonged chappals. He got up quickly to receive her. Brief formalities exchanged, his daily offer of a cold drink declined as usual, they got down to business.

Annette now sat on the dried-out chair and looked through the entries in all the ledgers whilst Hussain rummaged about in the store weighing up and measuring out the grain for the birds and the fruit for the monkeys. Madam preferred to check the weight of the fish and the meat herself, so he would only weigh that when she'd finished reading all the entries of food delivered into the stores that day. It took about forty minutes to get all the food ready and then the two boys who also assisted the head gardener to keep the drying lawns tidy would come to help him feed the animals under the watchful eye of the Memsahib.

He wondered about her sometimes. Who she was, where she

came from and what kind of love of animals this was that brought her out in the afternoon sun when most other women of her class still drowsed in darkened rooms. He knew that he had this job because of her in a way. It was common knowledge that the previous superintendent had been sacked because of her intervention. The gate-keeper had told him the story many times . . . how she came to visit the zoo about two years ago, saw that the animals looked thin and under-fed and decided to complain. She wrote letters, made approaches and got them to change the super. She was there with a letter from the governor himself the day Hussain took charge saying she had permission from him to 'inspect' the food before it was given to the animals and that she would personally make sure that the animals had a proper diet. To this day she had not been late. Hussain got into a routine of being ready for her, terrified of what might happen if she became angry again. The gate-keeper, Maaja, thought her an interfering busybody. 'Poor Nawaz Sahib who got turned out with his family of eight in such disgrace had still not found a job, and was such a good man really!' he always ended with a sigh. At this point in the conversation Hussain would lose interest in the story and walk off remembering something important that needed doing.

Annette, exhausted with the heat that day, summer dress clinging to her body stickily, sat down to rest herself on a bench shielded by a grove of jasmine and hibiscus bushes, as she trailed Hussain on his round to feed the animals. The heavy perfume battled with the odour of the animal cages; water was a problem in the summer months and the cages smelt foul two-thirds of the time. She was worried about Heera. He seemed even more listless than he'd been the day before, quite disinterested in the meat that had been pushed unceremoniously by Hussain into the cage. She opened her manual wondering if they should be getting in touch with the vet, or whether she should just observe him more closely. She was fond of him. He was popular with many of the staff too. It was they who had nicknamed him Heera because of the diamond glint to his eyes at night. He was as lively and mischievous a cheetah as any you could find in the Sundarbans, but this summer had really knocked it out of him. She picked up her bag and started walking slowly, unthinkingly, back towards his cage, her footsteps muffled by the soft mud.

Instinctively she drew back out of sight when she saw the woman. She had not seen or heard Annette. She was intense, absorbed, circling the cage slowly, carefully moving round inside the forbidden inner perimeter of the white railings. Only the staff were allowed into that area. Even Annette respected that boundary. She watched awestruck.

The woman had an eye on Heera but she didn't seem unduly worried. Annette almost gasped as she saw her lower her body, lean forward and put her arm through the bars to lift a couple of hunks of meat and slip them speedily into a limp polythene bag. She was a tall woman, thin, lithe; her mission accomplished she rose and dashed swiftly away with a speed that would have done Heera some credit. In the dusky gloom Annette felt aware of a frantic need to sit down as her body swayed, liquid and weak. She waited to collect herself for a few moments wondering what had held her back from challenging the woman. Surely she should have yelled at her. That was what she was supposed to be doing, preventing the pilfering and thieving that had been going on in the place. Heera got up slowly and ambled towards his dinner, sniffing the meat delicately before applying himself to the effort of eating. It was later than usual when she finally summoned her energies to leave. The men were hanging about the gate waiting to wish her and see her off. It wasn't altogether unusual for her to leave a little late. She found the quiet and peace of the after hours at the zoo sustaining and sometimes sat watching the animals settle down as long as the light permitted.

Darkness always fell suddenly as the sun dropped behind the high mud walls of the aviary at the western boundary of the zoo, forcing her to drag herself slowly away. Today she felt drained as the car drove past the gate and she lifted a limp hand to acknowledge their salutes.

She found herself desperate to talk it over with Saleem that night. He seemed absorbed and distant over dinner, but she raised it all the same. His laugh sounded curt and cold, 'Didn't you ring the police?'

174

'No.' Annette felt uncomfortable as she faced his sardonic amusement.

'What's so funny?'

'Your policing: the kind of moral crisis you've come to.' His laughter had an unpleasant chilly edge to it, widening the distance between them.

'Moral crisis?'

'I think that's what they call it.' He seemed intent on the food, picking the bones out of his fish with his fingers. She looked away. He added after a pause, 'Did I ever tell you the story about Mrs Howe?'

'I don't think you did. Who is she?' Annette was beginning to feel irritated by his tone of superior detachment.

'Was. Yes. Mrs Howe, was the wife of the Consul-General in Mashad, when Papa was posted there, back in the forties. She loved horses; loved them very much indeed. Her routine was to go out every afternoon, round the city, such as it then was, in search of any sick and maltreated horses and take them in. She'd go round in her jodhpurs, whip in hand, personally whiplash the guilty owner, and then take the horse away. She became a dreaded sight. The owners usually got treated worse than the horses, ended up in jail, and lost a working animal without recompense.'

'So?'

'So, nothing.' The tension mounted. Then. 'Mind you those were days when a British man-of-war would steam up to the shores menacingly, if, say, five men gathered in protest over the price of sugar.'

'I don't know what you're suggesting Saleem. What I'm trying to do here is different.'

'Yeah. I hope so. You weren't in your jodhpurs and you didn't get the police down. I was only eleven then, much purer in my sense of iniquity than I am now; always for the underdog. I can tell you though that I, for one, was never sure if the horses were the real underdogs.'

Annette felt a hopeless, voiceless rage against his cruel remoteness from her own feelings. Hostility, polarisations, oversimplifications. What had happened to them? She hated scenes. But her chair scraped angrily as she dropped her napkin and rose to leave the dining table. She stepped out onto the verandah gazing abstractedly at the fireflies in the still, suffocating darkness outside, remembering the past. The radicalism of their Cambridge days had faded for both of them. In her case it had dissolved into a vague defensiveness about her own realities. It had become his style, she thought angrily, to rub in the entire guilt of the white nations into her soul with a personal venom. Controversies and anger rankled, hung solid in the air between them.

He knew well enough, she thought sadly, how she felt about the animals at the zoo. They were special to her, like family, her babies almost. It was as if someone had deprived one of her own children. A wrong had been committed, and here he was confusing issues, blurring the boundaries between wrong and right, trying to set up a parallel which wasn't really a parallel at all. Just to humiliate her, show her up. Not a glimmer of the old passion remained between them to buffer differences of opinion.

There were other women in Lahore she knew, white women she could have talked to, but there, too, were gaps in convictions and assumptions that always yawned in the space between them intensifying her aloneness in this teeming, torrid city. He was reducing her, cutting the ground from under her feet, putting her on the defensive again. She knew now that she'd been foolish and weak. She really should have called, well, the men, the staff, if not the police; that was the logical course of action. That night she decided she'd take it up with Hussain first thing tomorrow.

Her resolution wavered the next afternoon though, as she looked for a suitable moment to raise the question. She forced herself to utter, almost under her breath, 'There's something I need to ask you, Hussain.'

'Yes, Madam,' he was alert and politely attentive.

'How many families live inside the compound of the zoo?' she asked.

'Three, Madam. Mine, the gate-keeper's and the gardener's.'

He'd anticipated her next question correctly. Somehow she could not connect that woman with Hussain. She began reluctantly, 'I saw a woman stealing meat from Heera's cage yesterday.'

He seemed genuinely shocked. 'A woman? Was she tall or short, madam?' he lowered his voice carefully.

Annette was aware of the curious eyes of the two boys who were hovering in the verandah. 'Tall,' she said briefly.

'That's Tara, madam, Maaja the gate-keeper's wife. Shall I call her?'

'Yes, please. Afterwards. But you'll have to stay and talk to her for me.'

She was already dreading the interview.

It was certainly not easy. Tara came, a poorly dressed but strikingly good-looking woman. A mangy, snot-stained baby perched on her hip and a dust-encrusted toddler trailed by her side holding on to her faded yellow shalwar. She stopped to deposit them both on the patch of grass outside before she came in and stood before them, looking rebellious and defiant rather than evasive or contrite. For a few moments it seemed as though she would say nothing by way of explanation or apology. She had turned her face away. Annette could feel a righteous throb of anger building up inside her head. But then, quite suddenly, the woman launched into a voluble emotional speech. Annette could not make much of the words. She looked at Hussain for explanation. He coughed in some embarrassment and tried to respond to Tara, but Annette held him back. 'Tell me first,' she spoke imperiously.

'She says something about Heera, madam; she says he wants her to take some of his food,' Hussain muttered, his disbelief of that theory filtering clearly through his intonation.

'What makes her say this?' The angry throb pounded even more impatiently in Annette's head. She looked intently at the woman's face as she chattered on whilst Hussain looked more and more irritated and anxious to dissociate himself from this episode.

'She says, Heera won't go near his food, till she's taken some of it and, she says, madam, you can stay tomorrow night and see for yourself.'

'That's maybe because of the heat and partly because he's not been well.' Annette gestured to Hussain to interpret; but her mind latched on to those words. She was less sceptical than he was. Before her eyes was a picture of Heera, sitting in the shadows, seemingly disinterested in the food, allowing the woman to pinch it without pouncing or even batting an eyelid.

'Madam, she says Heera is an animal with the spirit of a saint. He knows that her children often have to go hungry, so he can't eat. He waits for her to take something and if, if, she doesn't take it the meat will lie around and rot.' Hussain's lip was distinctly curling up with cynical disbelief even as he narrated this fantastic story.

A part of Annette wanted to believe it but, officially, she felt obliged to contradict the proposition. 'Tell her she's mistaken, would you Hussain. And tell her she mustn't do it again,' she repeated in an attempt to bring the incident to a dignified close.

Hussain felt disappointed at a certain lack of firmness in Madam as he conveyed this to the woman. She was not impressed. She was arguing, torrents of words pouring out of her, as if she were egged on by the success of her initial defence. Annette looked at her face once again, more closely. It was an open, honest face, her dark skin glowed with an earnest intensity which completely banished the righteous throb from her head. Her story about Heera was like the confirmation of genius in a child prodigy to an admiring doting mother. Annette concluded the interview with a mild warning and turned to leave, intrigued but more satisfied with the outcome than she had expected to be.

That day was Thursday, barbecue night at the Lahore Gymkhana Club. She usually joined Saleem there for dinner at about eight and they returned late in the evening, together. She sat nursing her soft drink, waiting for him to come out of the showers. He'd been playing golf. The usual crowd was there, usual gossip, usual meaningless pleasantries. Annette waited with some impatience, her spirits sodden with the emotional exchange of the evening and her mind tortured by the larger question mark which hung over her marriage, a question she had blinked away for so long. Plain as daylight that it was all over. Children and mortgages, the aspic which magically holds marriages together, had both been denied them. The house they lived in had belonged to Saleem's father and came to them unencumbered; and children they could not have . . . It had not really been a deep regret, not to her, not so far, but she felt aware of a secret fear that in this society it could easily become one. She'd thrown herself with energy into other things, the zoo had been one of them. But Tara had shaken all her certainties. And Heera, of course. She thought of her coming up the burning concrete pathway with her two children, of her conviction that Heera wanted them to share his food. She saw herself in the verandah of the depot, with Hussain, checking, weighing, inspecting all the food and cringed a little.

Saleem forgetting her dilemma of the night before asked her absently about her day as the waiter piled the barbecued dishes in ritualistic sequence before them; chicken breasts followed by kebabs and spicy lamb tikkas, maybe worth a day's wages for Hussain, two days' wages for the gate-keeper.

She watched the food mesmerised as the appetising glaze vanished along with the charcoal flavour and it turned into bloody hunks of tough fibrous beef. She could smell the raw wetness dripping down its sides. The morsel nearly stuck in her throat choking her with the obscenity of it all. She rounded on Saleem with a bitter vehemence.

'It's over, isn't it?' was all she could manage to say.

ANJANA APPACHANA

Anjana Appachana was born in India and educated in Delhi. In 1984 she and her husband left for the United States; they now teach at Arizona State University. Several of her short stories have appeared in journals, both in India and the United States. 'Her Mother' first appeared in *The 1989 O. Henry Festival Stories* (Greensboro, N. Carolina, 1989).

Her Mother

W hen she got her daughter's first letter from America, the mother had a good cry. Everything was fine, the daughter said. The plane journey was fine, her professor who met her at the airport was nice, her university was very nice, the house she shared with two American girls (nice girls) was fine, her classes were OK and her teaching was surprisingly fine. She ended the letter saying she was fine and hoping her mother and father were too. The mother let out a moan she could barely control and wept in an agony of longing and pain and frustration. Who would have dreamt that her daughter was doing a Ph.D in Comparative Literature, she thought, wiping her eyes with her sari palla, when all the words at her command were 'fine', 'nice', and 'OK'. Who would have imagined that she was a gold medallist from Delhi University? Who would know from the blandness of her letter, its vapidity, the monotony of its tone and the indifference of its adjectives that it came from a girl so intense and articulate? Her daughter had written promptly, as she had said she would, the mother thought, cleaning her smudged spectacles and beginning to reread the letter. It had taken only ten days to arrive. She examined her daughter's handwriting. There seemed to be no trace of loneliness there, or discomfort, or insecurity – the writing was firm, rounded and clear. She hadn't mentioned if that overfriendly man at the airport had sat next to her on the plane. The mother hoped not. Once Indian men boarded the plane for a new country, the anonymity drove them crazy. They got drunk and made life hell for the air-hostesses and everyone else nearby, but of course, they thought they were flirting with finesse. Her daughter, for all her arguments with her parents, didn't know how to deal with such men. Most men. Her brows furrowed, the mother took out a letter writing pad from her folder on the dining table and began to write. Eat properly, she wrote. Have plenty of milk, cheese and cereal. Eating badly makes you age

181

fast. That's why western women look so haggard. They might be pencil slim, but look at the lines on their faces. At thirty they start looking faded. So don't start these stupid, western dieting fads. Oil your hair every week and avoid shampoos. Chemicals ruin the hair. (You can get almond oil easily if coconut oil isn't available.) With all the hundreds of shampoos in America, American women's hair isn't a patch on Indian women's. Your grandmother had thick, black hair till the day she died.

One day, two months earlier, her daughter had cut off her long thick hair, just like that. The abruptness and sacrilege of this act still haunted the mother. That evening, when she opened the door for her daughter, her hair reached just below her ears. The daughter stood there, not looking at either her mother or father, but almost, it seemed, beyond them, her face a strange mixture of relief and defiance and anger, as her father, his face twisted, said, why, why. I like it short, she said. Fifteen years of growing it below her knees, of oiling it every week, and washing it so lovingly, the mother thought as she touched her daughter's cheek and said, you are angry with us . . . is this your revenge? Her daughter had removed her hand and moved past her parents, past her brother-in-law who was behind them, and into her room. For the father it was as though a limb had been amputated. For days he brooded in his chair in the corner of the sitting-room, almost in mourning, avoiding even looking at her, while the mother murmured, you have perfected the art of hurting us.

Your brother-in-law has finally been allotted his three-bed-roomed house, she wrote, and he moved into it last week. I think he was quite relieved to, after living with us these few months. So there he is, living all alone in that big house with two servants while your sister continues working in Bombay. Your sister says that commuting marriages are inevitable, and like you, is not interested in hearing her mother's opinion on the subject. I suppose they will go on like this for years, postponing having children, postponing being together, until one day when they're as old as your father and me, they'll have nothing to look forward to. Tell me, where would we have been without you both? Of course, you will only support your sister and your brother-in-law and their strange, selfish marriage.

Perhaps that is your dream too. Nobody seems to have normal dreams any more.

The mother had once dreamt of love and a large home, silk saris and sapphires. The love she had got, but as her husband struggled in his job and the children came and as they took loans to marry off her husband's sisters, the rest she did not. In the next fifteen years she had collected a nice selection of silk saris and jewellery for her daughters, but by that time, they showed no inclination for either. The older daughter and her husband had had a registered marriage, refused to have even a reception and did not accept so much as a handkerchief from their respective parents. And the younger one had said quite firmly before she left, that she wasn't even thinking of marriage.

The mother looked at her husband's back in the verandah. That's all he did after he came back from the office – sit in the verandah and think of his precious daughters, while she cooked and cleaned, attended to visitors and wrote to all her sisters and his sisters. Solitude to think – what a luxury! She had never thought in solitude. Her thoughts jumped to and fro and up and down and in and out as she dusted, cooked, cleaned, rearranged cupboards, polished the brass, put buttons on shirts and falls on saris, as she sympathised with her neighbour's problems and scolded the dhobi for not putting enough starch on the saris, as she reprimanded the milkman for watering the milk and lit the kerosene stove because the gas had finished, as she took the dry clothes from the clothes line and couldn't press them because the electricity had failed and realised that the cake in the oven would now never rise. The daughter was like her father, the mother thought – she too had wanted the escape of solitude, which meant, of course, that in the process she neither made her bed nor tidied up her room.

How will you look after yourself, my Rani Beti? she wrote. You have always had your mother to look after your comforts. I'm your mother and I don't mind doing all this, but some day you'll have to do it for the man you marry and how will you, when you can't even thread a needle?

But of course, her daughter didn't want marriage. She had been saying so, vehemently, in the last few months. The father blamed the mother. The mother had not taught her how to cook or sew and had only encouraged her and her sister to think and act with an independence quite uncalled for in daughters. How then, he asked her, could she expect her daughters to be suddenly amenable? How could she complain that she had no grandchildren and lose herself in self-pity when it was all her doing? Sometimes the mother fought with the father when he said such things, at other times she cried or brooded. But she was not much of a brooder, and losing her temper or crying helped her cope better.

The mother laid aside her pen. She had vowed not to lecture her daughter, and there she was, filling pages of rubbish when all she wanted to do was cry out, why did you leave us in such anger? what did we not do for you? why, why? No, she would not ask. She wasn't one to get after the poor child like that.

How far away you are, my pet, she wrote. How could you go away like that, so angry with the world? Why, my love, why? Your father says that I taught you to be so independent that all you hankered for was to get away from us. He says it's all my fault. I have heard that refrain enough in my married life. After all that I did for you, tutoring you, disciplining you, indulging you, caring for you, he says he understands you better because you are like him. And I can't even deny that because it's true. I must say it's very unfair, considering that all he did for you and your sister was give you chocolates and books.

When her daughter was six, the mother recalled, the teacher had asked the class to make a sentence with the word, 'good'. She had written, my father is a good man. The mother sighed as she recalled asking her, isn't your mother a good woman? And the daughter's reply, daddy is gooder. The mother wrote, no, I don't understand – you talk like him, look like him, are as obstinate and as stupidly honest. It is as though he conceived you and gave birth to you entirely on his own. She was an ayah, the mother thought, putting her pen aside, that was all she was; she did all the dirty work and her husband got all the love.

The next day, after her husband had left for the office, the mother continued her letter. She wrote in a tinier handwriting now, squeezing as much as possible into the thin air-mail sheet. Write a longer letter to me, next time, my Rani, she wrote. Try and write as though you were talking to me. Describe the trees, the buildings, the people. Try not to be your usual perfunctory self. Let your mother experience America through your eyes. Also, before I forget, you must bathe every day, regardless of how cold it gets. People there can be quite dirty. But no, if I recall correctly, it is the English and other Europeans who hate to bathe. Your Naina Aunty, after her trip to Europe, said that they smelled all the time. Americans are almost as clean as Indians. And don't get into the dirty habit of using toilet paper, all right?

The mother blew her nose and wiped her cheek. Two years, she wrote, or even more for you to come back. I can't even begin to count the days for two years. How we worry, how we worry. Had you gone abroad with a husband, we would have been at peace, but now? If you fall ill who will look after you? You can't even make dal. You can't live on bread and cheese forever, but knowing you, you will. You will lose your complexion, your health, your hair. But why should I concern myself with your hair? You cut it off, just like that.

The mother laid her cheek on her hand and gazed at the door where her daughter had stood with her cropped hair, while she, her husband and her son-in-law stood like three figures in a tableau. The short hair made her face look even thinner. Suddenly she looked ordinary, like all the thousands of short-haired, western-looking Delhi girls one saw, all ordinarily attractive like the others, all the same. Her husband saying, why, why? his hands up in the air, then slowly, falling down at his sides, her son-in-law, his lazy grin suddenly wiped off his face; she recalled it all, like a film in slow motion.

I always thought I understood you, she wrote, your dreams, your problems, but suddenly it seems there is nothing that I understand. No, nothing, she thought, the tiredness weighing down her eyes. She was ranting – the child could do without it. But how, how could she not think of this daughter of hers, who in the last few months, had rushed from her usual, settled quietness to such unsettled stillness that it seemed the very house would begin to balloon outwards, unable to contain her straining.

Enough, she wrote. Let me give you the news before I make

you angry with my grief. The day after you left, Mrs Gupta
from next door dropped in to comfort me, bless her. She said
she had full faith you would come back, that only boys didn't.
She says a daughter will always regard her parents' home as
her only home, unlike sons who attach themselves to their
wives. As you know, she has four sons, all married, and all,
she says, under their wives' thumbs. But it was true, the mother
thought. Her own husband fell to pieces every time she visited
her parents without him. When he accompanied her there he
needed so much looking after that she couldn't talk to her
mother, so she preferred to go without him. With her parents
she felt indulged and irresponsible. Who indulged her now?
And when she came back from her parents the ayah would
complain that her husband could never find his clothes, slept
on the bedcover, constantly misplaced his spectacles, didn't
know how to get himself a glass of water and kept waiting for
the postman.

With all your talk about women's rights, she wrote, you
refuse to see that your father has given me none. And on top of
that he says that I am a nag. If I am a nag, it is because he's
made me one. And talking of women's rights, some women
take it too far. Mrs Parekh is having, as the books say, a torrid
affair with a married man. This man's wife is presently with her
parents and when Mrs Parekh's husband is on tour, she spends
the night with him, and comes back early in the morning to get
her children ready for school. Everyone has seen her car parked
in the middle of the night outside his flat. Today our ayah said,
memsahib, people like us do it for money. Why do memsahibs
like her do it? But of course, you will launch into a tirade of
how this is none of my business and sum it up with your
famous phrase, each to her own. But my child, they're both
married. Surely you won't defend it? Sometimes I don't understand how your strong principles co-exist with such strange
values for what society says is wrong. Each to her own, you
have often told me angrily, never seeming to realise that it is
never one's own when one takes such a reckless step, that
entire families disintegrate, that children bear scars forever.
Each to her own, indeed.

Yes, she was a straightforward girl, the mother thought, and so loyal to those she loved. When the older daughter had got married five years ago, and this one was only seventeen, how staunchly she had supported her sister and brother-in-law's decision to do without all the frills of an Indian wedding. How she had later defended her sister's decision to continue with her job in Bombay, when her husband came on a transfer to Delhi. She had lost her temper with her parents for writing reproachful letters to the older daughter, and scolded them when they expressed their worry to the son-in-law, saying that as long as he was living with them, they should say nothing.

The mother was fond of her son-in-law in her own way. But deep inside she felt that he was irresponsible, uncaring and lazy. Yes, he had infinite charm, but he didn't write regularly to his wife, didn't save a paisa of his salary (he didn't even have a life insurance policy and no thoughts at all of buying a house), and instead of spending his evenings in the house as befitted a married man, went on a binge of plays and other cultural programmes, often taking her younger daughter with him, spending huge amounts on petrol and eating out. His wife was too practical, he told the mother, especially about money. She believed in saving, he believed in spending. She wanted security, he wanted fun. He laughed as he said this, and gave her a huge box of the most expensive barfis. The mother had to smile. She wanted him to pine for her daughter. Instead, he joked about her passion for her work and how he was waiting for the day when she would be earning twice as much as him, so that he could resign from his job and live luxuriously off her, reading, trekking and sleeping. At such times the mother couldn't even force a smile out. But her younger daughter would laugh and say that his priorities were clear. And the older daughter would write and urge the mother not to hound her sister about marriage, to let her pursue her interests. The sisters supported each other, the mother thought, irritated but happy.

Yesterday, the mother wrote, we got a letter from Naina Aunty. Her friend's son, a boy of twenty-six, is doing his Ph.D in Stanford. He is tall, fair and very handsome. He is also supposed to be very intellectual, so don't get on your high horse. His family background is very cultured. Both his parents are lawyers. They are looking for a suitable match for him and Naina Aunty who loves you so much, immediately thought of you and mentioned to them that you are also in the States. Now, before losing your temper with me, listen properly. This is just a suggestion. We are *not* forcing you into a marriage you don't want. But you must keep an open mind. At least meet him. Rather, *he* will come to the university to meet you. Talk, go out together, see how much you like each other. *Just* meet him and try and look pleasant and smile for a change. Give your father and me the pleasure of saying, there is *someone* who will look after our child. If something happens to us who will look after you? I know what a romantic you are, but believe me, arranged marriages work very well. Firstly, the bride is readily accepted by the family. Now look at me. Ours was a love marriage and his parents disliked me and disapproved of our marriage because my *sister* had married out of the community. They thought I was fast because in *those* days I played tennis with other men, wore lipstick and bras. I wonder why I bore it. I should have been cold and as distant as them. But I was ingratiating and accommodating. Then your father and I had to marry off his sisters. Now in an arranged marriage you can choose not to have such liabilities. I am not materialistic, but I am not a fool either. I know you want to be economically independent, and you must be that, but it will also help if your husband isn't burdened with debts. I am not blaming your father. Responsibilities are responsibilities. But if you can help it, why begin married life with them? Now don't write back and say you're sick of my nagging. You think I am a nag because it is I who wield the stick and your father who gives those wonderful, idealistic lectures. Perhaps when you marry you will realise that fathers and husbands are two very different things. In an arranged marriage you will not be disillusioned because you will not have any illusions to begin with. That is why arranged marriages work. Of course, we will not put any pressure on you. Let us know if it is all right for the boy to meet you and I will write to Naina Aunty accordingly. Each day I pray that you will not marry an American. That would be very hard on us. Now, look at your father and me. Whatever your father's faults, infidelity isn't one of them. Now these Americans, they will divorce you at the drop of a hat. They don't know the meaning of the phrase, 'sanctity of marriage'. My love, if you marry an American and he divorces you and we are no longer in this world, what will you do?

When the milkman came early this morning, he enquired about you. I told him how far away you are. He sighed and said that it was indeed very far. I think he feels for us because he hasn't watered the milk since you left. I'm making the most of it and setting aside lots of thick malai for butter. When the postman came, he said, how is the baby? I replied, now only you will bear her news for us. He immediately asked for baksheesh. I said, nothing doing, what do you mean, baksheesh, it isn't Diwali. He replied, when I got you baby's first letter, wasn't it like Diwali? So I tipped him. Our bai has had a fight with her husband because he got drunk again and spent his entire salary gambling it away. She is in a fury and has left the house saying she won't go back to him unless he swears in the temple that he will never drink again. Your father says, hats off to her. Your father is always enraptured by other women who stand up for themselves. If I stood up for myself he would think he was betrayed.

Betrayal, betrayal, the mother mulled. His job had betrayed him, his strict father had, by a lack of tenderness betrayed him, India herself had betrayed him after Independence, and this betrayal he raved against every evening, every night. He told her that sometimes he felt glad that his daughter had left a country where brides were burnt for dowry, where everyone was corrupt, where people killed each other in the name of religion and where so many still discriminated against Harijans. At least, he said, his daughter was in a more civilised country. At this the mother got very angry. She said, in America fathers molested their own children. Wives were abused and beaten up, just like the servant classes in India. Friends raped other friends. No one looked after the old. In India, the mother said, every woman got equal pay for equal work. In America they were still fighting for it. Could America ever have a woman president? Never. Could it ever have a black president? Never. Americans were as foolish about religion as Indians, willing to give millions to charletons who said that the Lord had asked for the money. She was also well read, the mother told her husband, and she knew that no Indian would part with his money so easily. As for discrimination against untouchables in India – it only happened among the uneducated, whereas discrimination against blacks was rampant even among educated Americans. Blacks were the American untouchables. The mother was now in her element. She too had read *Time* and *Newsweek*, she told her husband, and she knew that in India there had never been any question of having segregation in buses where Harijans were concerned, as was the case in America, not so long ago.

Don't rant, her husband told her, and lower your voice, I can hear you without your shrieking. The mother got into a terrible fury and the father left the room.

The mother wrote, you better give us your views about that country – you can give us a more balanced picture. Your father thinks I'm the proverbial frog in the well. Well, perhaps that is true, but he is another frog in another well and Americans are all frogs in one large, rich well. Imagine, when your aunt was in America, several educated Americans asked her whether India had roads and if people lived in trees. They thought your aunt had learnt all the English she knew in America.

The mother made herself a cup of tea and sipped it slowly. Her son-in-law hadn't even been at home the night her daughter had left. It upset the mother deeply. He could have offered to drive them to the airport at least, comforted them in their sorrow. But he had gone off for one of his plays and arrived a few minutes after they returned from the airport, his hair tousled, his eyes bright. He stopped briefly in the living room where the mother and father sat quietly, at opposite ends, opened his mouth to say something, then shrugged slightly and went to his room.

Selfish, the mother thought. Thoughtless. The daughter hadn't even enquired about him when she left. Had she recognised that her fun-loving brother-in-law had not an ounce of consideration in him?

The two months before her daughter had left had been the worst. Not only had she stopped talking to her parents, but to him. It frightened the mother. One can say and do what one likes with parents, she told her silent child once, parents will take anything. Don't cold shoulder him too. If he takes a dislike to you and your moods, then you will be alienated even from your sister. Remember, marriage bonds are ultimately stronger than ties between sisters. The daughter had continued reading her book. And soon after, she had cut off her hair. Rapunzel, her brother-in-law had said once, as he watched her dry her hair in the courtyard and it fell like black silk below her knees. Rapunzel, he said again, as the mother smiled and watched her child comb it with her fingers, Rapunzel, Rapunzel, let down your hair. Oh she won't do that, the mother had said, proud that she understood, she is too quiet and withdrawn, and her daughter had gone back to her room and the next day she had cut it off, just like that.

The mother finished her tea and continued her letter. Let me end with some advice, she wrote, and don't groan now. Firstly, keep your distance from American men. You are innocent and have no idea what men are like. Men have more physical feelings than women. I'm sure you understand. Platonic friendships between the two sexes does not exist. In America they do not even pretend that it does. There kissing is as casual as holding hands. And after that you know what happens. One thing can lead to another and the next thing we know you will bring us an American son-in-law. You know we will accept even that if we have to, but it will make us most unhappy.

Secondly, if there is an Indian association in your university, please join it. You might meet some nice Indian men there with the same interests that you have. For get-togethers there, always wear a sari and try to look pleasant. Your father doesn't believe in joining such associations, but I feel it is a must.

The mother was tired of giving advice. What changed you so much the last few months before you left? she wanted to cry, why was going abroad no longer an adventure but an escape? At the airport, when the mother hugged the daughter, she had felt with a mother's instinct that the daughter would not return.

There had been a brief period when her child had seemed suddenly happy, which was strange, considering her final exams were drawing closer. She would work late into the night and the mother would sometimes awaken at night to hear the sounds of her making coffee in the kitchen. Once, on the way to the bathroom she heard sounds of laughter in the kitchen and stepped in to see her daughter and son-in-law cooking a monstrous omelette. He had just returned from one of his late night jaunts. An omelette at 1 am, the mother grunted sleepily and the two laughed even more as the toast emerged burnt and the omelette stuck to the pan. Silly children, the mother said and went back to bed.

And then, a few weeks later, that peculiar, turbulent stillness as her daughter continued studying for her exams and stopped talking to all of them, her face pale and shadows under her eyes, emanating a tension that gripped the mother like tentacles and left the father hurt and confused. She snapped at them when they questioned her, so they stopped. I'll talk to her after the exams, the mother told herself. She even stopped having dinner with them, eating either before they all sat at the table, or much after, and then only in her room.

And that pinched look on her face . . . the mother jerked up. It was pain, not anger. Her daughter had been in pain, in pain. She was hiding something. Twelve years ago, when the child was ten, the mother had seen the same pinched, strained look on her face. The child bore her secret for three days, avoiding her parents and her sister, spending long hours in the bathroom and moving almost furtively around the house. The mother noticed that two rolls of cotton had disappeared from her dressing table drawer and that an old bedsheet she had left in the cupboard to cut up and use as dusters, had also disappeared. On the third day she saw her daughter go to the bathroom with a suspicious lump in her shirt. She stopped her, her hands on the trembling child's arms, put her fingers into her shirt and took out a large roll of cotton. She guided the child to the bathroom, raised her skirt and pulled down her panties. The daughter watched her mother's face, her eyes filled with terror, waiting for the same terror to reflect on her face, as her mother saw the blood flowing from this unmentionable part of her body and recognised her daughter's imminent death. The mother said, my love, why didn't you tell me, and the child, seeing only compassion, knew she would live, and wept.

The omniscience of motherhood could last only so long, the mother thought, and she could no longer guess her daughter's secrets. Twelve years ago there had been the disappearing cotton and sheet, but now? The mother closed her eyes and her daughter's face swam before her, her eyes dark, that delicate nose and long plaited hair – no, no it was gone now and she could never picture her with her new face. After her daughter had cut her hair, the mother temporarily lost her vivacity. And the daughter became uncharacteristically tidy – her room spick and span, her desk always in order, every corner dusted, even her cupboard neatly arranged. The mother's daily scoldings to her, which were equally her daily declarations of love, ceased, and she thought she would burst with sadness. So one day, when the mother saw her daughter standing in her room, looking out of the window, a large white handkerchief held to her face, the mother said, don't cry my love, don't cry, and then, don't you know it's unhygienic to use someone else's hanky, does nothing I tell you register, my Rani? And her daughter, her face flushed, saying, it's clean, and the mother taking it out of her hand and smelling it and snorting, clean what rubbish, and it isn't even your father's, it's your brother-in-law's, it smells of him, and it did, of cigarettes and after shave and God knows what else and the mother had put it for a wash.

The mother's face jerked up. Her finger's grip on the pen loosened and her eyes dilated. Her daughter had not been crying. Her eyes, as they turned to her mother, had that pinched look, but they were clear as she removed the handkerchief from her nose. It had smelled of him as she held it there and she wasn't wiping her tears.

The mother moaned. If God was omniscient, it didn't seem to hurt him. Why hadn't He denied her the omniscience of motherhood? Oh my love, my love, the mother thought. She held her hand to her aching throat. Oh my love. The tears weren't coming now. She began to write. Sometimes when one is troubled, she wrote, and there is no solution for the trouble, prayer helps. It gives you the strength to carry on. I know you don't believe in rituals, but all I'm asking you to do is to light the lamp in the morning, light an agarbatti, fold your hands, close your eyes and think of truth and correct actions. That's all. Keep these items and the silver idol of Ganesha which I put into your suitcase, in a corner in your cupboard or on your desk. For the mother, who had prayed all her life, prayer was like bathing or brushing her teeth or chopping onions. She had found some strength in the patterns these created, and sometimes, some peace. Once, when her husband reprimanded her for cooking only eight dishes for a dinner party, she had wanted to break all the crockery in the kitchen, but after five minutes in her corner with the Gods, she didn't break them. She couldn't explain this to her child. She couldn't say, it's all right, it happens; or say, you'll forget, knowing her daughter wouldn't. If you don't come back next year, she wrote, knowing her daughter wouldn't, I'll come and get you. She would pretend to have a heart attack, the mother said to herself, her heart beating very fast, her tears now falling very rapidly, holding her head in her hands, she would phone her daughter and say, I have to see you before I die, and then her daughter would come home, yes, she would come home, and she would grow her hair again.

SUNITI NAMJOSHI

Suniti Namjoshi was born in India in 1941. She has published poetry, fables, articles and reviews on literary and women's studies journals in India, Canada, the USA and Britain. Her first book of fables *Feminist Fables* was published by Sheba in 1981. This was followed by *The Conversations of Cow* (Women's Press, 1988). 'Dusty Distance' comes from *The Blue Donkey Fables* (Women's Press, 1988).

Suniti Namjoshi has held various academic posts in India and Canada, and now lives in England.

Dusty
Distance

O ne of the stories the Blue Donkey tells – there's a contro-
versy raging about whether to classify it as fact or fiction
– is about the first time she set off on a long dusty road to make
her fortune. In no time at all she met a woman who offered her
a carrot, a place to stay and an occupation. 'No thank you,'
replied the Blue Donkey. 'You see, I'm a poet, and I have a long
way to go.' 'What is a poet?' enquired the woman. This so
disconcerted the Blue Donkey that she muttered and mumbled
and managed to utter a hasty goodbye and marched onwards.
In consequence she nearly ran down a fellow wayfarer.

The Blue Donkey apologised profusely, and to show that she
was genuinely sorry and genuinely interested she asked him
who he was and what he was doing and what was his purpose.
'Oh,' he answered sternly, 'I'm on my way to encounter Life.
When I find her, I shall take her by the throat and grapple with
her.' 'And then?' asked the Blue Donkey, enthralled by this
account in spite of herself. 'And then I shall bind her hand and
foot and take her home.' 'And then?' The Blue Donkey was
almost whispering now. 'And then,' he responded magnifi-
cently, 'I shall chop her up and grind her down and put her
into delicate mince pies which shall go on the market at
fourpence a dozen.' His teeth were gleaming. He turned on
her. 'And who are you?' he enquired suddenly. 'Oh, I'm only a
poet,' the Blue Donkey murmured with what she considered
suitable modesty. But her fellow traveller grew highly indig-
nant. 'Rubbish!' he cried. 'I am a poet. Why you, you are only a
bit of Life.' As he said this his eyes grew round with specu-
lation. The Blue Donkey didn't wait for more. She says that her
readers can call her a coward if they like, but she galloped off
fast and left him behind in the dusty distance.

Eventually the countryside grew greener. There were land-
scaped gardens, immaculate woods, and in one of these woods

there was a Beautiful Lady reclining gracefully against a convenient tree trunk. She was reading a book. As the Blue Donkey approached, the Lady looked up and smiled at her. 'Hello,' said the Blue Donkey. 'What are you reading?' 'Poetry,' sighed the Lady. 'I think poetry is so beautiful. I feel I could live on poetry and fresh air for ever.' The Blue Donkey edged closer. 'Well, as it happens,' she ventured diffidently, 'I am a poet. Perhaps you would like me to recite some of my verse?' 'Oh. Oh no,' the Lady replied hastily, then she recovered herself. 'The fact is,' she explained, 'that though I have studied many languages and my French and German are both excellent, I have never mastered Blue Donkese. And though I have no doubt whatsoever that your poems are excellent, I fear they would fall on untutored ears. 'But please, I speak English.' The Blue Donkey could hear herself sounding plaintive. 'Oh,' murmured the Lady. 'But surely as a Blue Donkey, integrity requires that you paint the world as it appears to you. And consider: what have a lady and a donkey in common?'

'Nothing at all,' said the Blue Donkey sadly and she turned away and retraced her steps. At last she came to the door of the woman she had first encountered. 'Please,' she enquired humbly, 'would you settle for a part-time worker for half a carrot?'

GLOSSARY

Where the language is not shown, it is Hindi or Urdu (which have much in common) and is often found in other Indian languages as well. The transliteration is not consistent, because writers follow different conventions.

aapa: elder sister.

aarti (arati): part of the ceremony of worship when the sacred flame is circled round the holy image.

abba: father.

abhisheka (Sanskrit): daily anointing of the stone image in milk, honey, sandalwood paste and rose water.

akka (Kannada): elder sister.

Adaab: Muslim greeting

agarbatti: incense stick.

ajjayya (Kannada): grandfather.

Allah ho Akbar: God is great! (Muslim call to prayer).

Anarkali: dancing girl with whom the prince Salim, later the Mughal emperor Jehangir, fell in love.

anna: small coin, no longer in use, sixteen to the rupee (8 annas = ½ rupee); (Urdu) nurse.

Antarjanam (Malayalam): the secluded ones. Nambudiri women were known by this title.

appaiah (Kannada): father.

Arubathimoovar (Tamil): the sixty-three canonised Saiva saints of the Periya Puranam.

atte (Kannada): aunt.

Azan: congregational prayers at the mosque.

avil (Malayalam): beaten rice.

ayah: nurse, maidservant.

baba, babu/baabu: father.

baji: elder sister.

barfi: milk sweet.

basti: town neighbourhood.

beti: daughter.

begum: (Muslim) lady.

behen: sister.

bibi, bitya: young woman (respectful Muslim forms of address).

bhajans: Hindu devotional songs, sung in chorus.

bidi: Indian cigarette.

Bismillah: 'In the name of God'. The day of the Bismillah is when a child begins formal lessons in the reading of the Koran.

Brahmasvam (Sanskrit): that which belongs to Brahmin

buqchi: a cloth used to wrap best outfits, special fabrics with gold threat etc., and also to store odd bits and pieces of material.

burqa: long cloak worn by some Muslim women when they went out, completely covering the face and body

chappals: sandals.

chaitya: Buddhist caves meant for congregational assembly.

Chauthi ka Jaura: the dress worn by the bride on the fourth day of the wedding celebrations, on her first visit to her maternal home after the consummation of the marriage.

chenar: Kashmiri maple.

chilla: a vow lasting a specified length of time.

chikki (Kannada): father's younger brother's wife.

Chingam (Malayalam): first month of the Malayalam (Kerala) calendar, when the festival of Onam takes place.

chhota hazri: breakfast (especially used by the British in colonial times).

churidar: trousers which are tight from ankle to knee.

dai: birth attendant, midwife.

dal: lentils.

Devi: goddess.

Diwali: Hindu festival of lights, celebrated in October.

Dhruva: the pole star. According to legend, a boy was rewarded for his goodness and faith by being turned into this symbol of constancy.

doddajjayya (Kannada): grandfather's elder brother.

doddatte (Kannada): grandfather's sister.

dosa: breakfast dish, like a pancake made of ground rice and lentils.

dhobi: washerman.

dhoti: length of cloth tied at the waist and pleated in various ways, worn by men.

dupatta: long scarf worn over the shoulders by women.

eekh (*ikh*): sugar-cane.

emli (*imli*): tamarind.

Fatehpur Sikri: sixteenth-century fortress and walled city built by the Mughal emperor Akbar

Ganesha: elephant headed god, son of Shiva and Parvati.

ghagra: long full skirt.

gharara: trousers worn by women, falling in full gathers from the knee.

ghee: clarified butter.

ghora hospital: 'horse' hospital or veterinary hospital.

goli: sugar sweets.

goonda: hooligan.

Gopalji: another name for the god Krishna, worshipped as a young boy.

halwa: special sweet, made during celebrations and festivals.

Harey Ram: names of God.

Harijan: 'God's children' (Gandhi's name for the Untouchables).

ikkada e (Marathi): 'come here'.

jalali wazifa: a special series of prayers.

kala log: black people, 'natives' (used by the British).

Kaliyug: the age of moral decay, basest of the ages in the Hindu cycle of time.

Kamala Jharia and *Kalu Qawwal*: popular singers of the 1940s.

kameez: loose shirt.

kanyakumari: virgin girls, also virgin goddesses.

karuka (Malayalam): herbal grass grown in Kerala.

khadi: homespun cloth.

kheema: minced meat.

Khuda hafiz: God be with you! (Muslim farewell).

koi hai: QUI-HI: the popular distinctive nickname of the Bengal Anglo-Indian, from the usual manner of calling servants in that Presidency, viz. *'Koi hai?'* 'Is any one there?' (H. Yule and A. C. Burnell, *Hobson-Jobson: a glossary of colloquial Anglo-Indian words and phrases . . .*' 1903). 'Anglo-Indian' is used here in the earlier sense: a 'European' in India.

kumkum: vermilion powder applied both to images and devotee.

kuvalam (Malayalam): small heart-shaped green leaf used in the worship of Shiva.

Lakshmi: goddess of wealth.

maama: mother's brother.

maami: mother's brother's wife.

maasi: mother's sister.

Mahabharata: one of the two great Sanskrit epics.

malai: cream.

masaalchi: kitchen-hand, usually given the job of grinding spices.

mehr: the amount of money settled upon at the time of marriage, paid to the bride by the bridegroom, sometimes over a period of time.

memsahib: madam; (in colonial times) a white woman.

miswak: a fresh twig of the neem tree, used to clean the teeth.

Muhurram standard or Muhurram Alam: the spear-headed banner of Hasan and Hussain carried in procession during the Muhurram festival, celebrated by the Shi'a sect of Muslims. (Excessively tall and thin people are often compared to the Muhurram Alam.)

mundu (Malayalam): straight piece of cloth, worn around the lower part of the body, like a sarong.

Murugan: eldest son of Shiva, also known as Skanda, the god of war.

naani: grandmother.

namaaz: Muslim prayers.

Nambudiri (Malayalam): Brahmans of Kerala.

namkeen: salty biscuits.

Navagriha (Sanskrit): the nine planets of Hindu astronomy.

neivillakku (Malayalam): lamps lit with ghee, offered on special occasions by devotees.

paan: betel nut and spices wrapped in a betel leaf.

paandan: box in which betel leaves and nuts are kept.

pandal: canopy under which the marriage ceremony is held.

pallav, palla, pallu: end piece of a sari.

parippu vada (Malayalam): savoury snacks, made of ground lentils.

Parvati Swayamvaram (Malayalam): title of a song sung by Nambudiri women when they danced the traditional folk dance during the festival of Tiruvadira. The theme of the song is the marriage of the goddess Parvati to Lord Shiva.

Parasurama: one of the ten incarnations of Vishnu, who threw his axe into the ocean and raised a piece of land which came to be known as Kerala.

pati devata (Sanskrit): husband god.

pati vrata (Sanskrit): husband worshipper.

phat-phati: motor-cycle (onomatopoeic).

pheriwalla: itinerant salesman.

Pilpili Sahab: nickname for Eurasians (Anglo-Indians).

pir, pirji: Muslim saint and teacher.

poovan (Malayalam): much-prized variety of bananas.

prasad: food distributed to devotees after worship.

pratyaksha deivam (Malayalam and Sanskrit): visible god.

puja: ceremonial worship.

Rabindra sangeet (Bengali): musical compositions of the poet Rabindranath Tagore.

Ramayana: one of the two great Hindu epics, the other being the Mahabharata.

Ravi Varma: well-known romantic portrait painter of the early twentieth century

Sahib aa gaya?: 'Has Sahib arrived?'

Seelavati Charitram (Malayalam and Sanskrit): song relating the story of Seelavati (Silavati), who ordered the sun not to rise in order that she might save her dying husband.

Salaam: Peace! (Muslim salutation)

seh dari: literally, three doored room, opening into the courtyard and used as an informal sitting-room by women.

shalwar: loose trousers.

shehnai: the main musical instrument at north Indian weddings and wedding processions, with a distinctive wailing sound.

Shivalinga: stone symbol of the god Shiva.

slokas (Sanskrit): sacred verses in Sanskrit.

surahi: earthenware water pot.

taal: the beat or measure in music.

tarawad (Malayalam): matrilineal household and its house, of the Nayar caste of Kerala.

tekkini (Malayalam): room facing south.

Tirumalai: sacred mountain in the temple town of Tirupati, upon which the temple is situated.

Tirupati: one of the richest temple towns of south India, the abode of the 'lord of the seven hills'.

tola: a measure for weighing gold; two and a half tolas equal an ounce of gold.

tonga: two wheeled horse-drawn carriage, seating three to four passengers.

tulasi mala: necklace of holy beads, sometimes simulated in gold.

tumba (Malayalam): small white flowers grown in Kerala, used in the worship of Shiva.

va'al-e-qum: peace be with you! (Muslim greeting).

vadakkini (Malayalam): room facing north.

Vadakkunatha: Lord of the North, Lord Shiva. Deity of a famous temple in Trichur, which faces north.

variyam (Malayalam): the house of the Variyar, a half-Brahman caste who were in the payroll of the temples as assistants to the Nambudiris.

veshti (Malayalam): a piece of cloth worn on the shoulders, covering the upper part of the body.

Yakshagana: popular folk theatre of the west coast of Karnataka, in which all-night performances are held, of episodes from the Ramayana and the Mahabharata.

zari: gold-thread work.

Other books of interest from Virago

THE BINDING VINE
Shashi Deshpande

From the author of *That Long Silence*, winner of one of
India's most prestigious literary prizes, the Sahitya
Akademi Award, comes a new, equally haunting novel.
The narrator is the clever, sharp-tongued Urmu,
grieving over the death of her baby daughter, and
surrounded by, but rebuffing, the care of her mother
and her childhood friend, Vanaa. Instead, she becomes
caught up in the discovery of her long-dead mother-in-
law's poetry, written when she was a young woman
subjected to rape in her marriage; and in Kalpana, a
young woman hanging between life and death in a
hospital ward, also the victim of rape. Yet in this web
of loss and despair are the glimmerings of hope. Shashi
Deshpande explores with acuity and compassion the
redemptive powers of love.

INCANTATIONS AND OTHER STORIES
Anjana Appachana

This is the first collection of fiction from a writer of remarkable talent. Written with a raw and vibrant energy, Anjana Appachana's stories capture the funny, poignant, unexpected and optimistic moment. Every story is a social encounter fiercely accurate in tone and relentlessly attentive to detail as she strips her characters of illusions and scratches away at the fragile surfaces of respectability and convention.

Her characters strain for a place beyond the boundaries of a prescribed way of life in urban India: a hapless college student gets gated a few days before an abortion apppointment; a disgruntled clerk philosophises gloomily about his place in the scheme of things; a young girl, against all the odds, decides to keep her sister's deep dark secret. By turns warm, gullible, arrogant and bigoted, they live their lives amid contradictions and double standards, superstitions and impossible dreams, but ultimately usurp their familiar landscape and imbue it with an idiosyncratic vision.